MARY JAAY

Broken, Beautiful Lies

For the ones who love in silence,
Carried the weight of secrets,
And still chose to protect what was fragile and
Real.
This is for you-
The broken, the brave, the beautifully flawed.

Contents

Foreword

At seventeen, Clara Monroe vanished from her hometown without a word. For eight years, she built a new life far from the heartbreak she swore she'd never face again. But one phone call changes everything: her mother is in a coma, and Clara must return to the place she vowed never to see again.

No one knows the real reason she left, except the one person who can't speak. Now, surrounded by the family she abandoned and the boy she was never supposed to love, Clara is forced to confront the past she buried and the lies that tore everything apart.

Beautiful, Broken Lies is a gripping story of forbidden love, shattered trust, and the haunting power of secrets.

Trigger Warning

- This is a taboo Romance (step-siblings)
- Speaks on parent trauma
- Talks of pregnancy
- Mental Health
- One scene of sexual interactions where characters are 16/17 years old

One

Ghost

CLARA

Eight years is a long time to stay gone. Long enough for people to forget the sound of your voice, but not the weight of your name. I told myself I'd never come back, not for holidays, not for funerals, not even for her. But now my mother was in a coma, and this town was calling me home like it knew I still had something to hide.

The Emerald City hadn't changed, but I had, leaving with a secret curled deep in me, so quiet, I almost convinced myself it wasn't real.

The streets were scarcer than I'd remembered. I glanced outside the car window, taking in the sight of greenery passing us by. The trees blurred into one another, drenched in mist. Seattle's rain hadn't forgotten me. The road seemed never-ending. Seeing that I'd lived in New York City for so long, it was a drastic change. I missed the liveliness of it already.

The closer I got to the place I once called home, the more anxious I grew. My fingers drummed on my thigh, doing ten-second counts in my head. *1,2... I can do this... 3,4... I can get through this... 5,6... I'll be fine... 7,8... I'm fine... 9,10... I'm fine.*

"We're here," Jamie's voice cut through my chant. I flinched, fingers still drumming on my thighs.

The house loomed beyond the windshield like a ghost itself, all sharp lines and ivy, untouched by time.

"You okay?" She twisted toward me in the driver's seat, voice gentle, but somehow her eyes didn't match it. Pity oozed off of her. Pity that felt rehearsed, followed by a smile too polished.

Jamie tucked a strand of honey-blonde hair behind her ear. She looked so different from the girl I remembered.

"Yeah," I lied, lips curving up in what I supposed was a smile.

We'd known each other since I was eleven, back when I still believed my home was a safe space. She messaged me out of the blue, not too long after I left Seattle. Said she missed me. Said she wouldn't tell anyone. And she hadn't.

Something about her now, though, felt…I don't know. I couldn't put my finger on it.

"Well," she said. "Good luck in there. She didn't offer to come in, just gave my hand a quick squeeze, too tight to be comforting.

"Thanks."

I stepped out before I could change my mind. The gravel crunched beneath my boots, and rain slicked my coat. The house stared back at me, three stories of memories wrapped in damp light and silence.

My feet didn't seem to want to move, like they were being weighed down by freshly cast cement. Jamie's engine hummed in the background. *She hadn't left.* Taking that as a sign that she was waiting for me to go in, I used that as motivation to move my ass.

One step at a time, I walk on the gravel pavement up the driveway. My mind was in overdrive with thoughts of my arrival. Would they be happy to see me? Would they turn me away?

Everything's fine. I'm fine.

What seemed like an hour later, I stood face to face with the hardwood door. Knuckles raised, my heart pounded, and my hands trembled. Before my fist could hit the wood, the door opened from the inside.

My breath caught as we locked eyes. My grip tightened on my suitcase handle to anchor myself. Eight years collapsed on themselves as memories of the young and carefree me flooded: barefoot in the grass, lips swollen from first kisses, whispering secrets in the dark.

Denver.

He looked… different. Taller, broader. His hair was shorter than it used to be, swept back as if he did not have time to let it fall across his eyes anymore. His jaw was angular, with a few days' worth of stubble, and his arms crossed over his chest, tattoos curling down the muscles in stark black ink I didn't recognize.

But it was his eyes that hit the hardest.

Those green eyes used to look at me like I was the only person in the world.

Now, they didn't even flinch.

"Denver," I whispered, his name sounding foreign to my tongue.

His face stayed hard. "What are you doing here?" His voice was gravelly with a slight bite to it.

Ouch.

I blinked, swallowing hard. "I-I just got here. My dad called. He said she was—"

"I know why you're here." His tone was flat as he let out a tired sigh, as if he'd just asked a question he'd known the answer to. "I just didn't think you'd show up."

"I came as soon as I could. I didn't know what else to—"

"To what?" he snapped. "Pretend none of it happened? That you didn't disappear?"

My throat tightened. "I didn't have a choice."

He shook his head, the muscles in his jaw ticking. "There's always a choice."

The words cut deeper than I expected. I looked away, trying to breathe past the sting in my eyes. I'd imagined this moment a thousand times. None of them ended like this.

"Denver," I started again.

But he was already brushing past me.

"Wait," I said, turning after him. "Please don't walk away like this."

"I'm sorry that this is what brought you home." The apology carried a bite, but underneath it was something more raw.

The words pressed against my chest. I wanted to tell him I was sorry too, for leaving, for the silence all these years, for everything. But I stayed quiet.

"I have somewhere to be. Dad's inside," he said flatly.

He dragged his hand through his damp hair and moved down the driveway without another glance. Only when his figure cut through the mist did I notice Jamie was still here because of him. My stomach turned. Of course. That's why she hadn't left.

She was still behind the wheel, leaning toward him as he pulled open the passenger door. For a moment, he hesitated, one hand on the frame, rain slipping down his temples. Then he slid inside. Her hand brushed his arm, and the sting of it caught me by surprise.

I had almost forgotten how close they used to be when we were children. I left while they stayed. I didn't have the right to feel any way. It wasn't my place. Not anymore.

Drawn back to the open door, I heard the clinking of pots. The scent in the house remained unchanged. The air held the smell of cedarwood, old money, and something faintly floral that my mother always insisted wasn't perfume. I moved through the front hall like a ghost as my fingers trailed the walls I'd once marked up while playing with colored pencils. The dim overhead light of the living room shed light on the masterpiece, which was plastered on the wall. Guitars of all shapes, sizes, and colors, decorated so well, were a sight to see. It was new, but I knew whose work it belonged to. Denver's big idea was always to put them up where he and everyone else could see. *I want every guitar I touch to remind me how much I love to play. So, why not hang them where I can walk past every day and smile?"* His eyes filled with glee the night he mapped out this bright idea to me. His love for music had always been profound. My chest warms at the memory of *him*.

The smile vanishes when I don't see a specific guitar. *It should be up there.*

"Clara?"

I whipped around, almost losing my balance, my long hair hitting my arms like a striking lash.

Red-rimmed eyes stared back at me like *he'd been crying*.

"Clara, you came."

His voice was soft, stunned. My stepfather looked at me like he was seeing a ghost, his eyes scanning over me, like he couldn't quite believe I was standing in front of him. His hands, dusted in flour and thyme, wiped absentmindedly on the apron tied around his waist. The scent of my mother's favorite soup filled the room, rich and nostalgic, making my throat tighten.

He opened his arms, hesitant at first, like he wasn't sure if I'd step in.

I did.

For a moment, I let myself fall into the warmth of his hug. It was safe and familiar. But it wasn't simple. Not anymore.

Did he know? Did she tell him the reason why I left? Tell him what I'd done?

His arms tightened around me for just a second before he pulled back, studying me again. He harbored the same eyes Denver had inherited. Warm. Kind. Loving.

"Yes," I mumbled. "I came."

"I wasn't sure you would, but I hoped."

I nodded, swallowing hard. "I wasn't sure, either. When my dad called and told me what happened, it just felt right… to come." I couldn't deal with the awkward silence. "You're making her favorite soup."

His gaze softened. "She always said it could fix anything: Head colds. Heartbreak. Bad days. Thought maybe…" He trailed off, clearing his throat. "Maybe if she could smell it, she'd remember she had something to come back to. People to come back to," he said, trailing off.

The ache behind my eyes threatened to spill over. "I understand." Like a full-blown Cinderella story, where a kiss, a song, or the smell of something warm and good could break the spell.

It was wishful thinking.

"Well, um, you can get settled if you're staying. We turned your old room into a guest bedroom, but it's still yours. Once I finish up, we can go visit your mom."

"Yeah, of course. Thanks, Tom."

Nodding, my feet didn't move at first. I was waiting for the hammer to drop, for him to tell me he knew it all.

But it didn't.

"Thanks," I murmured. He called my name, stopping me as I turned to follow the stairway upstairs.

"I'm happy you're home. For however long that is. I know she'll be happy to see you when she wakes up." The comfort of the smile he gave me tightened something in my stomach.

I tried my best to return it and then continue on my way up. I couldn't muster a response to that. It'll come out wrong, rude even.

She wouldn't be. Not really. I'd fought with myself about coming here for days.

The woman lying in that hospital bed, the one everyone spoke about like a saint, was the reason I left. Or, more accurately, the reason I ran. Out of this house. Out of this town. A life that was never really mine to begin with.

She'll be happy to see you.

The truth weighed down on me like it always had. This house, this town, just being back here. Everything I'd run from was still here, waiting. And so was the reason I left, the only thing I could never undo.

Two

Echoes in the Walls

CLARA

The door creaked open when I walked into the room. Without all the space being taken up by my things, it looked bigger. The bare cream walls lacked the posters I had nailed there years ago. Instead of pink everything, the color of the bedding, dressers, etc., was beige. Dust stuck to my fingers as I skimmed them across the dresser and then the headboard.

Memories of running in and out of this room appeared so vividly. This was my sanctuary until it wasn't.

The bed dipped beneath me as I sat on the edge. Running my hands over the delicate comforter, I thought about my plan from here.

When my dad called me and told me about my mother's condition, it shook me to my core. It took a few days to decide. It seemed selfish if I didn't.

Seventeen. I was so young. Moving from Seattle to a big city like New York gave me whiplash. I was a small girl in an enormous world that was ready to eat me up at every turn. *The classic runaway destination.* It almost ate me up whole. *Almost.* I found a decent school and got my bachelor's in marketing by twenty-one. I climbed the ladder at the digital marketing company where I've worked for over five years. It was a rough start; I felt lost. For the first few months, I'd felt myself slipping into the unknown.

Then came Ethan. A friend who had become more than that. He helped pull me back to reality, no matter how much I'd tried to push him away. I'd indulged in something so wrong that I felt like I didn't deserve any kindness. *My mother sure didn't show any.* We'd forged a bond so strong that, to this day, nothing could break it. Pulling me back from the edge of my sanity, I found something to live for again. My son. My entire world. I built a life, one that was *ours.*

I was examining my past, even though I knew it would only cause me pain from wounds I'd worked so hard to heal.

I retrieved my phone from my pocket and hit call when I found the contact I was looking for.

"How is he?" I didn't let Ethan get a word in.

Soft laughter filtered through.

"He's fine," he said, his husky voice putting my mind at ease. "We had homework time, and now he's passed out. The kid could sleep."

I sink into the bed with a sigh of relief.

"I should've never left."

"Don't start doubting yourself. You needed to be there. Plus, he's in good hands. Did you forget?"

"Of course not. I just… I don't think it was the brightest idea. It's already too much, and I haven't seen my mother yet."

The idea of seeing her again scared me. Seeing her in a coma… it just didn't sit right with me.

"You're going to be plucking gray hairs soon if you keep working yourself up," he joked.

"Oh, dealing with that kid of ours, I already have a few," I humored him.

"No shit. On a serious note, Clara, don't think too much about it. Family needs you, no matter how it may seem now. You've been away for eight years. Just be there. That's all you need to do while I take care of Eric."

I fell silent. His words of encouragement always did wonders, but my mind was hearing something else entirely.

While Tom was delighted to see me, Denver, on the other hand? I didn't think so. That interaction hit hard. He's the one I owed something to. I disappeared before the sun could catch me. *Before he could.*

My mother was another tough pill to swallow.

"Are you there?" Ethan's voice pulled through my thoughts.

"Yes, I've got to go. I'll call to speak to him before bedtime."

"Okay, you do that.. And Clara…I'm here."

"I know." I paused. "Bye."

I hung up before the tears sprang free. Taking a deep breath, I ran my hand through my hair, tugging the strands.

A sudden knock on the door broke through my train of thought.

"Clara, are you all set?"

I wasn't, by any means, but I responded with a *yes* anyway.

When I opened the door, Tom was still there, with a lunch bag with the soup he'd made clutched under his arm.

"Wow." He scanned me from head to toe, a smile curving at his lips. He'd gotten older. More gray hairs appeared throughout his hair, and small wrinkles pronounced themselves whenever he smiled, as he was doing right now.

I stiffened under his gaze, not knowing what to do or say. Coming back here made me feel like a stranger among people I'd known my whole life.

"I'm getting déjà vu," he continued. "Feels like just yesterday you were flying through that door, tracking mud and laughter behind you." His eyes wandered over me, into the room, as if he were picturing the memory.

"Yeah… feels like a different lifetime." I tried to smile, but it wobbled, too thin to cover the ache.

I was eleven when my mother moved us across town to live with Tom and Denver. It was the first day I met them both. I was under the impression that it was just a daughter meeting her mother's new boyfriend. Boy, was I in for a rude awakening. We were over the pleasantries when Denver was told to show me to my new room. There wasn't room for questions, because she shooed me away before I could utter a word. I was angry at first. I was leaving my friends, home, and school behind without a heads-up.

Denver gave me a tour and observed that I appeared distressed. When I informed him, he assured me he would show me around, introduce me to his friends, and ensure I never felt out of place. For an eleven-year-old, you'd take his words with a grain of salt. Yet, he fulfilled his promises. Within a month, I had felt completely at home.. *Because of him.*

"So… how are you holding up?" I'd forgotten to ask him when I first arrived. This line of conversation seemed more doable instead of taking a joyride down memory lane. It wasn't the time.

He let out a deep sigh as his expression softened. The bags under his eyes indicated he wasn't doing well. He worshiped the ground my mother walked on. That had never been a doubt when I first met him. I was sure it didn't change during my absence.

"Taking it a day at a time. It's all you can do, I guess." His hand shuffled with the lunchbox under his arm. He paused and looked away for a moment, then met my wary eyes again. "How about you? I know this isn't easy."

I pondered the question. Normal people would fall to their knees, praying to God to get their mother through this. I'd yet to cry. Maybe it was the fact that I hadn't spoken to her in so long that she'd become a distant memory to me. I dropped everything and came; that had to count for something.

"I'm fine," I said, my voice a little too steady. "I'm handling…handling it the best I can. It's just a lot, you know? I didn't want to come back home like this."

I was surprised at how easy it was to lie. How effortlessly I could slip into the mask I'd discarded a long time ago. It'd found me as soon as I stepped off the plane, like it was just waiting for its owner's return.

"I know. I'm sure you'd like to see her now. We can catch up later." His pointed look gave me the impression that catching up later was going to happen one way or another.

I acknowledged with a nod and followed him to his car, parked in the garage.

I wasn't ready

Three

Fractures

DENVER

The guitar case sat in the corner of my room, untouched since my last gig at the Rusty Note. Every time I looked at it, I heard the voicemail again. My dad's voice, hollow and breaking.

A drunk driver. A red light. Heleen.

Time hadn't stopped. It turned on me.

I'd already lost one mom. Losing another wasn't something I could wrap my head around. Heleen wasn't just my stepmother. She raised me, loved me like I was hers. Now she was in a hospital bed surrounded by wires. I kept telling myself she'll wake up. That she had to.

But today, all I could do was pretend that was still true.

Rain slid down the windshield of Jamie's car as we pulled onto Main. I told her I needed to make a stop before heading to the hospital, and she insisted she would drive no matter how much I told her I was fine to do it on my own.

My foot tapped against the floorboard, restless, the tension running through me with nowhere else to go. My hands wouldn't stop flexing in my lap.

"You're shaking," Jamie said quietly, eyes on the road.

13

I hadn't realized it. My knee bounced harder. My head wasn't in the car right now.

Clara.

She'd walked back into our lives like no time had passed. Like she hadn't ripped the ground out from under me and disappeared before the sun could catch her. Eight goddamn years gone, and in one second, I felt like I knew her again. Same honey-brown eyes that saw too much. Same pull I'd spent years trying to sever ties from.

And I hated that she still had that power.

"Denver?"

Jamie's voice tugged me back. I blinked at the blurred shapes outside.

"Is this about Clara?" she asked. Her tone was careful—too careful. Like she already knew the answer to her question.

Her name in the air was a spark to dry wood. My pulse jumped. I didn't answer, staring harder at the rain sliding sideways across the glass. Leave it to Seattle weather to match your mood.

Jamie gripped the wheel tighter. "What happened between you two?"

The words cut through the quiet. She didn't look at me, just kept her eyes locked forward.

I turned my head. "You don't need to ask that."

"I'm not asking to pry. I saw the way you looked at her. That's not nothing." She hesitated, her voice edging sharp. "Most people would be glad their stepsister came home."

Stepsister. She said it like it burned her tongue.

My chest tightened. She wasn't wrong. Clara coming back was not nothing, it was everything I'd tried not to think about for years. Then again, she came back for her mother's sake. I'm sure that's the only reason.

I let the thought sit just as we pulled into the parking lot of Daisy's Palace. I listened to the faint ding of the bell as an older couple walked out, the older woman holding a bouquet close to her chest.

"Listen. I just think—"

"Maybe just stop thinking for a second, Jamie." My voice came out harder than I meant.

I shoved the door open before she could answer. The slam echoed in the wet air. Guilt snapped at me even as I stalked into Daisy's.

That was a dick move. She didn't deserve that.

But Clara being here… it was going to undo me.

Inside, the shop smelled like damp earth and lilies. I picked out a bouquet of white daisies, Heleen's favorite, before placing it on the counter as the clerk rang me up.

Back at the car, Jamie was waiting, her hands locked around the wheel even though the car was off. She didn't look at me when I slid back in.

"Sorry," I muttered, rubbing my palms against my jeans.

Jamie stayed quiet at first. That was her way. She never rushed to fill silence, never pushed unless she thought she had to. Maybe that was why she'd always been easy to have around. She knew when to talk and when to just sit with you in the mess. It'd been like that since we were kids.

"I pushed when I shouldn't have," she finally said.

I shook my head. "Doesn't matter. I shouldn't have snapped."

I wanted to tell her that it wasn't her fault that my greatest weakness showed back up unexpectedly, and I was freaking the fuck out on top of having to worry about my stepmother and dad's well-being. 'Sorry' had to suffice.

Her mouth twitched, almost a smile. "So we're both assholes, then?"

A laugh slipped out before I could stop it.

Her hand landed on my shoulder, a quick squeeze before she pulled back to the wheel. "Glad we have that understanding," she said before the engine rumbled to life.

Moments like this reminded me why she was one of the few people I let close. She called me out, but she never left me hanging there.

The tension cracked just enough for the air to shift between us, lighter for the first time all day.

Four

The Beginning

C LARA
11 Years Old

Mom's perfume hit me before we even pulled into the neighborhood. It was the kind that clung to everything in the close vicinity. The strong, flowery scent burned the back of my throat. She'd sprayed too much. She always did when she wanted to impress someone.

At first, I thought I'd be sad about her dating again. But after Dad left, the house had felt too big, too loud with just her anger in it. Their fights used to rattle the walls. I never understood why they fought, only that my chest went tight every time they did. When he finally packed up and left, Mom said he was a bad husband and an even worse father. He still sent me letters, always written in the same blue ink, little doodles in the corner like when we used to play games together. I asked her why he bothered. She said it was guilt. Nothing more.

"Now, remember, Clara," Mom said, steering into a wide, tree-lined driveway, "be on your best behavior. I really like Tom, and who knows, maybe he'll be your new dad someday."

My face scrunched up. "I already have a dad."

"Barely," she muttered. Like always, she thought I wouldn't hear her. But

I did. I always did.

The car rolled to a stop in front of a house that looked like something from a magazine. The grass was perfect, the trees lined up in neat rows, like even they had manners.

"Wow," I whispered, even though I didn't mean to.

Her smile flashed like she'd won something. "I know, right?" She fixed her hair in the mirror before stepping out. I followed slowly, my shoes dragging against the stone path.

The front door swung open before we reached it. A tall man stepped outside, arms wide, smiling brighter than the sun. His hair was white, not gray, but striking white, like fresh chalk. He moved with the kind of ease that made it feel like he'd been waiting for us all day.

"Heleen, my love!" His voice was warm as he greeted Mom. He kissed her cheeks, wrapped her in an embrace that lasted too long for my taste. When he finally let go, he crouched down to my level.

"And you must be Clara." His hand extended.

I hesitated, then slid my small palm into his. "That's me."

His smile deepened, a crease forming near his eyes. "Denver!" he called toward the open doorway.

Seconds later, a boy came skidding out, his uniform shirt half tucked, his hair sticking up like he'd wrestled with his pillow and lost. He looked around my age as I got a better look at him when he stopped beside Tom, chest heaving and grinning. He looked like the mini version of him, aside from the white hair.

"This is Clara," Tom said. "Clara, my son, Denver."

"Denver… like the state?" I blurted before I could stop myself. Geography was fresh in my head.

"City," Denver corrected, still grinning.

My cheeks warmed at my mistake.

Tom's laugh was soft, breaking through my embarrassment. His eyes had the same warmth as his voice. "Denny, why don't you show Clara to her new room?" Tom suggested.

My head snapped toward Mom. "New what?"

Her arm slid around me, too tight to shake off. "We talked about this, Clara. We're moving in with Tom and Denver."

No, we hadn't. I would've remembered something this big.

"Now go on," she said, already turning back to Tom with her perfect smile.

I stood frozen until Denver jerked his head toward the stairs. "Come on. I'll show you."

Inside, the house smelled of faint lemon polish. Everything gleamed: the banister, the chandelier overhead, the polished floor that made me afraid to step too hard. My old house smelled like vanilla and candles and Dad's aftershave. The floors creaked when I ran, and my posters peeled from the walls. This place felt… untouchable.

"Are you coming?" Denver was halfway up the stairs, waiting.

I hurried after him, trailing behind until he stopped at the last door on one end of the hallway.

"This one's yours."

When he swung it open, my jaw dropped. Pink everywhere. Pillows, lamps, curtains, and even a rug. It looked like someone had raided a princess's diary and built it into a room.

"Your mom must've told my dad you liked pink." Denver snickered behind me, watching me take it all in.

I touched the comforter, silky, stiff, and nodded.

He plopped down on the edge of the bed like it was his. "Wanna see my room?"

His was nothing like mine. Clothes piled into corners, books stacked sideways on shelves, video games half-open on the desk. A framed photo sat on the dresser: a woman holding a baby with eyes that matched his.

"Who's this?"

"My mom and I." His voice softened.

"Oh. Where is she?"

"She died a few years ago."

The floor seemed to tilt under my feet. "I'm sorry. I didn't mean to…"

"It's fine." His eyes lingered on the photo. "I don't remember much. But Dad tells me stories. Keeps her alive, you know?"

I nodded, throat tight. My kind of missing: friends, my school, Dad's doodles, felt small in comparison.

"Wanna see something cool?" he asked suddenly.

"Yes."

He ducked down into his closet and dragged out a black guitar case. Sitting cross-legged, he unlatched it and pulled out a shiny guitar, sleek and heavy-looking.

"I don't really know how to play yet," he admitted, plucking at the strings.

"Then why do you have it?"

"Dad took me to a concert. The guitarist, John Somebody, was amazing. I told him I wanted to learn. Some day, I'm gonna start a band with my friends. We'll play in places even bigger than this house." His grin stretched wide, alive with too much dream for one kid.

"I like that," I said, as he continued to pluck the strings.

The mention of friends reminded me of my new reality. I was leaving mine behind.

"Hey," he said when I stayed quiet. "What's wrong?"

"I don't know anyone here."

"You know me."

"I just met you."

He shrugged. "You live here now. We'll get to know each other."

Tears pricked my eyes, but I blinked them away, picking at the hem of my dress and not wanting to look like a baby.

But I couldn't help but feel blindsided by Mom. Did Dad even approve of this? Ugh.

"I know it sucks," Denver said. "Leaving your friends, your house. But I've got you. I'll show you around, make sure you don't sit alone at lunch. Stuff like that."

He gave my shoulder a playful shove. I tried rolling my eyes, but my chest eased a little.

"You're like my sister now. That means I've got your back. Always."

"Promise?" I held out my pinky.

He grinned, shaking his head like it was silly, but hooked his pinky with mine anyway.

"Promise."

He let go first, springing toward the door with an energy I couldn't help but mirror. "Come on, I'll show you the kitchen next. My dad says it's the best part of the house.

This time, I didn't drag my feet. I hurried after him, lighter somehow, like the pinky-promise had lifted a weight off me. His chatter filled the hallway, every word tumbling out fast. I didn't catch it all, but I liked the sound of it, like he already counted me in on things.

Before we reached the stairs, something below caught my eye.

Mom and Tom stood near the wide entryway, their voices carrying upward. Tom's hand rested gently at the small of her back as she laughed. Like, really laughed. I'd never seen her laugh like that with Dad. I watched as Tom leaned closer, murmuring words I could only catch in pieces: new start, family.

My grip tightened on the railing.

"You've already given us more than I could imagine," Mom told him.

He brushed a strand of hair from her face with such tenderness. *Cringe.* "It's nothing compared to what I want for you. For both of you."

I swallowed and looked away, heat crawling into my cheeks when I realized I was intruding.

Denver nudged my shoulder, his grin pulling me back. "They'll be like that forever if we don't interrupt."

The words made me laugh, and he smiled at the sound.

We continued down the stairs, his shoulder brushing mine on purpose. Their voices trailed after us, but I wasn't listening anymore.

I was still wary of mom's actions, but it felt like maybe I wouldn't have to face this new life alone.

Five

The Unspoken

CLARA
Present Day

A sterile chill clung to my skin when I stepped into the hospital. The sharp tang of antiseptic thickened with each breath until it turned metallic at the back of my throat. Voices were hushed, movements clipped. Doctors in pale coats slipped past like shadows. A man coughed into his sleeve. Somewhere down the hall, a monitor beeped, steady and merciless.

Tom spoke to the nurse at the desk. She gestured with plump hands down a long hallway, and he didn't waste words— just nodded, then passed me a visitor's badge. I pressed it against my chest like it might steady my heartbeat.

Each step dragged. My fingers tapped against my thighs, trying to match the quick rhythm of my pulse.

Would I even recognize her? Would she recognize me if she opened her eyes? And if she did, would she want to?

The closer I got, the more the years fell away. I wasn't the woman who built a life in New York. I was seventeen again. Ashamed. Bruised in places no one could see.

Tom opened the door and went inside. I froze on the threshold. The room

21

was dim except for the glow of machines. My stepfather stood bent over the bed, his shoulders shaking. Denver was beside him, one hand gripping a bouquet, the other pressed firmly against his father's back. His gaze was fixed on the bed, on her. Jamie was there too, tucked close, like she had every right to be.

Then my eyes landed on my mother. She looked impossibly small. The starched white sheets swallowed her body. Tubes ran from her nose and arms, tethering her to machines that did the work of keeping her alive. Her chest rose and fell with a mechanical rhythm, too steady, too foreign. Tears blurred my vision before I even realized I was crying. I didn't see the woman who cast me out. Not the one whose eyes turned to glass the night she discovered the truth. I saw someone broken, barely hanging on.

My body swayed. My silence pressed down harder than the air in that room. And then…Denver's eyes. They lifted and locked with mine. The years didn't matter. The anger didn't matter. His gaze burned through it all, softening in a way that made my chest cave in. For one moment, we were only two people who used to be everything to each other. Then my phone rang, slicing through the silence. Heads turned, and I bolted. The air outside hit me like a slap, damp and cold. Rain tapped against the pavement in restless patterns.

I stumbled to a sheltered bench just beyond the doors, hands shaking as I answered the call.

"Clara?" Ethan's voice was tight with alarm. "What's wrong? Talk to me."

I pressed my face into my hands, my shoulders shaking. "I…" My voice cracked; words strangled.

"Okay," he said softly. "Let it out. I've got you." So, I did. My sobs filled the line, unsteady, raw. He didn't rush me. He just stayed, his breathing steady, waiting me out.

When I finally found my voice, it was a rasp. "I'm at the hospital." A pause. "How is she?" "Bad. I barely recognized her. I couldn't even step inside." Silence stretched, only broken by the rhythm of rain drumming against the shelter roof.

"You don't have to push yourself," he said gently. "You showed up. That matters. I'm proud of you."

Fresh tears spilled. "I'm not going anywhere," he added. "You're stuck with me, remember?" A shaky laugh slipped out of me. "And don't even think about loopholes. No refunds. No exchanges." His grin came through the phone, and this time, my laugh was real. "There she is," he breathed. "Hey, if you're up for it, our little one's awake. He's been asking for you."

For the next fifteen minutes, I let my son's voice fill me. His questions tumbled out fast, eager, his laughter pulling me back from the edge.

By the time the call ended, I felt hollowed out but steadier. The sliding doors whooshed open. I looked up.

Denver.

His hands were shoved deep in his pockets, shoulders hunched against the drizzle. I expected him to keep walking, but instead, he crossed to the covered bench and sat at the far end. Silent. My pulse tripped over itself. Eight years apart, and suddenly he was sitting close enough for me to hear the quiet drag of his breath. We used to sit like this all the time. Back when things were simpler. Back when it didn't hurt to look at him. For a moment, neither of us spoke.

Then he said, almost gently, "Remember when your mom tried to teach us how to bake a cake?" The memory rushed in before I could stop it. Flour dusting the counter, Denver sneaking a spoonful of batter, my mother actually laughing as she swatted at us with the wooden spoon. She'd pulled me into her side, her arm heavy around my shoulders, and for the first time in forever, it felt like I belonged to her. I swallowed hard. "She ended up ordering dessert instead." His mouth twitched, like he was fighting a smile. "She said we made the kitchen look like a crime scene."

I laughed softly. "I miss that." My voice betrayed me. What I really meant was I missed this. Sitting next to him. Sharing memories that belonged to us both. Even missing the moments my mother chose to show me affection, rare enough that I hoarded them like treasures. The quiet stretched, but it wasn't easy anymore.

Denver turned his head, and his eyes found mine. The softness was gone, replaced by something sharper. "Why, Clara?" His voice was low, rough.

"Why did you leave the way you did?" The air between us thickened. My throat closed, words clawing for a way out but never making it past my lips.

I wanted to tell him everything. That I'd missed him in ways that went deeper than just old memories. That sitting this close to him, sharing even a scrap of laughter, reminded me of a life I'd once let slip through my hands. But all I managed was silence. His jaw tightened, disappointment flickering across his face like a shadow.

The sound of footsteps broke the moment. "Hey, you two." Jamie's voice was too smooth, too well-timed. She stepped out of the sliding doors, eyes darting between us before settling on me. Her hand brushed Denver's shoulder, lingering. "The doctor's about to give an update. Your dad sent me to get you."

Denver pushed to his feet quickly, scrubbing a hand through his hair. "Let's go." He walked past me without another glance. Jamie fell in step beside him, her hand still at his back. I stayed behind, my chest aching, watching the two of them disappear into the hospital.

For a second, I couldn't tell what stung worse, the way Denver had looked at me just now, or the way Jamie looked at him. I drew in a shaky breath and forced myself to stand. My legs carried me forward, back toward the sliding doors.

Six

When the Dam Breaks

D ENVER

Jamie's voice followed me down the hall, light but probing. "What was that? You two looked…tense."

"Nothing," I muttered.

"Doesn't look like nothing." She bumped her shoulder into mine, a smile tugging her mouth like she wanted to lighten things. "You can't just leave me out of—"

I threw my arm over her shoulder, cutting her off and pulling her into a half-hug as we walked. "Relax, Jamie. Not everything's worth prying into."

She laughed under her breath. "Fine. But if something's up, tell me. I'm always here for you."

I kissed the top of her head. "I know."

I left her in the waiting area and stepped into Heleen's room.

Dad sat at her bedside, her hand locked in his, whispering words she couldn't answer. His thumb brushed over her knuckles like the smallest touch might wake her up. My chest tightened, the sight tearing me in two.

"You okay, son?" he asked, looking up.

"Yeah."

His gaze lingered before he nodded and turned back to her. "Where's

Clara?"

"She'll be in soon." At least, I hoped she would.

The door creaked again, and Clara stepped in, hovering just inside the threshold, shoulders squared but body taut as if she might bolt at any second.

I didn't understand why.

Dad gave her a soft smile, one I knew by heart. "Come closer. The doctor said she might be able to hear us if we talk to her."

She didn't move at first. Her eyes fixed on Heleen, then darted to Dad, then to me. Something in her expression twisted, a mix of fear, anger, and grief, I couldn't place it. But they were all fighting for space on her face.

Dr. Chambers entered the room then, clipboard in hand, voice steady and clinical. Pushing his glasses up from his nose, he looked over the paperwork in his hand. "There's been no new bleeding," he began, voice even. "That's the good news. The swelling is still present, but it's stable. Her body's responding to the medication as we'd hoped. The next step is time. Continuing to monitor, watching for signs of improvement."

Dad leaned forward, a loud breath releasing from him. He gripped Heleen's hand a little tighter. "So, nothing's worse?"

"No," Dr. Chambers assured him with a smile. "At this point, no news is good news. It means her condition hasn't declined. What we're waiting for now is responsiveness. Even the small movements, such as eye flutter, finger twitch, would tell us she's starting to come back."

A hopeful smile crossed Dad's face, and I was so happy to finally see him smiling. Losing his mom had been hard on him. It took him a long time to open up again. When he finally did, it was Heleen. Seeing him at another bedside with the notion that he could lose her fucked me up a little. I might've been too young to grasp the nature of my mother's passing from cancer, but he'd lived through it all.

"I know the waiting is the hardest part, but talk to her," Dr. Chambers continued. "Keep talking to her. Familiar voices, stories, those things matter."

He gave a polite nod, then slipped back into the hallway when we didn't have any more questions for him.

"You hear that, honey, you're going to be alright," Dad whispered to Heleen. "Clara's here," he continued, looking over at her.

I watched as she shifted near the door, arms folded across her chest.

Dad turned back to Heleen, his thumb stroking across her hand. "She came back to you. She's home."

Her feet carried her forward, slow and careful, until she stopped at my side, looking down at her mother.

"Talk to her," Dad said gently.

I glanced down just as Clara's fingers twitched at her side, her face almost pale as they didn't leave Heleen's. She opened her mouth, but no sound came out. Her lips pressed tightly together.

Before I could think better of it, I reached for her hand. She startled, but didn't pull away. Her hand was trembling in mine, and I held on, giving her something steady.

This must've been a nightmare for her.

Dad looked between us and let out a quiet breath. "It's alright. She knows you're here. It's a shock, seeing her like this."

Her gaze never faltered. I felt the weight of her silence more than any words she might've said.

Time blurred after that. Jamie eventually slipped back in for a little while, and we all sat and listened while Dad told story after story as the beep of the machines played in the background.

"I'll stay a bit longer," Dad looked over his shoulder and said, pressing his keys into my hand. "You two should take the car and head home. She needs rest. You both do."

Clara didn't argue. Neither did I. I grabbed the keys from him before we said our goodbyes.

The ride back was muted, save for the wipers swiping the rain away. Streetlights bled into streaks against the wet windshield. Clara curled toward the window, her reflection broken by the glass.

I tried to keep my eyes on the road as my unanswered question gnawed at me. By the time I pulled into the driveway, I couldn't hold it back.

"Why, Clara?"

Her head turned slowly, her eyes studying mine as if she was contemplating answering me. Her lips pulled into her mouth before she averted her gaze.

"Because she knew," she whispered. I almost didn't hear her.

My chest locked. "What are you talking about?"

"My mother." Her voice cracked on the word. "She found out about us. She confronted me. I couldn't stay after that." She motioned to open the car door before I reached my hand out to stop.

"Wait. Wait." My mind was racing. It felt like the world had just tilted on me. Heleen knew? All this time. Family dinners, holidays, vow renewals, and she'd never said a thing. She'd let Clara vanish and left me in a wreck.

It seems crazy that that's the part I'm most shocked about, rather than my stepmother knowing the nature of Clara and I's relationship.

"She knew," I repeated, letting the words sit on my tongue. "And she didn't tell me?" I asked, more to myself.

We sat with the truth while I tried to make sense of it. *No. No.*

"You don't understand," Clara continued, voice cracking.

Anger rolled through me. "And you didn't think to tell me?"

She pulled her hand from my grasp. "What was I supposed to say, Denver? That I couldn't stay because what we had was wrong? That my mother looked at me and saw something she couldn't forgive?" I almost reached for her hand again. "I was seventeen and scared."

I shook my head, bitter heat rising in my chest. "You still could've told me. You could've given me something. Instead…Instead, you left me here wondering what the hell I did to push you away! And you're telling me you left for what? To protect me?"

A dry laugh rolled out of me.

Her jaw tightened. "And what good would that have done? You think your life would've been easier carrying that kind of shame, too? You didn't need to wear the weight of how wrong it all was. I did."

The words hit like a blow. For a moment, neither of us spoke. Just the sound of our breathing in the dark car..

The urge to reach for her resurfaced. To brush her hand, to tell her she wasn't alone anymore, to undo eight years of whatever pain she'd been carrying. But she was already pulling inward, shoulders rigid, gaze fixed on anything but me.

So I swallowed it back. I opened the door, the night's cold rushing in, and left her there.

Did Dad know too? Were they all just playing some fucking trick on me for eight fucking years? Heleen had known this entire time. This entire fucking time.

Upstairs, my door rattled in its frame when I slammed it. Too hard. I paced, fists clenched, heart hammering. Heleen was lying in a hospital bed, and all I could think about was how furious I was with her. How confused. How ashamed.

And then there was Clara. The girl I couldn't stop loving, even when everything screamed that I should. The girl I lost because of something we both chose, but only she paid for.

I sank onto the edge of the bed, my eyes dragging over the room.

Two guitars hung in a neat row, each one a memory: the battered acoustic I wrote my first song on, the vintage electric I bought at eighteen. The dark cherry Les Paul leaned untouched by the door, waiting for a gig that never came.

A dusty amp slumped in the corner. Sheet music littered the desk. A faded photo of my band clung to the mirror above it.

This room was supposed to be a sanctuary. Tonight it felt like a museum.

My gaze fell on the family photo on the dresser. Heleen, Dad, Clara, and I were at the fourth vow renewal. We were all smiles. Clara in a blue dress, looking like a dream I could never hold onto.

I picked it up. My hands shook.

I should've told someone. Fought harder. Seen that Heleen knew. Seen that Clara was breaking.

But I didn't.

The frame shattered against the wall. Glass splintered like the years between us.

Eight years. All of it on me.

Seven

Shattered

CLARA

Seconds passed as I sat in the dark car, frozen in place. The slam of the front door still echoed in my chest. I'd thought giving him part of the truth might ease the weight between us, but the look on his face told me otherwise.

My hands rubbed furiously on my thighs, as if I just stayed here long enough, I could keep everything from spilling open. But the longer I sat, the more I saw him at sixteen, slouched beside me on the roof, whispering about how every star had a story. He used to make me believe we were infinite, untouchable. And now? We couldn't even look at each other without breaking.

I shoved the passenger door open and got out, the night air damp against my skin. Inside, the house was too quiet. Not even the hum of the refrigerator reached me.

Then the crash.

Glass shattering. A hollow thud, again and again.

My chest caved.

I followed the sound upstairs, my heart pounding faster with each step. His door was cracked open, light spilling through. I pushed it wider and froze.

A picture frame lay shattered near the dresser. His knuckles were raw, blood streaked across the white drywall where he'd been punching. His chest rose and fell like he couldn't catch his breath, eyes unfocused, as if he wasn't even here.

"Denver?" My voice caught.

No answer.

I shut the door behind me and stepped between him and the wall, forcing myself into his line of sight.

"Denver," I said again, stronger this time, and wrapped my arms around him.

He went rigid, then collapsed into me, his weight crushing and desperate. A guttural cry tore from him, rattling through both of us, and my own throat burned from holding back tears.

"I'm so sorry, angel." His voice broke on the words, repeating them, over and over.

Angel. I hadn't heard that nickname in years.

I pressed closer, whispering against his shoulder. "It's okay. It's not your fault."

Tears welled in my eyes to see the pain he was in. I did this. It was all on me.

He trembled, his mumbled words falling apart in my hair.

When I pulled back, the sight of his hand, the one he played guitar with, made my stomach twist. I led the way as we moved in sync towards his bed. When he sat down, I pulled away just enough to grab a towel from the bathroom, then knelt in front of him. My hands worked carefully around his, wrapping the bleeding knuckles. He didn't even flinch. His eyes were glassy, lost somewhere far away.

"Denver," I called.

Nothing.

"Do you remember that summer?" I asked softly.

His gaze flicked to mine.

I needed him here with me. He seemed like he was pulling away.

"The one where we used to sneak out after our parents went to bed." My voice shook, but I kept going. "We'd climb onto the roof, and you'd make up stories about the stars."

A breath shuddered out of him.

"You told me one of them was mine."

"The one that flickered the most," he rasped.

I nodded. "You said it reminded you of me. Restless. Bright. Always running."

His breath hitched, and finally, finally, he looked at me fully.

"I never stopped loving you…" The words broke from him, ragged and bare, and they hung there between us, heavy as stone.

I couldn't answer. My throat locked tight. My eyes dropped to his hand instead, the makeshift bandage clumsy against skin, because staring at the damage was easier than facing the truth in his voice.

"I had to leave, Denver," I whispered.

"Because of your mother," he finished, bitterness apparent in his tone.

I let that truth sit. Let it rest between us, because if I said more, there wouldn't be any coming back from it.

More tears stung before I could stop them. "I'm sorry." My apologies seemed pointless, but it was all I had to offer. "I'm so, so sorry."

He reached up, his thumb brushing a tear from my cheek. The smallest touch, but it almost undid me.

I stood before I could stop myself, wrapping my arms around him. His good hand pressed hard against my back, holding me like he needed to anchor both of us.

When his grip finally loosened, I didn't step away. I sank beside him on the bed, my head finding his shoulder. His injured hand rested in mine, carefully, but I held it anyway.

"There wasn't a day that went by that I didn't think about you, that I didn't know my leaving was going to ruin everything we were trying to build. But I couldn't—"

"It's okay," he murmured.

We sat like that for I don't know how long. My head on his shoulder, our breathing slow, the room finally quiet. Nothing between us was fixed. Not even close. But in that moment, with his hand in mine, all I could feel was the truth pressing in. Leaving hadn't saved him. It only left us *both* broken.

I told myself I was only staying to make sure his hand was alright. He'd refused to get it checked out, insisting it was nothing, and aside from a few scrapes and swelling, he wasn't wrong. Still, I couldn't bring myself to leave.

One moment bled into the next, and somehow we ended up stretched across his bed. My head rested on his chest, his breathing slow and steady beneath me, his uninjured hand absently resting over my hair.

It was innocent, but the quiet we'd settled into was tense. What seemed like peace was really a space filled with questions we hadn't asked and words we hadn't spoken. They lingered there until my eyes slipped closed.

Eight

Angel

LARA
12 Years Old

"Clara! You better not be running after Denver." Mom's voice echoed up the stairs like a warning shot.

I stuffed my diary into the small backpack I kept under my bed and bolted into the hallway, where Denver was waiting, bike helmet in hand, a grin already plastered across his face.

"Ready?"

I nodded, but didn't speak. If Mom heard me agree, I was toast. She was always going on about how I shouldn't be "chasing behind boys," especially older ones. Even if they were only a year older, and one of them lived under our roof.

Denver and I had grown close since I moved in a little over a year ago. Wherever he went, I wasn't far behind. Like today, Saturday band practice at Eli's. It was becoming a regular thing.

Just when I thought I was going to make it out undetected, Mom stepped into view at the bottom of the stairs, arms crossed and eyes narrowed. Denver zipped right past her, leaving me to face the music.

I pasted on the most innocent smile I could muster. *Didn't work.* It never did with her.

"Where do you think you're going, young lady?"

"Uh… to watch band practice?" I fiddled with my fingers behind my back, praying she'd let me go.

"Don't you have homework?"

"It's done."

She didn't budge as her foot tapped and her eyebrow raised.

We play this song every weekend. I always made sure my homework was finished so I could hang out. This was an example of why I did that.

"Honey, let the girl go play," Tom chimed in, stepping in from the kitchen.

"She doesn't need to be running around with boys older than her." Her eyes stayed on mine as I held my breath, just hoping that she'd let up.

"They're only a year older," I rushed out. "Jamie's going. Katie might be, too, and they're both girls."

Her red lips formed a thin line. *I don't think she liked that.*

Tom slipped an arm around Mom's waist and kissed her cheek. "See? It's fine. We'll get some quiet time."

I gagged a little inside. Mom's blush grew deep red on her cheeks. It was gross.

She sighed, the hard line of her mouth softening. "Fine. But don't stay out late."

I made a mental note to thank Tom later and bolted for the front door before she could change her mind. I didn't miss her muttering, "She never listens."

Denver was already on his bike, a pink helmet held out for me in one hand, his guitar strapped awkwardly across the handlebars.

I hopped on the back pegs and held on tight to his shoulders as we pedaled toward Eli's house a few blocks over. He rambled on about a new set list, mostly John Mayer again, and some chords he'd been practicing. I nodded, the wind blowing my loose hair as he peddled down the street. I was only half-listening. Mom's words still played in my head. *She never listens.*

"Okay, spill." Denver unclipped his helmet and kicked the bike stand out once we got to Eli's.

"What?" I asked.

He gave me a "don't act stupid" look as he waited.

Looking down. I kicked a few loose rocks around with the tip of my sneakers.

"I know something's up." He nudged my elbow with his arm.

"It's mom." I knew better than to keep it in. If I didn't tell him, he'd eventually drag it out of me. It had been like that since the beginning.

"What about her?"

"She said I don't listen and that I shouldn't be running around with you guys. Like I'm doing something bad. She doesn't even know I heard her." She'd always been like that. Nitpicking at everything. There'd be moments where we're bonding, and the next, she's scolding me for something.

Don't wear your hair like that, Clara. You're a lady, Clara. Clara. Clara. Clara. Ugh.

He was quiet for a beat, hovering over me, blocking the sun from beaming down on me.

"She's just being a mom," he said, then looked down at his sneakers. "But you? You're an angel."

My face grew hot. "What?"

"You are." He shrugged, mumbling now. "Don't let her make you feel like you're not."

I stared at him, heart racing.

He lifted his pinky. "Promise me you'll always remember that."

I squinted. "Didn't you say pinky promises are childish?"

The second time I tried to do it, he'd said those exact words. I tend to take them very seriously, thank you very much.

"I'm making an exception," he said, rolling his eyes.

Smiling, I put my pinky up to his. "Promise."

He slung an arm around my shoulders. "Now come on, angel. Band practice awaits."

The weight of Mom's words had vanished, but I knew it wouldn't be the last of it.

Inside Eli's house, chaos reigned. Amps and cords were scattered everywhere; someone had tossed the pillows aside. The living room had become the unofficial practice space. I sat on the edge of the couch, diary on my lap, while the boys tuned and fussed with their instruments.

Jamie plopped beside me, legs swinging off the edge, shoelaces untied as always.

"What are you writing in there?"

"Stuff," I said. "Things I don't want to forget. My dad used to say, 'Writing helps when you want to remember things.'"

"Mr. Stone?"

"No. My real dad. Tom's just my stepdad."

"Oh." She frowned, like she wasn't sure what to say, then shrugged. "My mom says we've got too many people in our house to keep secrets."

That made me laugh. I'd been to her place. Five siblings, three dogs, and a parakeet. Chaos. But it was always fun over there.

"Can I see?" she asked, leaning over the open pages.

I slid it onto her lap as she flipped through the ink-filled pages.

"Clara, you're on drums today," Denver called out.

"What? No."

"Hey! I play drums!" Jamie shot back immediately, loud enough to cut through the noise.

"Clara needs a turn."

Jamie's smirk turned competitive, like she wanted to argue but also wanted to watch me fall on my face. "Go ahead. Let's see if you can even keep a beat."

I crossed my arms, glaring at Denver. "Fine. Just once."

He winked, and the boys scrambled into place. Eli hunched over the keyboard, Mason twirled a drumstick before handing it off to me, and Mark slouched into his bass.

I sat behind the kit, heart hammering like I was about to flunk a test.

"Hold the sticks like pencils," Denver coached. "Not too tight. Just follow me."

The song started. Loud. Messy. I missed the first few beats, but Denver nodded at me like I was killing it. By the third chorus, I actually caught on.

By the time we stopped, I was sweaty, laughing, and a little proud.

"Not bad," Jamie said, smirking again. "For your first time."

Her tone made it sound less like a compliment, more like a challenge.

I rolled my eyes and scribbled in my diary while the boys argued about the next cover. Denver gave in first, as always. He'd do anything to keep the peace.

I kept sneaking glances at him, still hearing his words.

You're an angel.

Nine

What We Don't Say

D ENVER
Present Day

The past few days blurred together: hospital chairs, white noise, and hope slipping through the cracks one hour at a time.

The house was quiet when I woke up. Too quiet. The smell of coffee cut through it as I stepped into the kitchen, where Dad sat at the table, his phone in hand like he could bring good news into existence.

He looked up when I came in. Since the night I messed my hand up, he'd been watching me. Not just because of Heleen. Because of me. He was worried.

Clara's been avoiding me since that night, too. We'd fallen asleep together, and it was innocent, but she acted like it wasn't. She slipped out of my room before I woke, leaving me with bandaged hands and more confusion that I couldn't shake. We hadn't talked about it since. Not the things we said. Not about her revelations. Not the way she breathed steady beside me, like it was the only thing holding me together.

I reached for a mug. Pain shot up my arm, and I hissed, the ceramic slipping against the counter.

"Still hurting?" Dad asked, not looking up.

I nodded.

"You know you could've torn a tendon, hit the wall wrong. Ended everything you've worked for."

He wasn't wrong. The reality of it had hit me the next morning. Playing was part of me. If I lost that, I didn't know what would be left.

Dad set his phone down. "I'm already losing sleep over Heleen. Don't make me worry about you, too."

I crossed the room and squeezed his shoulder. "I'm fine."

The words felt heavy in my mouth. As the days went by since Clara came home, I realized Dad didn't know about Clara and me. He valued honesty, and I doubt he would've kept something like that in. Which leaves me to realize that Heleen's been keeping this a secret.

But why? I mean, yes, having a relationship with my stepsister could be seen as forbidden or morally wrong, but to keep this in and allow her daughter to run away from it? It didn't make sense. None of it did.

I poured coffee and sat. His eyes stayed on me a moment longer than usual.

Footsteps came from the hall. My chest tightened before I even saw her.

Clara paused in the doorway like she wasn't sure she was allowed to enter. Her hair was tied back, loose strands falling anyway. She looked like herself, but not like the girl who held me in the dark the other night.

Her eyes found mine, and for a moment, the kitchen went still.

"Morning," she said softly.

"Morning."

Dad smiled. "You're up early."

"Didn't sleep much."

Yeah, me neither.

She passed close, and I caught the faint trace of lavender. Familiar. Like her.

"Coffee?" Dad asked.

"Tea," we both said at the same time.

She blinked, surprised. I didn't look away.

"She said it makes her heart race," I added. "It always felt like bad news was coming."

Her face shifted, quick and unguarded, before she nodded. "Still true."

Dad moved to the cabinets. "I think we've got that lemon ginger blend you liked."

"You remembered?"

"This house remembers the people who matter." He smiled. She returned it, small and brief.

I wanted to say I remembered too. All of it. Every detail.

She sat, curling into herself, fingers tracing the phone that seemed glued to her hands.

I sipped coffee and kept my eyes on the chipped edges of the mug, because if I kept staring at her, I'd give everything away.

Dad set the tea in front of her, and she thanked him without looking up. I was about to say something, anything, when a voice cut in.

"Sorry, hope I'm not interrupting," Jamie called as she walked in.

I leaned back in my chair. "Interrupting's your thing."

She hugged Clara and dropped into the seat beside her. Then she pointed at my hand. "I'd hate to see the other guy."

"Well, he was silent, cold, and made of drywall," I said.

Jamie winced. "Ouch."

Clara laughed, quick and quiet. My chest pulled tight. That laugh had been mine once.

Dad stood again. "Coffee, Jamie?"

I went back to staring at my mug, trying not to look at Clara's smile. Trying not to feel like a fool for missing it this much.

Jamie accepted coffee. Dad sat again. "I was just about to ask Clara about life in New York."

Clara stiffened.

"It's good," she said, eyes wavering from her tea to her phone. "Different from Seattle, but I like it."

"And work?"

"Marketing. Small firm."

Clipped answers. Just enough to keep us at a distance.

Dad smiled. "Any husband or boyfriend I should worry about?"

My grip tightened on the mug.

She shook her head. "Not really my focus."

Relief loosened my hand.

Jamie leaned forward. "And your kid?"

The room froze.

Clara's head snapped toward her. "Uh… yeah, I have a son."

Four words, and the air left my lungs. My eyes went to her, searching for her to meet mine. She didn't. That cut deeper than the words themselves.

Dad found his voice first. "Wow. A son. How old?"

Her fingers traced her mug. "He'll be six soon."

A whole life I didn't know about.

Dad whispered, "I've got a grandson." Pride in his voice.

Clara flinched at the word.

I looked at Jamie. My voice came low. "How'd you know?"

She shrugged. "With the amount of nieces and nephews I have, you start noticing how someone checks their phone. It's either a boyfriend or a kid."

Clara gave a bitter laugh. "Didn't know you were a detective."

Her bite caught me off guard. She hadn't wanted this out.

Jamie backtracked. "Sorry if I overstepped."

The tension stayed thick.

I broke it. "What's his name?"

She finally softened, but her eyes stayed away from mine. "Eric."

Dad asked the next question. "And his father?"

Her pause was long enough.

"His name is Ethan. We're not together. It was never that kind of story. Things were heavy back then. I couldn't breathe. He was there. He saw me when I didn't know how to be seen. Then Eric came, and we made it work."

The words tore at me. He saw her when I hadn't.

Dad nodded, impressed. "Sounds like a good man."

Jamie agreed too quickly.

"Yeah," I said, the words like ash on my tongue.

Clara's eyes flicked to me then, like she knew exactly how much it gutted me.

The doorbell rang. I shot out of my seat before anyone else could move.

"I'll get it."

I needed the air.

When I opened the door, I froze. "Mr. Monroe."

Clara's dad stood on the porch, tired eyes and hands shoved in his pockets.

"Is Clara here?"

"Yeah. Right this way."

I stepped into the kitchen just in time to hear Clara's chair scrape against the floor.

"Dad?"

Her voice broke, sharp as glass.

He didn't answer.

And Clara looked like she'd rather be anywhere but here.

Ten

Too Close, Too Far

CLARA

My dad's presence filled the doorway, making silence feel like a decision.

I hadn't expected to see him. I meant to, really. But meaning to and being ready are two different things. I'd kept in contact with him over the years, mostly through screens. He hated it. But after a while, he stopped pushing and accepted it. Like he accepted everything.

His smile was soft, but his eyes didn't match it.

He looked around the kitchen and gave a simple nod to everyone. Observing. I hated how he could read a room in seconds.

"It's good to see you again, James," Tom said, standing and offering a handshake.

Again?

"You too," Dad replied. "How is she?"

Always the better person, especially between him and my mother. I used to think kindness made him weak. I learned a long time ago that it just made him brave.

The buzz of conversation faded as the reality of what I'd revealed set in. *Eric. My son. My secret.*

My eyes found Jamie's. Something sharp stirred behind her usual warmth. I wasn't sure if it was curiosity or calculation. *Had I been that obvious?*

I dropped my gaze, only to find Denver's instead.

He leaned against the doorway, his good hand toying with a guitar pick. His eyes were sharp and unreadable, searching for something in me I wasn't sure I had left to give. He used to look at me like I was music. Now, it felt like he couldn't recognize the melody.

I looked away. My throat burned.

"Clara?"

My dad's voice pulled me back. He tilted his head, concern etched in his brows like he'd called my name more than once to get my attention.

Tom was back in his seat. *When did that happen?*

"Can we talk for a minute?" he asked.

"Sure." My voice barely cleared my throat.

I followed him out of the kitchen, my back prickling with every step. I felt seventeen again, scared, and one breath away from unraveling.

The morning air made chills run down my spine. The sun beamed down on us as birds chirped in the nearby trees.

We stopped at the edge of the driveway. Dad looked older. The kind that didn't show up on camera. Lines deeper and hair grayer.

"So… you're really here," he finally said, a ghost of a smile on his lips.

"I can't believe it either," I admitted with a short laugh.

He nodded as if he understood. Maybe he did.

"I meant to stop by. I just… haven't found the time."

"Why do you think I'm here?" he said. "How are you holding up, kiddo?"

I exhaled. "I'm fine. Just trying to get used to being back. Seeing her like that…"

I still haven't found the courage to speak to her. Even though she won't be able to talk back, it's just… I don't know. Being in the hospital room has been good enough so far.

Dad didn't hesitate. "Ah, come here." He pulled me into his arms. Warm. Fatherly. I let my head rest against his chest, holding back the tears burning behind my eyes. He'd held me like this the day I left, too. Like he didn't want to let go.

"I know you and your mom haven't always seen eye to eye, but she'll be okay. Maybe you two will get the chance to fix things between the two of you." Wishful thinking. "But you're not alone, you have me, your stepfather, and Denver."

But I was. Even standing in his arms, I'd never felt more alone.

"Thanks, Dad," I whispered, stepping back.

He studied me, as if he were searching for the right thing to say.

"So… Is Eric here with you?"

"No. He's in New York with Ethan."

His brow furrowed.

Then, quietly, "Are you even going to let him meet his family?"

My heart stuttered. *Family.*

"He has a family," I bit out, the words brittle as glass.

"You know what I mean, Clara." He threw his hands up. "Your mother is in a coma, you don't think it'll be good for Eric to be here, too? I know you said you didn't want her in your life for reasons I don't understand, but I'm here. You've been pulling away for years. I want to know my grandson. Claire wants to know her nephew. Not just through a phone screen."

Tears stung, but I turned away, swiping them before they could fall.

"I wasn't trying to hurt anyone," I said, voice low.

"I know. But don't you think he deserves to know where he comes from?"

He was breaking. And it was breaking me.

"I missed out on so many years with you," he continued. "Don't make me miss out on him, too."

"I can't." I shook my head. "I barely know where I stand in this family. I'm not dragging my son into this mess."

He inhaled slowly. "Clara, eventually, you'll have to stop running."

I clenched my jaw, a wave of anger washing over me. I wish people would stop acting like they know what's good for me.

"Thanks for stopping by, Dad." I turned and walked back toward the house. The weight in my chest didn't ease. Not even a little.

"Clara!"

I didn't stop.

I may have come back here, but it didn't mean everything was okay. And to bring Eric here? Where I could barely breathe without feeling like I'm doing it wrong, was out of the damn question.

I ignored the kitchen chatter and went straight for the stairs, two at a time. I needed out. Out of their voices. Their questions. Their eyes.

This was all a mistake.

I paced the old room upstairs. The idea of packing my suitcase and hightailing it out of there sounded like the best idea.

I'll just be running... again.

A soft, tentative knock halted my steps.

"Come in," I said, already bracing myself.

I half-expected my dad. It wasn't him.

Denver stepped in, quiet and unsure, and shut the door behind him. He didn't come closer.

"Are you okay?" he asked, eyes drawn tight with concern.

Some of the tension in my chest loosened. Just a little. Being in the same room with him after the other night had been confusing. Unless it was the hospital, I'd been avoiding it. Avoiding him.

"I'm okay," I lied, fingers clinging to the hem of my sleeve like it could anchor me.

His eyes studied mine, as if he could see past my lies.

I swallowed, waiting for him to call me on it.

Instead, he asked, "So... a son, huh?"

I let out a hollow laugh. "Yeah."

He was quiet, but his eyes didn't leave mine.

Then, gently. "I bet you're a great mother."

"You don't know that."

"I don't need to. I know you."

I shook my head, chest aching. "You knew who I was before I...before everything."

"I knew the girl who loved hard, who kept pinky promises, and would've burned the world down to protect someone she loved."

She didn't exist anymore.

"You're still her," he mumbled.

My stomach twisted. I didn't know what to say. How do you tell someone they're wrong when you want them to be right?

"You're still her," he repeated, like he wanted me to believe it.

I couldn't.

"You know, he's lucky to have you."

His words lodged in my chest. I laughed—small, broken. "No. I'm lucky to have him."

"I meant his father."

Everything in me went still. I blinked too quickly.

"How's your hand?" I asked, deflecting.

Talking about it felt wrong. I couldn't go there with him.

There was a time when the only guy I noticed was him. He'd been my first love, my first for many things. If I asked myself all those years ago if I'd be standing in front of Denver discussing another man, I would've laughed.

He lifted his injured hand slightly, gauze still wrapped tightly around it. "Nothing I can't handle."

This was easier territory.

"That's your playing hand."

"So, everyone keeps reminding me. Stupid, right? Doesn't matter, anyway."

"Why?"

"My priorities have changed," he said simply.

My mother. Of course.

"Did you ever make it to the big world?" I asked, forcing lightness.

He smirked. "If you stick around, you'd see the guys and me are pretty big here. We get slots to open for some artists, and hold a few shows on our own. I teach, too. Not exactly John Mayer status."

I cracked a laugh. "Surprised he hasn't filed a restraining order."

"God forbid a guy be a fan."

"You dedicated your life to him," I deadpanned.

"He makes heartbreak sound like a lullaby," he shrugged, "who could've resisted that?"

I folded my arms. "You were a sucker for sad songs."

"And you always pretended you weren't."

I raised a brow. "I'm not the one who wrote *'Empty Room'* after getting grounded."

He grinned, the sound of his laugh making something inside my chest do back flips. "A masterpiece."

"You rhymed pain with game, Denver."

He stepped closer, playfully. "It was symbolic."

"Of what? Xbox withdrawal?"

"Exactly."

The distance between us disappeared before I noticed it.

I meant to keep it casual, but he was so close I could see the flecks of gold in his green eyes, the scar on his jaw.

My breath stalled as I felt the red creeping into my cheeks. Memory tugged at me like a thread.

I didn't move

Neither did he.

"You always did get under my skin," I whispered.

"You never told me to stop."

"I didn't know how," I admitted. "Back then, you were everything and nothing."

"And now?"

Now felt dangerous.

The kind that twisted in my stomach and refused to be ignored.

"I don't know." My voice came out in a whisper, his frame eating up the rest of the distance between us.

"Clara," he whispered, so close. *So damn close.*

My name on his tongue sounded like a man starved. His eyes devoured me, lips parted enough that I could almost taste the coffee on his breath as it ghosted over mine.

Something in me snapped. I didn't mean to lean in, but I did.

So close.

And then…

Knock knock.

I recoiled as if a sire bond had just snapped, like whatever invisible force tying me to him had finally broken.

Denver jerked back, too, like the contact burned him.

Not again.

Panic surged.

I could not fall back into his arms. Not now. Not when everything-everything-could come undone.

I didn't chance a look at him as shame filled me. My breathing picked up when another knock came to the door.

Tom and Jamie were right downstairs, and I was…

"Clara, are you in there?" Jamie's muffled voice was loud on the other side.

My heart raced.

I felt a sickening feeling in my stomach as the door slowly opened.

Even though Denver was across the room, looking out the window, I still felt like a child being caught with my hand stuffed inside a cookie jar after I'd been told not to touch it.

"Oh, there you are," Jamie said, a tight smile tugging at her lips.

I swallowed, shifting from one foot to the other.

Neither Denver nor I said anything. I wondered if he was freaking out like I was.

I tried smiling at her, but it felt robotic, plastic, even.

Her eyes shifted from me to him, brows knitted together as if she was trying to piece something together.

"I hope I'm not interrupting," she intoned.

She's been doing a lot of that lately.

"You're fine," I laugh, shrugging it off with a wave of my hand.

Definitely not guilty at all.

"Oh, and Denver." She pulled out her phone. "Can you please get back to Sadie? She's been blowing up my phone, asking how you're doing."

Jamie must've noticed the confusion on my face, because she continued.

"Denver's girlfriend," she laughed.

I opened my mouth, but the words got stuck in my throat. My throat, which had gone dry at the mere mention of a *girlfriend.*

After we'd just almost kissed? Jealousy coiled in my stomach. I had no right to be.

"Don't be ridiculous, Jamie," Denver finally spoke, tone filled with boredom.

I still didn't turn to face him, the robotic smile still playing on my lips, as Jamie didn't take her eyes off me.

"Sadie's in the band. When I found out about Heleen, I told everyone I needed some time, space. Been off the grid since." It felt like he was offering *me* an explanation. "And she's *not* my girlfriend, Jamie," he emphasized.

"Oh, sure," she said sarcastically, folding her arms across her chest. "Anyway, do you mind if I speak to Clara alone?"

I eyed her, partly relieved to not be in the same space as him right now.

"Yeah, I was leaving anyway."

Then, he was gone.

"I really hope I didn't overstep earlier." She closes the gap between us, placing a hand on my shoulder.

"You didn't. I'm just very protective of my son, and I haven't had a chance to bring it up to everyone yet. It just... caught me by surprise, that's all."

I squeeze her hand over my shoulder for reassurance.

It was true. I didn't expect to mention my son and Ethan like that. I didn't expect to mention them at all.

"Well, I'm sorry either way. I'm surprised you didn't tell us. Well, since we talk every so often."

"I know, I'm sorry. I've been a shitty friend, haven't I?" I joked.

"No. I may not know the entire story behind your leaving, so I don't hold anything against you. I just hope we can catch up while you're here. It'll be like old times."

"We will. Thanks for understanding."

I released her hand, and she moved to leave the room before I stopped her.

"We're good, right?" I asked.

"Of course we are. Why wouldn't we be?" Her head tilted to the side as she eyed me.

"Right," I nodded.

Jamie lingered after her apology, eyes flicking toward the hallway.

"A few people just stopped by," she said. "Close friends of the family. They brought flowers, food, and the usual. You know how people get when they don't know what else to do."

Her voice carried a teasing note, but it didn't ease the knot in my stomach. People. Downstairs. People I hadn't seen in eight years.

By the time we reached the kitchen, voices filled the air, warm but heavy. Tom stood near the counter, thanking everyone as if gratitude alone could keep him standing.

How long had Denver and I been upstairs that I missed the sound of an entire band of people? So many familiar faces.

Mrs. Greene, the next-door neighbor with fifteen cats, pulled me into a hug before I had the chance to dodge. "Clara, sweetheart. It's been too long."

I forced a smile. "Yeah, it has."

The Carters pressed a casserole into Tom's hands, their words soft and rehearsed. "We're praying for Heleen's recovery."

Others offered flowers, quick touches to my arm, words I couldn't fully process. They were familiar, but I felt like a stranger among them, their sympathy pressing down on me more than comforting.

I kept my thanks short, my smile tighter.

Across the room, Denver leaned against the wall, silent. His eyes found mine once, then again. That look made it impossible to forget the closeness upstairs.

Jamie was beside him, too close. Her laugh brushed against his shoulder, her hand grazing his arm as she whispered something I couldn't hear. My chest tightened, though I didn't let it show.

Tom's voice filled the silence. "The doctors are hopeful. They've stopped the bleeding. We just have to wait."

Denver stayed quiet, his jaw rigid. His hand toyed with the bandage like he couldn't keep still. For a moment, I wondered if he was thinking what I was. If his father knew. If my mother had carried this secret alone all these years.

My phone buzzed in my pocket. *Ethan.*

I found Denver's eyes one last time before I slipped toward the stairs, before anyone could stop me.

By the time I answered, my chest ached with relief.

"Mom?" Eric's voice came through, bright and steady.

I sank onto the edge of the bed, closing my eyes. "Hey, baby."

Eleven

Half-Finished Songs

⚛

DENVER

The sun was low by the time I pulled into the driveway, bleeding gold through the trees and making everything look softer than it felt. I killed the engine and sat there for a second, fingers still curling around the steering wheel.

I'd stopped by the hospital earlier. Didn't stay long, just enough to drop off food and check in on Dad. And Clara, who'd been ignoring me since our near-kiss two days ago.

I let out a breath and rubbed my thumb along the callus on my index finger. She shouldn't still have this effect on me. So, why was I replaying our almost-kiss like I was a teenager about to score for the first time? It should've made sense. Eight years was a long time. People move on. People grow up. Now, Clara had a kid and someone whom she cared about deeply.

I got out of the car and headed straight to the garage. Well, studio. When I came back home after college, Dad had it renovated into a studio. I planned to stay in Florida after I got my degree at FU and set something up myself. By that time, adulting should've meant moving out, but something kept me home, so I came back. I had my space in the big house we lived in, a studio to work on my music, so it wasn't an issue. I loved being close to Dad and

Heleen, anyway. Most of the time, I was out traveling with the band, so I was barely home.

Dad's words replayed in my head. *Don't stop everything just because Heleen's in the hospital.* He didn't say it like a demand. Just a reminder. A quiet push to keep living when it's easier to stall out.

The studio smelled of wood and old sound. Photos filled the walls with memories of being on the road with the guys and Sadie. There was a leather couch that was a little worn, but held so many memories of late-night writing and practicing that it never crossed my mind to get rid of it. A freshly made bed, because I did crash here on occasion.

I flipped the lights on, grabbed my acoustic from the wall, and sat on the stool. My hand was still messed up, but less so than the morning after my caveman-like wall-punching.

I took out my phone and tapped open FaceTime. If I didn't reach out now, I'd talk myself out of it, which would lead to these animals barging in and making sure I wasn't dead or drowning myself in my sorrows.

The screen rang twice before Eli's face popped up, half-lit, as always, surrounded by lyric pages and empty mugs.

"You good?" he asked, without a hello.

"I'm here, at least."

Mason leaned into the frame from the other side of the couch, hoodie up, eating cereal out of a mixing bowl. "He lives."

"I thought we agreed not to let you disappear for more than ten days at a time," Eli added.

I gave them a tight smile. "I should've called. Sorry."

They didn't press. They didn't need to. They knew how I felt about family. We grew up together. From little boys making noise in the middle of Eli's living room to living out our dream. They knew the weight behind my silence.

Sadie's face appeared next, her curls wild, and her expression serious. "Hey."

We met her a few years ago when she crashed an open mic night and left the crowd silent. But she'd stuck, fit herself right in the middle like she always belonged. She added just what we needed, and her range was ridiculous.

I'd be lying if I denied being drawn to her when we first met. We may have gone on a date or two, but that was as far as we went. I didn't know where Jamie got the impression about Sadie being my girlfriend when she knew all of this. Sadie was cool and beautiful, but you never shit where you eat. Plus, she doesn't do it for me. It doesn't stop her from flirting here and there.

"Eli's mom saw your dad at the hospital," Mason said. "You okay?"

I hesitated. "She's stable, so, yeah."

They nodded. Not much to say when someone you love is stuck between waking and not.

"We're here for you if you need anything. Remember that," Eli added.

"Thanks, guys."

"And don't worry. We've been holding down the fort. We carried that last gig with pure chaos and charisma," Sadie added, pulling a laugh out of me.

"I don't doubt that at all."

Mason snorted. "Sadie carried that gig. I was so stressed I forgot the second verse of Winterlights and just repeated the first."

"That was a creative choice," Eli said.

I reached for my guitar, keeping my hand out of frame. They'd have a fit if they knew I was being careless. "You guys worked on anything new?"

Eli perked up. "Got something in D minor. Feels like a bruised kind of love song. Might be trash. Sadie's been working on harmonies."

It was fair to say that I was a sucker for love songs. Clara had been right.

"It's not trash," Sadie chimed in. "It's just not finished."

Mason was already digging around for the chord sheet. "Want us to send it over?"

I adjusted the guitar in my lap. The weight of it, familiar, grounding. "Yeah. Let's see what you've got."

When they sent it over, I pulled up the PDF. The chords were rough, the lyrics a work in progress, but there was something there. A heartbeat. A question hung in the last line.

I strummed once. It was difficult with my hand, but I strummed again.

Felt rusty, sure, but not gone. I played through the progression, filling in the gaps with muscle memory and instinct. Halfway through, Sadie started humming, Eli added the missing line, and Mason tapped out a soft rhythm against his cereal bowl.

It wasn't a gig. It wasn't perfect. But it was us. And it felt like breathing again.

I don't know how long we played. Long enough for my fingers to remember the calluses they used to wear like armor. Long enough for the song to shape itself into something that almost felt finished.

I leaned back against the couch after we hung up, the guitar in my lap, my head tilted to the ceiling. I wasn't planning on moving anytime soon.

I jolted at the sound of a soft knock on the door.

I set the guitar down, pushed to my feet, and moved to the door. I hesitated a second before opening the door.

And there she was.

Standing on the other side, arms wrapped around herself, the light above cast her in a soft amber. She couldn't be more beautiful. Her hair was pulled back; A usual style for her, but messy, like she'd been running her hands through it. She looked up, eyes wide, caught somewhere between nerves and whatever it was that lived between us now.

"Hey," she murmured, a slight blush creeping onto her cheeks. Just like they did when we almost kissed.

I gripped the door frame. "Hey."

She glanced past me toward the glow of the studio. "Wow, you really styled this place up."

I nodded. "Yeah."

Silence stretched between us, heavy but not hostile.

"I came back from the hospital and heard the music."

"You… You wanna come in?"

Her eyes widened, just slightly. "You sure?"

"Yeah." I stepped aside for her to step in.

Her eyes roamed the room, landing on cluttered shelves, tangled cords, and the worn-out rug in the middle of the floor. Then her gaze lifted to the walls, to all the photos scattered. Some framed, some taped up crooked.

She moved closer to one, tracing the edge of a picture with her fingers. "I remember this night," she said, in almost a whisper. "The rec center show. You broke a string during the first song and kept playing."

"Didn't have a choice. I was trying to impress a girl."

Her shoulders tensed as her eyes flicked to mine, but she didn't smile.

Instead, she turned to the far corner of the room and stopped.

I knew exactly what she was looking at.

The guitar. Sunburst finish, slightly worn from years of use. The gold ink was still visible on the body: *Play the hell out of it—J.M.*

"You kept it?" She whispered, sounding surprised. She stepped closer, fingers hovering just above the surface. "That was your eighteenth birthday."

"You told me it took you six months and three different email aliases to get a response."

"I wanted it to be perfect. You were so happy."

I didn't say anything. Truthfully, I hadn't just been happy that night. I'd been seen.

By her.

My obsession with John Mayer when I was younger needed to be studied. But she found a way to surprise me with a guitar signed by him. I was ecstatic; I have no idea how she managed it.

She finally turned back toward me, arms folded across her chest.

"About last night…"

I waited.

"I shouldn't have let us get that close."

The blush creeping back on her face said otherwise, but my chest tightened at her admission.

"I wasn't thinking clearly," she continued. "There was so much happening, and God, Denver, I missed you, but—" Her voice trailed off. "We can't go there. Not again."

I nodded slowly, even though every part of me wanted to argue. "I get it."

I didn't.

"I think we should just…" she hesitated. "Try to be friends. Can we do that?"

The plea in her eyes begged me to agree. When every part of my being wanted to tell her that it was impossible. It was impossible to be this close to her when I was still in love with her. Impossible that she was this close in my grasp, and I didn't want to let her go again.

The last thought had me nodding in agreement. It hurt, but I couldn't lose her again. Even if it meant we would try to be a family again. "Yeah. We can try." It pained me to say, but the relief in her eyes told me it was the right thing to do.

She let out a breath as if she'd been holding it for hours. Then, with a small voice, she said, "I don't want to talk. Not tonight. I just want to sit. Can I do that? Just… listen to you play like old times?"

I gestured to the couch. "I have the best seat in the house."

She smiled. She crossed the room and sat, pulling her knees up and tucking her legs beneath her.

I picked up the guitar she gave me all those years ago, ran my thumb across the strings, then started to play. I fought against the slight pain in my hand. The way she relaxed into the couch, like this was the first time she'd been since coming back, was worth all the pain.

So, I kept playing. Nothing big. Nothing bold. Just the kind of song you play for someone who already knows where your ghosts live.

I didn't look up at her when I played. I didn't need to. I felt her there, her eyes on me as if I were her focus.

That was enough. She was here. There wasn't any tension, just contentment.

When I did finally look up, her eyes were closed, and she looked… at peace. I stood watching her for a moment.

She had no idea how much she wrecked me by just being here.

I grabbed the old throw blanket from the back of the couch and draped it over her slowly, carefully, not to wake her. Her nose scrunched up for a second, as if she felt it, but she didn't stir.

I stood there longer than I should've, heart pounding loudly in my chest.

Brain too loud in my skull.

Friends.

That's what she said she wanted.

That's what I said I *could* be.

I was so screwed.

How do you stay friends with the only person who's ever made your heart sound like music?

Twelve

Unsteady Ground

CLARA

The first thing I noticed when I woke up was the blanket. I didn't remember falling asleep, but Denver's voice and his playing lulled me into a peaceful state. It was some of the best sleep I've gotten in a few weeks, aside from the couch's stiffness.

The next thing I noticed was that I was alone in the studio. It was warm with early morning light, the kind that slid in gently.

I sat up, rubbing the side of my face where it had been pressed into the couch cushion. The blanket slid off my shoulders, pooling in my lap just as my phone started ringing.

I rushed to pull it out of my pocket as if I were expecting the most important call of my life.

When I swiped to answer the FaceTime call, a bright smile greeted me, almost as bright as Ethan's ginger hair. Hair slicked in place and dressed in his uniform, Ethan shuffled around on the other end.

"Morning," he grumbled.

"Daddy! Daddy! Is that Mommy?" a cheeky voice squeaked, making my smile widen immediately.

I almost got whiplash as the phone shook before my sweet boy's face appeared on the screen.

"Hi, honey," I cooed.

His smile was big, showing his missing bottom tooth.

"Are you coming home today?" he asked, voice hopeful.

I swallowed. "Soon, honey."

My chest pinched at the slight drop in his smile. I should've been there. Home.

"I had cereal!" he declared instead. "And Dad made me pour the cereal all by myself."

"Wow, that's amazing," I said, smiling so hard it almost hurt. "Did you make a mess?"

As long as he was smiling, I was fine.

"A little one," he giggled.

Ethan took the phone back. As if he could've sensed my guilt, he said, "He's good. Happy. You don't have to worry."

I sank into the couch. Ethan was my anchor. He didn't just save lives as a firefighter, but he also saved mine.

"I'm about to drop him off at school and head into work. I'll call you later," he continued..

"Love you, Mommy!" Eric yelled.

"Love you, too, honey. Have a good day at school."

He mumbled, *"I will."*

"Clara," Ethan called before I could hang up.

I didn't miss the pinch in his brows and the sad smile he offered me.

"You'll be fine. I love you."

I closed my eyes. "I love you, too." Then I hung up before I could break down. I've been trying to avoid that a lot lately.

I dropped the phone onto the couch and leaned forward, elbows on my knees, hands pressed to my face.

It wasn't just that I missed my son, though I did, painfully so. It was the guilt of knowing he was being raised in a house full of half-truths. Dad was right to call me out. Eric had a whole family he didn't know about because of *my* mistakes. He knew about his grandfather and the aunt he'd only seen through a phone screen. He was too young to understand, but I'd tried explaining the tidbits of it. Enough for a child to comprehend.

And my mother.

Each day I spent at the hospital felt like I was being pricked by needles. I haven't sat by her bedside or held her hand while she lay unconscious. I kept telling myself I was protecting myself, that she wouldn't know I was there. But deep down, I knew the truth.

I couldn't face her. Not after everything.

Yet, I was slowly letting myself fall back into orbit around Denver. *Again.*

I tasted gravel when I said, "Can we be friends?" last night. There was a sliver of hope that he'd tell me *no*. To rush me and claim the kiss we'd almost had.

The one I couldn't stop thinking about.

I'd almost kissed him. It would've been so easy. One more inch closer. One moment of weakness.

But it wouldn't have been a weakness for me.

It would've been everything I'd been trying to suppress since I landed back in Seattle. All the history, the longing, the love I never got to accept or enjoy. Not openly, at least.

A big part of me was relieved when he agreed to be friends. I couldn't suck him into the darkness that surrounded me. I was more screwed up than anyone could imagine.

It's one of the reasons I've not really dated throughout the years. Aside from Eric coming first, and some guys not liking the idea of how close Ethan and I were, even though I'd explained it was because we shared a son. Eric was the world to both of us, but some men didn't like it when the attention wasn't solely on them. It never bothered me. My heart had been stolen a long time ago for me to dwell on anyone else not sticking around.

Sighing, I stood, folded the blanket, and headed for the door. I didn't have the right to feel sorry for myself.

The main house was quiet when I stepped in until I heard loud laughter coming from the kitchen. I followed the smell before the sound. *Bacon. Eggs.* My stomach grumbled.

Denver's back was to me in front of the stove, his good hand stirring the sizzling bacon, while he laughed at a female voice coming from his phone propped up on the counter.

I almost backed away not to intrude. Was it the Sadie girl? The thought hit like a punch.

Just then, he turned, and the smile was gone.

"Hey, I'll call you guys back," he said before ending the call. "Morning."

"Hey, good morning."

The smile he gave eased the confusion I was just battling. *For now.*

It was soft and welcoming.

Friends.

He quirked a brow. "Breakfast?"

"Yeah, sure."

He tapped the tiled counter. "Take a seat."

I did and watched as he maneuvered around the kitchen.

"Since when do you cook?" I asked when a plate with bacon, eggs, a toasted English muffin, and tea was put in front of me.

"When you're on the road for days on end, with no restaurant in sight for the next ten miles, you learn to fend for yourself."

I laughed and dug in as he did the same across from me.

We ate. Talked about nothing for a while. The weather. The town. His band—he said they were playing in town soon, and he was looking forward to it since he missed their last show. About Eric and my job.

It was almost like we were us again.

Almost.

There was a lightness to it that felt fragile, like it might snap if either of us looked too closely. So we didn't. We kept it safe, kept it surface level.

I pushed my empty plate forward and started to stand. "I'll clean it up."

"I got it," he said, reaching for it.

His fingers brushed mine. Not intentionally, but just for a second.

But it was enough.

Just skin against skin, the lightest touch, and suddenly I was burning all over again. His hand lingered a fraction too long before pulling away, and I didn't dare look up. I couldn't.

Because I knew if I did, I'd see the way his jaw had gone tight. The way his forearm flexed as he picked up the plate, tattoos shifting along the lines of his muscles like they were breathing with him.

I swallowed hard and turned to the sink, pretending to adjust something on the counter. My hands were shaking. *God, why were my hands shaking?*

* * *

Later that afternoon, we found ourselves in his truck, windows down, the dusty sun pouring over us. Seattle's own *Fever Light* song drifted through the speakers, the kind of music that felt like it belonged in a moment frozen in time. Denver and the guys weren't just good. They were magnetic.

I hadn't planned on going with him to the grocery store.

I'd come back into the kitchen for my phone after rushing out of there before I did or said something I'd regret, only to find him already pulling on his jacket, muttering about restocking the fridge so Tom wouldn't have to worry about it.

And somehow, I ended up in the passenger seat, clutching a grocery list, with the kitchen moment hovering in the back of my mind. My gaze kept drifting to his hand on the wheel. Fingers curled, knuckles faintly pale, and each time, an illicit flicker ignited something I tried to suppress.

I was apprehensive about being seen in town. The notion of running into people from my past unsettled me, like ghosts brushing shoulders. But the moment we stepped into the grocery store, that anxiety dissolved under the fluorescent lights and hometown nostalgia.

Everyone seemed to stop Denver at every aisle we turned down. Giving him and *Fever Lights* praise.

When I tossed a grape at his shoulder in the produce aisle, it bounced harmlessly off, and he smirked without looking back.

"You're such a liar," I said lightly.

He shrugged, scanning a package of chicken. "What?"

"You're absolutely on John Mayer's level."

I may have done some late-night stalking on social media. Their fan base wasn't just passionate, it was ravenous. Ten states. Articles. A dedicated column in the local paper.

I threw another grape, but this time he caught it, casually, like he'd expected it. His smirk deepened.

"What can I say? I'm a humble guy," he said, voice rich with amusement.

Then, without taking his eyes off me, he brought the grape to his mouth.

The simple motion snatched the breath from my lungs. My pulse quickened, and I felt the warm juice oozing between my clenched fingers. I'd crushed the remaining grapes in my hand.

I was losing it, and he knew exactly what he was doing.

"Clara!"

I jumped at the familiar voice. Guilt flared, irrational, but burning. Watching your stepbrother eat a grape shouldn't feel criminal. But when your thoughts weren't exactly sibling-approved…

I turned.

Jamie's mother was pushing a cart toward us. Jamie was in tow behind her. I hadn't seen her in what? Eight years. Mrs. Evans looked elegant and polished, and her smile widened the closer she got.

"Mrs. Evans," I greeted, shoving the ruined grapes into my back pocket. *I'll deal with it later.*

"Gosh, I heard you were in town. Had to see it to believe it. You've grown so beautiful." She sidestepped around the cart and pulled me into a hug.

Jamie just hung back, arms crossed over her chest.

She pulled back, her eyes flicking over me with almost maternal pride. "How are you kids holding up?" she asked, glancing between Denver and me with something between sympathy and curiosity.

"Good," we both said in unison. I almost winced.

Mrs. Evans offered a pained smile. "You're all in my prayers." Her brows knitted, her lips tilted downward in a carefully composed expression of grief.

If there was anything I hated, it was pity.

I gave her a tight smile.

"And you, mister, we'll be seeing you Friday. Everyone's looking forward to it," she said, walking to Denver and patting his cheek.

Thirteen

The First Time We Fell

DENVER
14 Years Old
I shoved off the wall once Clara walked out of her class.

Walking her to class was just… what we did. No one told me to. It was something that fell in line, like a step. She waited for me even on the days she pretended to be annoyed by it. She always did.

"You know," she said, tugging her books closer to her chest, "someday I'm going to grow strong enough to carry my own stuff."

I looked down at the stack of her books in my arms. "Not today, though, right?"

"Obviously, not today." She laughed as we weaved through the students in the hallway. "Wouldn't want you to feel useless."

"Wow. Such kindness."

She bumped my shoulder. "It's a gift."

We reached her locker, and she spun the dial, hair falling across her cheek as she focused. I leaned against the locker next to hers, already half zoning out. Watching her do normal things, like opening a locker or complaining about math homework, was weirdly calming. If everything else around us was a mess, at least this wasn't.

"Denver," a voice sang out behind us.

I didn't even have to look to know who it was. Kayla strutted down the hall with her usual entourage. Some girl followed her everywhere she went, even to the bathroom, and Jamie trailed behind her, already looking like she regretted the decision to tag along.

"We're heading off campus for lunch," Kayla said, twirling the gum she was chewing around her fingers. "You coming?"

I shook my head. "Nah."

Her eyes slid toward Clara, who had not even turned around. "Still hanging out with your little sister?"

The dig was uncalled for, but that's who Kayla was. She wanted to be the center of attention. If no one complimented how good she looked in a new outfit, her hair, and other unnecessary stuff, she'd go out of her way to make sure all eyes were on her. When I noticed that last year, I distanced myself from her.

My fist gripped around the books I was still holding when I noticed Clara stiffen, her fingers pausing on her locker door.

Jamie glanced sideways at Kayla and muttered, "Knock it off."

She just shrugged, that knowing, smug look on her face. "Whatever."

They walked off without waiting for a response. Jamie cast a look back at me with this quiet, apologetic look before disappearing behind them.

I looked over at Clara just as she slammed her locker shut.

"Don't mind her, angel," I leaned over and whispered.

She turned slowly, jaw tight. "Stop calling me that. I'm not a kid." She snatched the books out of my hand.

I wanted to crack a joke about her being a year younger than me… but the furious look on her face told me it wouldn't go over well. Though I was taken aback. I'd called her that numerous times without receiving this reaction.

"Whoa, where is this coming from?" I questioned, confused.

"Angel." Her voice was sharp. "Why do you keep calling me that, anyway?"

Her face pulled into a scowl, but it was both adorable and funny.

I hesitated. Then shrugged a little. "I call you that because…" I trailed off, scratching my head. "Because when you're around, the noise stops. You're the only part of my life that feels like a song instead of static."

Her eyes shot open, the scowl deviating into confusion, like she didn't expect something real to come out of my mouth.

For a second, I let it hang there. Just long enough to feel like I'd said too much.

I cleared my throat and added, "Plus, you kind of have that innocent, floaty look. You know. If angels had sarcastic comebacks and permanent scowls."

The corner of her mouth twitched like she didn't know if she was supposed to smile or punch me.

She looked away fast; her cheeks flushed. "I have to get to class."

"Yeah...okay." I stepped back to give her room.

She turned and walked off without another word, her pace so fast, she almost ran into a kid.

I stood there, watching her go, trying to pretend I hadn't just said something I meant way too much.

I didn't see Clara for the rest of the day, deciding I'd give her a little space after freaking her out.

It messed with me more than I wanted to admit. We were always together. Between classes, after school, even on weekends, I practiced with the guys. It didn't matter where; we just were. She was my best friend.

By the time I got home, I couldn't sit still. I grabbed my songwriting book and went to her room. Not bothering to knock, I wrapped my hand around the knob and peeked my head in.

She was on her bed, legs crossed, with her book scattered in front of her. Her eyes darted up at the sound of my arrival, but she said nothing.

I held up the book. "Peace offering."

She gave a small shrug. "Depends on if it's any good."

She smiled, and the strange distance that had settled between us faded into nothing.

I sat on the edge of her bed and opened it. She leaned in, close enough that her hair brushed my arm. I flipped to a safe page.

She reached to grab it, about to flip the page.

"Not that one," I said quickly, flipping back.

She squinted. "What's that one?"

"Nothing."

"Then, let me see."

"No."

She lunged across me, reaching for the book. I leaned away, but she caught the edge.

"Clara, seriously."

"If it's bad, I'll only make fun of you a little," she said, half-laughing.

My heart hammered in my chest. I wasn't worried about her thinking the song was bad, but worried that she'd see what I wrote.

We tussled, knees bumping, arms overlapping, as we laughed, out of breath. She crawled over me, trying to wrestle the book free. It was stupid and loud.

She stopped moving when her struggle seemed futile. Her hair had fallen over one side of her face. It was wild and messy, but I didn't care. I couldn't stop looking at her. Her eyes weren't the same. Not like when we were laughing over cereal or making dumb jokes in the backseat of Dad's car. This was different. Suddenly, everything inside me flipped, like I'd touched a wire I wasn't supposed to. I didn't see my stepsister or my best friend. I saw… her. And I didn't know what to do with it.

My eyes widened when she leaned in. Barely, but just enough. Just enough for her lips to brush mine; soft and unsure, like she wasn't even sure she was doing it right.

It wasn't long, or anything more than lips brushing lips. But for a first kiss? It made me feel like I couldn't breathe.

It was over before it started.

Bang.

Her head slammed into mine when she pulled back. Sharp, stupid pain exploded across my forehead, making my hand jump to it immediately.

Ouch.

She gasped and scrambled back, limbs tangling in the bed sheet as she toppled onto the floor with a grunt.

I sat up, blinking. "Clara!"

She flinched. Not from the pain. From *me*.

One hand went to her forehead. The other shoved against the floor as she backed away. Her chest rose and fell too quickly, and her eyes, when they met mine, looked glossy and filled with tears. Her cheeks were a bright red.

She didn't speak, just stared; Mouth open and breathing like she'd just run a marathon.

Then, barely above a whisper, "Don't."

I froze.

Tears gathered at the corners of her eyes, but she didn't blink them away. She just sat there, stunned, shoulders curled in as if she was trying to disappear.

Her lips moved before the sound came. "Oh my God."

She shook her head, as if she were trying to undo the kiss we shared.

I reached out, just enough to let her know I was still there. That I wasn't mad. That I was just as confused as she was.

She pulled back. "Go."

My hand dropped.

Her voice cracked the second time. "Please."

That word hit harder than the headbutt.

"It's okay. You don't have to be upset," I tried cooing, but her head just shook left to right.

I stood, knees wobbling a little, but I didn't look at her again. I couldn't. I could've stopped her before she kissed me, but I didn't.

The hallway was too quiet when I stepped into it. Every step felt like I was being weighed down. My chest was tight, too tight, like I couldn't get a full breath. Like I might throw up or cry. Or both.

I touched my forehead as I descended the stairs. I stared at the little smear of her lip balm on my thumb. Cherry or strawberry, or something stupid. Something normal. But none of this was normal.

She kissed me.

And then she looked at me like I was the worst thing in the world.

I was grateful Dad and Heleen weren't home. I didn't know how I'd explain my need to get out of the house, as if I'd just left the scene of a crime.

Clara avoided me for weeks. At school, at home. She spent weekends at her dad's. Dinners turned quiet, with Dad and Heleen carrying all the conversation.

It gutted me.

Fourteen

Promises

CLARA
Present Day
"You want me to come in with you?"

I hesitated as Denver waited for an answer. Parked outside my dad's house, I debated whether to leave or get it over with. He'd been calling since he showed up at the house. I'd been ignoring him since our disagreement.

The more time I spent with Denver over the past few days, I've been thinking about the reasons why I came home. Yes, I came back because my mother was in a coma, but I wasn't just here for her. It's shitty to think that it took a terrible situation like this for me to return.

Everyone needs a family. Whether it's the one we were born into or the one we create for ourselves.

"No," I said, smiling at him. "You need to get ready for your show. I'll take an Uber to the venue when I'm done here."

"I'll be here," he assured me.

I didn't fight him on it, just nodded, and got out of the car.

Ethan was the only family I had over the years. His family took me in as their own, and for a long time, it felt like enough. Him, Eric, and me against the world. But coming back here made me realize there had always been a missing piece. Tom welcomed me back like I hadn't slipped out of their lives without a word, his kindness as steady as ever. With Denver, we had unfinished business, but somehow the weight of that felt lighter these past few days. Between late-night drives when neither of us could sleep, coffee runs that stretched into hours of talking, and him making me laugh when the hospital walls pressed too close, being with him felt natural in a way I'd almost forgotten.

I hadn't expected us to fall back into this rhythm. It wasn't intentional, but we did. And as much as it should've unsettled me, it was also a reminder of what could've been. I couldn't keep pulling away from dad when all he had done was try.

My guard was still up, but Denver had given me the push I needed when I eventually told him about Dad and I's disagreement.

The glasshouse I'd built around myself was bound to shatter. But I knew that before I decided to get on a plane and come back to Seattle.

It only took two knocks for Dad to come to the door. Even though I told him I was coming, he still looked surprised to see me. He masked it with a smile before pulling me into his arms. My hesitation washed away when little arms wrapped around my waist.

My dad remarried a few years after my mother did. It was refreshing to escape the arguments whenever I visited their house. It wasn't like the last few years of their marriage. Claire, my little sister, was born when I was fifteen. It was weird having that big age gap, but I got over it.

I didn't even get a word in as she tugged my arms behind her as she pulled me into the house, both of us laughing in tow.

We had a nice chat, Dad and I, ignoring any previous disagreements. I always admired that about him. His ability to let things go and not prod. Tom was like him in a sense. Growing up, Tom didn't hover or scold us. He consistently offered support, allowed us our independence, and always made us feel loved. That's why I took a liking to him so quickly, compared to my mother. Well, she definitely showed Denver love.

When I mentioned Denver was outside, Dad practically dragged him inside. It made me feel bad that I left him out there waiting. In a way, I felt like it would just cause questions from Dad that I didn't want to answer.

We sat around the table and talked as Claire sputtered question after question his way, and I couldn't stop my eyes from lingering on him too much.

Why are you so tall? Where do you live? Why do you have so many tattoos? She all but poked and prodded his arm like a detective.

It tugged at something in my chest I didn't want to name yet as I watched him entertain her. He smiled, ruffled her hair until she was having a laughing fit, and answered every question, shooting out his own. It was… nice. He was nice.

I didn't miss the wary glares Dad shot my way whenever my eyes lingered on Denver too long. Or the way I propped my elbow on the table, holding my head up as I smiled, seeing him like that.

By the time we left, I'd left Dad's on a promise that I'd bring Eric here. I wanted to crazy glue my mouth the moment I agreed.

When we reached the venue, I sat frozen in the passenger seat. Not because of the crowd trickling in, but because, inevitably, I'd run into people from my past.

"Here." Denver reached into the back seat and held up a T-shirt with his face plastered on it. It was a photo of mid-performance.

I covered my mouth to hide a laugh. "What am I, a groupie now?"

He hummed. "I like 'fan' better."

He joked casually as if he wasn't supposed to be here an hour ago to run through a practice. Instead, he had spent the evening at my Dad's place. He didn't even seem phased by the possibility of being late.

I swatted his shoulder, and he caught my hand.

"I'm kidding," he smiled. "You're not that."

His thumb moved absentmindedly across my palm.

I inhaled his warm touch against my skin, as heat crawled up my neck. I bit down on my lip to stifle a moan, and his eyes dropped to my mouth.

Suddenly, it was one hundred degrees here. He didn't say anything. Just kept moving his thumb, tracing the same area, while I fought to breathe correctly.

It was moments like these that made it hard not to cross the line with him. Sometimes it felt like old times, and those little touches were like memory reflexes of how we used to be.

A knock on the driver's window broke through the tension. I flinched, and his hand dropped, all traces of his touch fading with my confusion.

Outside the window, someone waved, but I didn't look. Couldn't yet. *Did they see anything?*

Denver moved first, opening the door and stepping out. I sat for another second, heart tight, willing myself to calm down. I picked up the T-shirt and threw it over my tank top. It smelled of him. Cedar and spice.

I forced the door open and stepped out into the breeze.

And there was Jamie. She was leaning against a car, her arms crossed over her chest. She wore an unreadable expression. She gave me a once-over, eyes stuck on the T-shirt.

"Hey," she said, voice even.

"Hey," I returned.

Her eyes flicked past me, and I didn't have to turn to know Denver had rounded the car. The shift in her posture was small, but it was there. Shoulders straighter, chin tilted slightly higher. I didn't know where this tension between us came from. I wanted to dissect it, but not right now.

"Clara," Denver called.

I turned and spotted Mason first. He was taller than I remembered, with wild blonde hair and a grin that looked like trouble waiting to happen. His energy filled the space like a loudspeaker.

"Holy shit," he said, making a beeline for me. "Didn't know you were coming. You look…" His gaze dragged down and up again, unabashed. "Let's just say I wouldn't have forgotten you."

I opened my mouth, unsure whether to laugh or run.

"Mason." Denver's voice was rough as he shot daggers at Mason.

Mason smirked. "Alright." He held his hands up in surrender. "Just being friendly."

I felt Jamie's gaze shift to Denver, then to me.

Behind them, Eli strolled up with his usual quiet ease. Dark curls fell into his eyes.

Then her. Sadie. She hung back, black boots planted firmly, arms crossed, sharp eyes taking everything in. Her presence was quiet but impossible to ignore.

Denver jerked his chin toward her. "This is Sadie."

She gave me a nod. "Nice to meet you."

"You too," I said, even if I wasn't sure yet.

I wasn't a jealous person, not really. Denver had explained that they went out a few times, but it didn't go anywhere. Still, seeing her, she was beautiful and kind've intimidating. I had no right to feel jealous where Denver was concerned.

"We should head in," Denver said, eyes skimming over the group before heading back to the car to grab his guitar. The rest had already set up inside.

The first thing I noticed as we headed toward the crowd of people filling in was how well they color-coded in black attire. Their style was effortless, not just coordinated. But not like they'd tried too hard. Just enough edge to make it look natural.

The second thing I noticed was Jamie. She walked beside Denver, not touching him, not even looking at him. But her pace matched his, like it always had. Like she knew exactly where to fall in step.

The rest of the group moved with the same kind of ease. The group exchanged jokes, shared quiet laughter, and gave shoulder nudges that conveyed more than words. Eli leaned in to say something to Sadie as Mason's voice cut through with a laugh. She rolled her eyes as if she were used to it.

They clicked.

I walked a half-step behind. I felt out of place.

Then, Denver glanced back, and instead of turning forward again, he slowed. I felt his hand brush my lower back before his arms slipped across my shoulders. He pulled me in like it was natural. His body was warm against mine, familiar in a way that made everything else fade for just a second.

"You good?" he asked under his breath.

I nodded, surprised by how fast my throat closed up.

Their appearance instantly prompted cheers. Unfiltered excitement rippled from the entrance to the stage. Someone shouted Denver's name. A girl near the front pulled out her phone, already recording and screaming.

They soaked it all in, Mason flashing a peace sign and grinning like he lived for this. Sadie reappeared beside him, drink in hand and unbothered, like she'd done this a thousand times.

They peeled off, disappearing backstage in a line.

Then, it was just Jamie and me.

"Drink?" she asked over the music, already moving.

We had beers in our hands in no time as everyone moved closer to the stage. We stood shoulder to shoulder for a moment as lights flickered above us. The low thrum of pre-show music buzzed beneath the surface of chatter and glass clinks.

The crowd went crazy when they came out. They introduced themselves before jumping right in. I didn't know the songs, but I didn't need to. The rhythm got inside me, shaking loose everything heavy. Beside me, Jamie jumped as she sang along. Every lyric.

I laughed as she grabbed my arm and pulled me closer to the stage.

My eyes couldn't leave Denver. He was made to be on stage. He moved and sang with purpose. The spotlight caught on the cut of his jaw; the way sweat started to bead at his temple, the way his fingers strummed the guitar as if it anchored him. He sang like it hurt, but meant everything all at once.

I couldn't look away.

I don't know how long they played. It was long enough for sweat to gather at the back of my neck, long enough to forget everything else. Each song bled into the next, the energy relentless.

And just when the lights dimmed again, just when the band pulled back, and the crowd started to chant for more, Denver stepped forward.

His voice came low through the mic. "This next one's not on the set list."

He looked around at the group, and they nodded as if they knew exactly what to do.

That earned a cheer from the crowd.

The first notes cut through, quiet at first. His voice settled over the noise.

"Sleepless nights on rooftops, watching stars fade slowly..."

My chest caved in.

The noise of the crowd kept going, but it felt miles away. His voice was quieter than on the last songs. Stripped down.

"You talked about the future. I was just trying not to let go."

Another twist to the gut.

His eyes scanned the crowd before they landed on me.

Time shrank. This noise faded until it was just him, just those eyes, steady and searching.

"Angel, you haunt the edges of my quiet, the place I never thought you'd find."

Angel.

His voice was raw.

"Angel, the nights we lost are still alive, and I can't leave you behind."

Tears burned behind my eyelids. I slipped through the crowd, past Jamie's call, out into the cold air.

I wiped my tears as I took off toward Denver's car.

It was too much. He shouldn't have done that.

The night air scraped against my skin as I leaned my head against the window.

Angel.

My chest ached. My eyes burned.

The song.

The past.

Him.

All of it. I ached for all of it.

Fifteen

Lie to Me

CLARA

Steady footsteps came up behind me.

"Clara."

"Go back inside, Denver."

"I'm not leaving you like this." His footsteps stopped behind me. Too close. *Not close enough.*

"Talk to me," he pleaded.

I laughed bitterly. "Now you want to talk?"

"What the hell is that supposed to mean?"

I whipped around, face hot and soaked. "You don't get to do that. You don't get to stand up there and pour out whatever the hell that was, like I'm not in the room. Like I'm not the one you were trying to gut." My chest heaved.

His jaw tightened. "I wasn't trying to hurt you."

"Well, congrats. You did anyway."

He stepped forward, voice hard. "I told the truth. For once. You want to punish me for that?"

"No," I said, shoving at his chest. "I want you to stop acting like this is simple. It's not a love song, Denver. It's fucking complicated. You and me,"

I waved my finger between us, " we were never meant to be this."

"Allowed by who?" His eyes narrowed. "Your mom? The world? Or you?"

"Everyone!"

"Why?" His voice cracked. "Because if you say it out loud, it becomes real again?"

I shoved him harder. "Because it already *was* real, and it ruined everything."

He grabbed my wrist, not roughly, but firmly. "We ruined nothing. We were kids, Clara. We didn't know what the hell we were doing."

"I knew," I whispered. "I knew exactly what I was doing. And I did it anyway. And when it all went to hell, I didn't stay. I left. I ran."

"I waited," he said, voice raw now. "I waited for you."

Tears welled again, too fast to stop. "I'm fucked up, Denver," I choked out, the confession clawing its way up. "You think this is love? It's guilt. It's shame. It's loving someone I shouldn't love the way I do."

His hands cupped my face. "Don't you *ever* call what we have shame." Hurt flicked behind his eyes.

What we have.

But it was.

And God, I hated how badly I still wanted it.

I still wanted *him.*

If my mother could see me right now, she'd freak out.

"You don't get it."

"Then make me get it! Tell me why you disappeared when I was here this entire time. Tell me why you look at me like you still love me. Tell me why the hell I still feel like you're mine.. Tell me… just tell me, *angel,*" he pleaded.

"Fuck this," I said before rushing him and pressing my lips to his.

The guilt I'd been holding for eight years, pinned beneath what was right and wrong, what I wanted and what I feared, it shattered in one damn moment.

My body moved before I did. I surged forward, grabbing his shirt, dragging him down into me like he was oxygen and I'd been drowning without it.

Our mouths crashed together. There was nothing soft about it. It was wild and desperate. It was a fight, a confession, a scream muffled by skin and heat and the years we'd wasted staying away.

His hands gripped my waist, fingers digging into my sides. My back hit the car with a thud, but I didn't care. I needed him closer. I needed him to erase every year I'd spent trying to forget this.

Trying to forget him.

His lips found mine again and again, deeper, harsher, like it hurt to stop. His teeth grazed my bottom lip, and I gasped against him, my fingers tugging at the collar of his shirt.

I should've pushed him away.

I should've screamed that we were a mess. Tell him that nothing has changed.

Instead, I kissed him again. Like it was the only thing in the world that made sense.

When we finally broke apart, our breaths mingled as our foreheads pressed together.

"I'm not sorry for any of it," he whispered.

I didn't answer, just kissed him again. Because if I said how I felt out loud, it would be my undoing.

Sixteen

Just One Time

D<u>ENVER</u>
My mind was reeling from what just happened. One minute, Clara and I were at each other's throats, and the next, she was kissing me. And I was kissing her back.

Fuck… I was kissing her back and fucking enjoying it. I didn't mean to play the song I wrote for her. Somehow, I thought it'd click to her how I felt when she left. How I still felt about her. We'd been tiptoeing around our feelings, and I hated it.

"I can't go back in there," she said against my lips.

"You don't have to." I held out my hand for her to take.

"Aren't you still needed in there?"

I shook my head. "They'll understand."

I hoped like hell they would. The gig was the last thing on my mind. We were done, anyway. That last song was just a bonus.

Without another word, I reached for the door and held it open. She slid in. I rounded the car and shot off a text to Eli. *He'd be the one to get it, without me going into detail.*

I drove us home.

I barely remembered the ride. My mind was spinning, still full of her. Her mouth, her anger, her voice breaking as she said she was fucked up.

She wasn't. She was *just* mine.

When I parked, she didn't move. I looked at her, and it hit me how young she looked when she was scared. How she carried the past in her posture still, and was waiting to be pushed away. And maybe it was selfish, but I needed to see her break for me. Needed to know I wasn't the only one walking around broken, lost, and fucking confused.

I opened the door and waited. Dad's car was there when we got back, so I led us to the studio.

I didn't turn on the lights. Just let the moonlight filter through the tall windows, painting the room in silver.

She turned toward me slowly, as if she was deciding if coming in here was a mistake.

"Clara," I said. "You don't have to—"

"I want to."

It stopped me cold.

She stepped closer and touched the hem of my shirt. "I've been wanting to for eight years."

My chest cracked open.

"Say something," she said, eyes burning.

I swallowed. "Uh, how much have you had to drink?"

Her eyes drank me in, filling with lust as she walked towards me.

"Not much. Say something else, Denver."

Fuck. Fuck. Fuck.

"I want you. Always have. Always will," I confessed. "Is that good enough?"

" And now what?"

"Now…" I slid my finger to her jaw, brushing my thumb against her cheek. "Now I'm just trying to survive you."

Her mouth opened, and I crushed my lips to hers before she could get a word out.

I swear, the second my lips touched hers, the world collapsed. Every fucking ache I'd ever felt, every dream I tried to let die, every night I'd reached for her in my sleep, it all lit up behind my ribs.

She undressed as if she were peeling away a past life.

So did I.

When we touched, it wasn't perfect. It wasn't smooth. It was trembling fingers and quiet gasps. It was hesitation laced with hunger. It was reverent.

Retrieving a condom from my wallet, I led us to the bed. I ripped it open and slid it over my aching cock before pulling her onto my lap. I held her, tracing every perfect curve of her body.

Her forehead dropped to mine, our noses brushing.

"I don't know how to come back from this," she whispered.

"Then don't come back. Just stay here. With me. For now."

She nodded, then sank onto me.

The sound she made wasn't loud, but it gutted me most beautifully. A soft, broken breath in my ear, like something holy had cracked inside her. My hands trembled as I held her hips, buried inside her sweet pussy deeper than I'd ever thought I'd be *again*.

She rode me slowly, and I met her rhythm with my own. I moved slow and deep, her name on my lips like a litany.

I wrapped my arms around her back, kissed her neck, and her shoulders. Whispered against her skin.

"You're still the most beautiful thing I've ever seen," I murmured. "You're my fucking angel, Clara."

She whimpered. "Don't let go yet," she said, cupping my face.

"I won't."

We came together. Not with fireworks, but with gravity. It was like a last release after holding your breath for too long.

She collapsed onto my chest. I held her gently, as if she were made of ash, terrified the wind would snatch her away again.

Minutes passed, even hours; I didn't know. But we didn't speak. I just brushed my fingers down her spine and pressed kisses into her damp hair. I prayed that tonight wouldn't be the last time she let me touch her like this.

Or touch her at all. For the first time in eight years, I felt whole again. Even though deep down, I knew it wouldn't last.

Even then, she was here. And I wasn't letting go. *No matter what.*

The next morning, I felt Clara's breath stuttering against my neck. Pale morning light spilled through the high windows, soft and golden, catching dust motes floating silently in the air. Outside, birdsong cut through the stillness.

For a moment, it felt like we existed outside of time. Just breath and light and the lingering heat of something sacred. I held onto it as long as I could.

Then, frantic rustling and the blanket being tugged away cut through the stillness.

Clara was sitting upright, clutching her phone to her ear. Her eyes were wild, half-asleep, and already spiraling.

"Hi, baby," she said into the phone, voice shaking.

The air turned cold, or maybe I just noticed it then. The way the studio held the chill of the night, how the warmth between us had been temporary. I sat up, instinctively reaching for her, but she was already curling away from me, wrapping the blanket tighter around her body like armor.

"Yeah, Mommy's okay… I know. I'm sorry. I didn't mean to miss your call." Her voice dropped to a hush.

The ache started slowly, then spread like a bruise. Not because I didn't know this call was coming. She talked about Eric as if he were the world. But because I could already feel her slipping. The way her voice softened for him, and the way her spine stiffened.

Because the life she built, the one without me, was calling.

There was a man out there, this Ethan guy, who got a version of her that I didn't get the chance to. Who touched her when she was soft and scared? Who held her while she carried his child? Who may have fallen in love with the idea of forever.

I didn't know much other than what she'd told us. She doesn't talk about him much.

But it hurt all the same. While I spent the last eight years trying to forget her, someone else inscribed themselves into her life. I hated the guy a little for it.

Still, even now, as I watched her hold the phone like it tethered her to another life, I wanted her. God, I wanted her.

She was someone's mom, but it didn't change how I viewed her. It never would.

She hung up and looked at me like I was the consequence of her worst decision.

"Clara—"

"I shouldn't have stayed," she muttered, putting on her clothes. "God, I knew better."

"It's fine-" I began, trying to stand and catch her before she disappeared.

"Your dad's in the house, Denver. What if he came out here? What if he saw?"

"He didn't," I said calmly, standing. "Clara, just breathe."

She wasn't hearing me. Her panic had already taken root.

"This was a mistake," she whispered, tugging her shirt over her head. "I just—I wasn't thinking."

That one landed hard. She didn't have to twist the knife, but she did.

"You don't need to run."

"It's easy to say for someone who didn't need to run."

My jaw tightened. "Come on, that's not fair."

"What's fair here?" She snapped, voice barely above a whisper.

"You don't think I know how complicated and fucked up this is?"

She looked at me like she wanted to believe me. Like some part of her hated this just as much as I did. But the wall was already back in place.

"I have to go."

I didn't stop her. I just watched her leave, the echo of her footsteps swallowed by morning light. All I had left was the fading warmth she left behind, burning me alive.

Fuck me.

Seventeen

Running

CLARA

I slept with him.

The reminder didn't whisper; it screamed. A low, constant wail at the back of my mind as I crept out of the studio barefoot, shoes in hand, heart still beating too hard for a morning that hadn't fully begun. The ache between my legs didn't make it easy to ignore either.

The sky was pale as my skin prickled, but not from the cold.

I could still feel him.

The way our bodies were glued together was like pieces of a puzzle. How his breath had turned ragged when he whispered my name, his mouth on my throat.

God, the way he touched me made me feel like he already knew every part of me. Like he'd been waiting years to memorize what I looked like coming apart in his hands.

Like I once did...

I pressed my fingers to my temple, as if I could scrub the memories away. But they weren't foggy or distant. They were vivid. Branded into me.

I stepped into the house and shut the door quietly behind me. I moved toward the kitchen, poured a glass of water with trembling hands, and tried not to think about how I'd buried my fingers in his hair. How, afterward, I hadn't pulled away. I'd curled into him like I belonged there.

Because I wanted to.

For the first time in years, I hadn't felt like a mother hiding a life or a girl running from the wreckage.

I felt like myself.

But the crash came quickly.

The phone call with Eric had brought me back to reality. I missed his call last night because I was engrossed in Denver.

I took a slow sip of water, then nearly dropped the glass when I heard the scrape of a chair behind me.

Tom stood at the edge of the table, mug in hand, hair still rumpled from sleep. His button-down hung open over a plain white tee. He looked more like a man who hadn't had time to breathe in weeks.

He studied me for a moment, then lifted his mug. "Couldn't sleep?"

I managed a small shake of my head. "Something like that."

He nodded, stepping into the kitchen. "You and I both. Tea?"

"I'm good." I set my glass down, ready to leave.

He moved the coffeepot, pouring a fresh cup, then leaned against the counter. "I feel like I've seen you a hundred times since you've come home, and still haven't actually seen you."

I looked down. "It's been a lot."

"Yeah," he said. "That it has."

He didn't ask where I'd been, though I saw the question flicker behind his eyes. I was still in yesterday's clothes, my hair was a mess, and my shoes weren't even on.

But he let it pass.

"How are you holding up?" he asked.

I hesitated. "Fine."

His mouth pulled into something like a frown. "Clara. You don't have to be fine. You don't even have to pretend."

I swallowed. "It's easier to pretend."

"I get that. But it's harder to come back when you forget how to tell the truth."

The truth. I felt it clawing at my throat.

If he knew what I'd just done, who I'd just done it with, would he still be standing here like this? So calm? So open?

"You've grown up," he continued after a pause. "I mean. But it's strange, having you here again and not knowing who you are now."

"You know who I was."

He exhaled. "I knew who I thought you were. But you left, Clara. And you didn't come back. Not really."

Why did it suddenly feel like I was under a microscope?

Did he even question my mother when I left? Attempt to find out where I went?

The questions angered me. Everyone seemed to have their opinions, but no one knows what hell I went through.

And it was all *her* fault.

I looked toward the stairs. "I should go get cleaned up."

He didn't move. "Can I ask you something first?"

I paused, bracing myself. "Okay."

"What pulled you away back then? I know it wasn't just college, or travel, or whatever your mom said. I always figured…something happened."

My throat tightened. "A lot of things happened."

"But what made you run?"

I didn't answer.

How was it possible that my mother left him in the dark?

"I'm not asking for the story. Just… if it was something we could've helped with."

I wanted to laugh. But I only stared at him.

He looked like he wanted to say more. He only gave a quiet nod. "If you ever want to talk, really talk, you know where I am."

I nodded and left.

After my shower, I packed a bag and texted my dad.

Me: Can you come get me?

That's all I sent.

Ten minutes later, he replied.

Dad: Be there in twenty.

No questions. No demands.

I sat on the edge of my bed with wet hair and numb hands, staring at the door like it might swing open and Denver would be there, asking me what I thought I was doing. But the house was quiet, and I wasn't ready for his voice.

I wasn't ready for anyone's.

When my dad pulled up, I slipped out without a word. My duffle hit the porch with a dull thud. I didn't look back.

He said nothing when I climbed into the passenger seat. He just reached across the center console and squeezed my shoulder. Then, he was driving.

I didn't cry. Not even when I wanted to. Not even when he played that soft rock station I used to hate, like it might soothe the ache in my chest.

It all felt too familiar.

This morning, this mess felt like a second act of the worst chapter of my life. Leaving the house in shame, packing my life into a bag, and running because staying meant suffocating.

Back then, I was seventeen and shattered.

I was older, now, twenty-six. But the fracture lines were all in the same place.

I stared at the blur of pine trees lining the highway and thought about how Denver looked last night. So open. So sure. His hands were on my skin, like he wasn't afraid. *But I was. Still am.*

And now that it's happened, now that I let myself fall apart in his arms, I'm more afraid than ever. Because it was too good. Too natural. Too much like something we'd always been heading toward, whether we wanted to or not.

Sitting in my dad's truck, I didn't feel powerful or bold. Or anything I'd pretended to be when I packed that bag and walked away.

I felt like *her* again. *A coward; disgusting and wretched.*

My dad's voice stopped my thoughts. "You want to talk?"

"No."

"Alright. But if you change your mind…"

"I know." I kept my eyes outside the window.

He didn't push. He never did.

When we got back to his place, he left me alone. Said something about work, about Claire being at school. I nodded through it all, barely hearing.

In the guest bedroom, I sat on the edge of the bed and unzipped my jacket. My eyes found the empty wall across from me and stayed there, unfocused.

I didn't mean to cry. It just happened, quiet at first, then harder, until I was curled around my knees with my face in my hands and no one there to see me fall apart.

My phone slipped out of my pocket. I stared at it for a long time.

Then opened the only thread that mattered.

Me: *I need you.*

I hit send.

Then cried until there weren't any tears left.

Eighteen

Almost

DENVER

She left.

Again.

I let myself believe for one second that things would be different. It had been three days, and my chest still tightened every time the front door opened, even though it was never her. Every time my phone buzzed, I reached for it like a reflex. *Pathetic.*

It's been fucking with my head. So much so that rehearsal was kinda sucking.

We were running the set for an upcoming acoustic show. It was just us—stripped back, raw vocals, softer edges. It should've felt good. *It didn't.*

I was off. And everyone felt it.

I missed the entrance to *"Paper Ghosts."* Came in late on *"Glass Spine."* Two of my favorite songs I'd written to date. My hands weren't steady. My voice kept catching. I dropped the pick again.

Eli finally stopped playing mid-verse.

"Okay," he said, guitar still slung across his chest. "We need to take five, because whatever this is, it's not working."

I sighed and set my bass down. "I'm good. Let's go again."

"You're not good."

"I said, let's run it again."

He didn't flinch. Just pointed at the door. "Outside. Now."

I hesitated, looking between Sadie and Mason. Sadie avoided my eyes while Mason was already pulling off his headphones, clearly glad someone finally said something.

I followed Eli out into the hallway. It was still early in the day when we didn't have to worry about much foot traffic coming in and out of the building.

Eli leaned against the wall, arms crossed, waiting.

"You wanna tell me what's going on?"

"I told you I'm fine."

He laughed, although it was dry. I knew he was being sarcastic, just like he knew I was lying through my teeth.

"You haven't been fine since the night of the show. Don't play me, man."

I was quiet for a beat. I trusted Eli like I trusted myself. But with the Clara stuff? That was unfamiliar territory.

"Okay, you wanna play it like this," he sighed, running his hand through his hair. "I saw you," he added, crossing his hands over his chest.

My eyes widened as I tried to keep my nerves at bay.

"After the set. The parking lot. With Clara."

Our eyes locked as the pounding in my chest picked up.

"She kissed you. And it didn't look one bit casual or a one-time thing."

I swallowed, running a hand across my face. "It's not what you think."

I was ready to hear how sick this was or the look of disgust from Eli.

It never came.

"Then tell me what it is," he shot back, "because I've been sitting on that for days, hoping you'd come to me. But now you're here, falling apart in front of all of us, and I'm done pretending I don't see it."

I ran a hand through my hair. "It's complicated."

"Yeah. No shit."

We stood in silence for a moment. He didn't look angry or freaked out by the fact that he caught me kissing Clara. Just frustrated, maybe.

"You know, you could've told me."

"Tell you what? That I have it bad for my stepsister? Come on, Eli. It's not as simple as that."

He blinked, eyes zeroing in on me. "Wait. You're in love with her."

Silence.

He blew out a breath. "Jesus."

"I didn't mean for it to happen."

"Doesn't matter. It happened."

I nodded.

"So, is that why you're playing like you haven't picked up a guitar a day in your life?"

I laughed. "Something like that."

"What happened?"

"Something happened, and she freaked out. I haven't spoken to her in days."

"Where is she?"

"At her dad's."

Eli straightened. "And you're here, why?"

"I don't know."

Maybe because she didn't want to see me. Otherwise, she wouldn't have bolted the first chance she got.

"Yeah, you do," he said. "You're afraid. For what? I don't know, but you should figure it out. It's clearly weighing on you; otherwise, you wouldn't be playing like someone just killed your puppy."

"I don't have a puppy."

He gave me a pointed look. "You know what I mean."

"I guess I do."

"So, go."

I nodded and turned to leave.

"And, Denver, we're not done with this conversation." He gave me a stern look before heading back into the studio.

Maybe I was scared. But she was still here. She didn't pick up and leave the state, and that had to count for something.

I took the long drive to Clara's dad's house, going over what the hell I was going to say. When I pulled up, I parked and didn't hesitate. The more I prolonged it, I would've just backed out.

When I knocked, it wasn't Clara who came to the door.

It was her dad.

Why was I shocked? It was his house.

"Denver," he greeted, brows lifted, like he hadn't expected to see me again.

"Hey," I said, clearing my throat. " I was hoping to talk to Clara. If that's okay."

He studied me for a second like he could see straight through the chaos I'd been carrying around since the other day. Then he stepped aside. "She's inside."

I followed him in, trying to ignore the way my pulse kicked up.

Laughter echoed faintly from the living room, small and bright. When I turned the corner, I stopped in my tracks.

Clara was on the couch, her head resting in someone else's lap.

Not just someone. *Ethan.*

I knew it before I could be introduced to him. Tall, red hair, an obnoxiously clean-cut look that screamed dependable. His fingers were in her hair, too casual.

For a second, I couldn't move. Couldn't breathe.

She didn't notice me right away.

He did.

His gaze landed on mine. It was unreadable, but I didn't miss the grip on Clara's hands for the slightest of a second when he leaned down and murmured something in her ear.

When she turned and our eyes met, she jolted upright.

"Denver."

My name in her mouth shouldn't have hurt. But it did. *Was this the reason she left the other day? For him?*

Something squeezed in my chest.

I forced a nod. "Hey."

She got to her feet, smoothing her shirt. Her whole body was stiff.

"This is Ethan," she said, almost too fast. "Ethan, this is…Denver."

He stood, not offering a hand, just giving me a nod. One of those practiced, polite things people do when they want you to know you're not a threat.

"Nice to finally meet you," he offered instead.

It didn't sound like he meant it, but I didn't miss the side eye Clara shot his way.

Before I could say anything back, a small voice came from down the hallway.

"Mom, grandpa said I could finish my cartoon."

A little boy padded into the living room. Barefoot, green eyes, and black curls falling into his face.

He stopped when he saw me.

Everything in me went still.

"Hey, little guy," I mumbled.

He stared at me. "You're tall."

An abrupt laugh escaped me. "So I've heard."

He turned to Clara, leaning into her side. "Can I watch now?"

"In a minute, Eric."

"Okay," he murmured, before giving me one more glance.

He wandered to the armchair and plopped down with a tablet, like this was normal. Like I was the only one who felt out of place.

I couldn't take my eyes off him. Something twisted in my chest. Something unfamiliar. He looked at me like he knew me. He favored Clara, as I glanced between him and this Ethan guy, jealousy etched in my gut.

I glanced at Clara. At Ethan. His hand was still hovering near her back.

"Can we talk?" I asked, words almost biting as I spoke.

She hesitated, as if she didn't want to.

Finally nodding, I followed behind her as she headed toward the front door.

"I didn't expect you to come here," she murmured.

"Yeah. I figured."

She stood still. She looked tired. Still beautiful, somehow worse for me because of it. Faint circles under her eyes, hair pulled back like she hadn't touched it all day. Her cherry lips parted like she had words, but didn't know which ones to use.

"I needed to see," I continued. "What I didn't expect was to come here and watch you act like nothing happened."

"I wasn't—I wasn't acting."

"Really? Could've fooled me. Because from where I was standing, you looked fine. Like everything between us got boxed up and put away."

"That's not fair."

I stepped forward. "Isn't it?"

Her jaw clenched. "You think I haven't been losing it, too?"

"I don't know what to think. You left, Clara."

Her voice was low. "I didn't plan to."

"But you did. No call. No explanation. Just gone."

She rubbed her hand over her arm. "I was scared."

"Of what?"

She met my eyes. "Of what it meant," she confessed, her voice fraying at the edges.

I remained still, suspended in the weight of her words.

"I've been trying to outrun it since the second we crossed that line. Because I knew once I let myself feel it, really feel it, there wouldn't be a way back."

"There isn't," I replied. "And I don't want there to be."

Her eyes lifted, and in them, resentment, longing, and devastation shone.

"This isn't just about what we did. It's about everything else. Everything that it would ruin."

"Then I'll be by your side when it's ruined to pick the pieces up."

Her breath caught. For a moment, she didn't retreat, but something in her eyes shut down.

And I felt it.

"I can't," she breathed.

"Why?" I pressed, my voice fraying now, too. "Why not?"

"You wouldn't understand."

I felt like we were on rotation on a broken clock.

"Then make me. Clara, I've been unraveling, trying to piece together everything, and I can't. So, please help me understand. That's all I'm asking. You don't just disappear and still act like you're protecting me."

"I'm not trying to hurt you."

"Then, stop."

She drifted closer without even realizing it, hands rubbing her sides like she wanted to bring them up to touch me, but couldn't. *Wouldn't.*

"I'm sorry."

"Don't do this," I pleaded.

"I have to."

I wanted so badly to shake her. To shake some sense into her. She was pushing me further away. If I had kept my hands to myself, this wouldn't have happened.

Fuck me.

It was at that right moment, her prince charming decided to pop his head out.

"Clara?"

"I'll be right in," she said without taking her eyes off me.

I shook my head. "Is this because of him? Are you two… together?"

"I already told you, we don't have that kind of relationship."

"Then what is it?"

"I'll see you at the hospital, Denver."

She stepped back, each move pulling her further from me. Like every time before, I let her. I stood there until the door shut.

I left there more confused than I was before.

Nineteen

The Pinky Swear

CLARA
14 Years Old

Birthdays weren't supposed to feel this heavy.

There were pancakes on the table. Slightly burned, slightly undercooked in the middle, and shaped like blobs. Tom made them, which was how I knew something was off. He rarely cooked. He wore a party hat as if it were the most normal thing in the world. When I walked into the kitchen, he grinned, which in turn made me smile.

It suffocated the tension between Mom and me. She handed me a glass of orange juice, already halfway out the door with her phone pressed to her ear. She smiled like she always did in front of people.

"Happy birthday, sweetheart," she said, before laughing at something the person on the phone said and stepping into the hall.

I took a seat without a word, picking at my pancakes, even though I wasn't hungry. I wasn't sure if raw pancakes were going to cut it.

Tom tried. He sat across from me and told a terrible joke about birthday candles and fire alarms. I forced a laugh, which was probably worse than silence.

Denver wasn't there. Thank God. Or maybe not. I didn't even know what

I wanted anymore.

We hadn't really spoken in weeks, not since that day.

Not since I kissed him and I freaked the hell out. Not since I looked at him like he did something wrong, when all he did was sit there and let it happen.

Ugh.

He had told no one, and I was lucky for that. Each day, I waited for Mom to call my name and tell me how disgusting I was for kissing my stepbrother.

I hated myself for doing it. I don't know what came over me. I also hated how much I missed him. He was my best friend, and I didn't have him to run to and talk his ear off about nothing and everything. I hated that the only thing I wanted for my birthday was the one person I was terrified of being around.

The day passed in a blur. I went to the movies with a couple of girls from school. We saw an animated movie that wasn't funny, and afterward, I sat quietly while they scrolled through their phones and compared lip gloss in the mall's food court.

Mom picked me up from the mall right on time. Fresh lipstick, and a new set of clothes on like she was going out, and a smile in place.

"You had fun?" She asked as I slid into the passenger seat.

"Sure."

I don't know why it was difficult to have a simple conversation with her. It always felt forced.

She didn't ask what I did or who I was with. I wasn't sure she cared, or if she just didn't want to know.

When we pulled into the driveway, Denver's bike was already there.

My heart skipped a beat.

He's home.

Dinner suddenly sounded like a punishment.

Inside, the dining room looked like a page from a lifestyle magazine. Silver trays, crisp white takeout bags from the fancy downtown steakhouse, and gently flickering candles adorned the table. And a chocolate lava cake was waiting on the sideboard. My absolute favorite.

Tom stood at the head of the table, wearing his relaxed "not a CEO tonight" button-down and holding a glass of bourbon. "Dinner fit for royalty," he said with a smile. "Happy birthday, Clara."

Denver sat at the far end of the table. His hoodie, half up on his head, his hair slightly messy, and his elbows resting on the table. That was until Mom gave him a look, and he muttered an apology before placing it on his lap.

I paused in the doorway, uncertain.

"Come on," Tom urged. "Filet, truffle fries, that weird kale salad you like; got it all."

Mom breezed past me, wineglass in hand. "We wanted to make it special."

I sat between her and Tom, while Denver sat across from me.

He wouldn't stop looking at me.

Not in a creepy way. Just… pleading in a way. Like he was waiting for me to say something, as if he could still feel what I felt and was too scared to see my reaction.

It wasn't like I'd acted in the best way after I kissed him. He was just leaving me alone like I wanted him to.

My appetite ceased to exist.

Tom talked mostly about a meeting with a sports agency looking for space. He asked us about school, and Denver chimed in, but only to echo something I said or to agree.

He was quiet. More than usual.

And I could feel the weight of his eyes every time mine dropped to my plate.

I laughed way too hard when I didn't need to. Answered their questions when asked, and just pretended like I wasn't freaking out inside.

The guilt ate at me more than the food did.

Until dessert came around. They sang Happy Birthday, and I stayed tight-lipped, like the awkwardness of being the center of attention wasn't nerve-wrecking. Chocolate cake, with chocolate frosting and gold lettering spelling my name, and candles, fourteen to be exact.

Tom lit them and stood back. "Make a wish."

I stared at the flames for a long moment, then closed my eyes.

Make me forget.

I blew them out.

Tom kissed my cheek and handed me a small necklace box. A gold chain with my name in cursive.

"Thank you," I mumbled.

Denver said nothing, but he was still looking at me. I could feel it more than see it.

"Opening more gifts upstairs?" Tom asked with a grin.

"Think I might." I stood quickly. "Thank you again. For all of this."

Mom gave a glossy smile and clinked her wine glass.

I looked over at Denver once more. His eyes flicked to mine, then down.

I slipped upstairs, necklace in hand, heart thudding.

I shut my bedroom door and leaned against it, letting out a shaky breath.

I set the necklace box on my desk without opening it again. Everything about tonight had been perfect on paper. Fancy birthday dinner with family, a pretty cake, and a gift with my name etched in gold. So why did it feel like I couldn't breathe?

A knock came.

I didn't answer, but I didn't tell him to go, either. I knew it was him.

The door creaked open an inch.

"Can I uh… come in?"

Denver stepped into view, the hallway light haloing behind him.

I nodded as he walked in. He glanced around like he was seeing my room for the first time, though he'd been in here a hundred times before. I think we both knew it hadn't felt like this… like something had broken between us. It was all my fault.

"I have something for you." He lifted a bag. "I wanted to give it to you earlier, but… You looked like you were barely holding it together."

"You're not wrong."

"I usually am. But not when it comes to you."

I sat down on the bed as he handed me a photo book, fingers brushing mine. A pulse jumped under my skin. I hated how nice that felt. It made me forget why kissing him was wrong, why my chest felt like it hurt when we didn't talk. I couldn't explain the feeling, and I was terrified of it.

The book was soft, like old linen with a ribbon that kept it tied shut.

I glanced up. "You made this?"

Denver shrugged, hands in his pockets. "Sort of. It's photos I've taken. I printed them and wrote stuff under some. I don't know, I thought maybe… You'd want to remember."

My throat thickened. "Remember what?"

He didn't look away. "The good parts. The real parts. Before everything got so complicated."

I untied the ribbon with careful fingers, flipped open the first page, and immediately saw a picture of the two of us from last summer. I laughed so hard that I was sunburned and had tears in my eyes. He was next to me, blurry and mid-laugh, too, arm slung behind me. It was candid. A moment I hadn't even realized was being captured. I traced the photo with a smile before flipping the page.

Each page after that was a thread. Photos of our long walks, nights sprawled on the rooftop, inside jokes scrawled in margins, a close-up of my hand holding a guitar pick, a photo of me asleep on the couch with a hoodie pulled over my head.

Under one: You fell asleep like this after eating all the sour gummies. I couldn't look away.

Under another: You said I was your favorite person and didn't even realize you said it.

By the time I got to the last page, I was a mess. Quietly undone.

"This is—" I swallowed. "I don't have words."

I was on the brink of tears. It was… beautiful.

"I didn't make it for words," he said, sitting beside me. "I made it because I thought you might need something to hold on to when you feel like pulling away. When you feel like pushing everyone away."

I pressed my hand over the closed book, feeling its weight. "You're not everyone."

"I know."

We sat in silence for a moment, the kind that stretches without snapping.

The kind that only exists between people who've memorized each other. This simple gift meant the most to me because I was pulling away from him, and these photos of the moments of nothing but happiness and laughter were everything.

"Come on." He nudged my knee with his. "Let's go up top. I brought more chocolate cake."

I laughed despite myself. "You're bribing me with my favorite poison?"

"Works like a charm."

The rooftop air was cool and sweet. I don't remember when we started climbing on top of here, but it sort of became a routine.

We lay back against the slope of the shingles, chocolate cake in hand, the city lights glittering in the distance like spilled stars.

"I'm sorry," I said eventually, my voice barely above a whisper. "About everything."

About the kiss, you idiot.

"You don't have to be," he replied. "I get it. You freaked out. I kind of did, too."

"I kissed you," I said pointedly.

It wasn't some boy I was gawking over in math class. It was him.

"You were scared," he shrugged, popping a piece of cake in his mouth.

"So were you."

"Yeah. But I was still glad it happened."

My eyes nearly bulged out of their sockets.

That stole my breath a little

I whipped my head toward him. "Denver," I breathed. "You're my stepbrother," I said finally, not accusing, just… trying to ground us. It seemed like saying it out loud might remind us both of what this was. Or wasn't.

"I know," he said.

That was it. Not a joke, no denial, just acceptance. He said it so casually that it scared me.

I could feel the weight of what we were teetering on. The what-ifs and the what-comes-next. The risk of someone overhearing, of a slip-up, of mom and Tom figuring out from the way I looked at him too long. It was a miracle they hadn't yet.

We weren't kids playing house. We were kids standing in the middle of a minefield, pretending like we knew where to step.

But all I could think about was him. How close he was, how quiet he got when he meant something, how the night stretched around us like a secret we hadn't finished telling.

I wanted to tell him I hated the way he looked at me after that kiss, because it made me want to kiss him again. I wanted to say I missed him over the past few weeks, even though we lived under the same roof, and how badly it ached not having him in my presence.

Instead, I said, "I hated how you looked at me after."

"Because I didn't look away?"

"No. Because you looked at me like you wanted me to do it again."

The air around us shifted.

"And you hated that?" he asked.

I didn't answer, just broke off a piece of cake with shaking fingers and popped it in my mouth.

"I don't want to keep pretending," I sighed.

"Pretending what?"

"That I don't think about it. That I don't think about you. About us."

I chanced a glance at him, half-expecting him to laugh. Or worse, pull away.

He didn't.

His voice dropped low. "Then don't."

Something lodged in my throat. I bit down hard on my lip, trying to keep the trembling in my chest from showing.

He sat up straighter, brushing his hand on the rooftop beside me, not touching, but close. "If we're gonna get through this... You can't keep icing me out. I get it's weird, but you can't keep ignoring me like I'm the one who did something wrong."

My heart tripped.

He held up his pinky. "No more ignoring me."

I stared at it, the night wind tugging at my sleeves.

"You're serious?"

"As a heart attack."

A corner of my mouth twitched, even as tears burned behind my eyes. "You're such a drama queen."

"Maybe," he smiled. "But you're still gonna pinky swear."

I hesitated, then placed mine beside his. It was just a pinky, just a promise, but something about this one felt enormous.

For a second longer, we stayed like that. Just two kids on a rooftop, caught in something neither of us had a name for. The wind hummed, the sky stretched wide and endless above us. Somewhere between the silence and the closeness, I knew this wasn't going away.

Not tomorrow. Not ever.

Twenty

Let Her See

CLARA

The sound of Denver's car faded slowly, swallowed by the quiet suburban street, and for a moment, I just stood there, hands still on the doorknob, forehead against the wood, trying to convince myself I was alright.

When he arrived, he looked like he hadn't slept in days. I hadn't either, but it hurt to see him like that.

This is what I did. *Run.*

Behind me, Ethan didn't speak. He was sitting in the armchair by the front window, elbows resting on his knees, watching me.

When I sent him that text, I never expected him to catch the next flight out. Yet, he and Eric were on my dad's doorstep, luggage in tow, just twenty-four hours later. It grounded me a bit, having Eric here. It was one less thing to worry about amidst the chaos I was dealing with.

It made me a little nervous. But I had promised Dad I'd bring Eric to see him. School was out for the summer, so what better time? After years of keeping my distance, I was finally closing it. The way he ran into Dad's hands like they weren't only communicating over a screen made me realize it was the right decision.

I swear I saw a tear fall from Dad's eyes, but he'd deny it if I brought it up. Seeing Dad and Claire bond with him was everything. It was good to know that from all the fucked up things I'd done, that I was making something right.

Baby steps.

"You're going to have to speak eventually," Ethan said.

"I know," I said.

Beyond the walls, the wind stirred the hydrangeas lining the porch. I stared at them until my vision blurred.

I finally turned to face him.

His red hair had grown longer since I left a month ago, curling at the ends like it always did when he let it go too long. Freckled arms folded across his chest, he wore a stern expression, though I knew he was waiting for me to speak. He always did. The person who absorbed everything before saying a word, he always had a read in the room. I used to envy that. Now, I rely on it.

"Eric's asleep," he said after a pause. "Out like a light, tablet on chest, mouth open. He's happy to be here."

I nodded, my eyes darting to the hallway. It was his way of signaling that it was safe to let go without Eric being there.

Ethan sat up on the chair and let out a sigh, and I braced myself for what he was about to say next.

"It's finally nice to meet the infamous Denver," he said, raising an eyebrow.

"Don't." I wagged my finger, watching as he bit his lips to suppress a laugh.

"What? Did you see how jealous that guy was?" he said with a laugh. "If he had lasers, I'd be a pile of ash right there in your father's living room." He was laughing uncontrollably now.

"You're an idiot," I said, unable to stop myself from laughing.

Had Denver really been jealous? I was too flustered by him showing up here, and Eric was thrown in the mix. It was hard to focus on anything else.

Ethan grinned like that was the whole point. It was his specialty. Cutting tension with humor, disarming me just enough to make space for the actual conversation underneath. He'd been through so much when he was younger, but he didn't let the past eat at him the way I did. Sometimes I wish I could be there for him like he always was for me.

The levity didn't last long.

"You know," Ethan said gently, "If you want him in your life, you can't keep shutting the door every time he tries to walk through it."

His words didn't cut; they settled. "I didn't mean to," I started, but the words fell short.

It wasn't giving in to Denver the other night that terrified me. It was what came next. What would still loving him cost?

The weight of what I'd kept hidden and the irreversible consequences of my actions terrified me. *I feared myself.* Being with him wasn't just about longing or love—it was about the layered secrets I'd built my life on. Letting him in now would mean risking everything, the ground beneath all of us splitting wide open.

Our parents were married, for god's sake. It wasn't something I'd ever forgotten. Not when I did a walk of shame from Denver's studio to the kitchen, where my stepfather had just tried to get me to open up.

The longer I threaded on that line, the harder it became to remember who I am outside of it.

"I don't know how to let him in," I whispered. "If I do—I just don't know how."

"You've spent years building a life that keeps the truth out. But Clara…" he paused. "It's already inside. All of it. You're just refusing to look at it."

I swallowed hard, pressing my hands into the sides of my thighs.

Ethan stood, trudging toward me, stopping just before the threshold, where I stood, frozen.

"You can't keep running. Not from him. Not from yourself. And not from her."

I didn't have to ask what he meant.

My mother.

Since returning to Seattle, I've visited regularly, like any daughter would. But I could never bring myself to sit by her bedside as she lay motionless. I always sat back, letting Denver and Tom do all the talking and comforting.

"I'm scared," I admitted.

And that was the truth. The one I kept dancing around.

It wasn't just about Denver or the past. It was what I'd have to face if I stopped running.

But more than anything, it was about her.

Even unconscious, she held power over me. Maybe that's what happens when someone shapes your entire identity from the start. You never stop fearing how they'll see you, even if they can't say it out loud.

"She's not even awake," I continued. "It doesn't matter."

"It matters to *you.*"

I looked at him, but he wasn't looking back. He was just staring out the window, hands tucked in his back pockets.

"You've been carrying this thing, this guilt, like it's the only thing holding you together. But it's not. It's what's holding you *back.*" His eyes found mine then, steady and sure. "You go talk to her. Not because she can answer, but because you need to get it off your chest. Out loud. Without fear."

"I'm afraid of what she might see. Even now. Especially now."

"Then let her see you. All of you. The part that stayed, the part that's trying, all of it. You're not a kid anymore, Clara. You don't need her permission to heal, move on, or to love who you decide to give your heart to."

Something in me loosened, but it wasn't love.

Was love enough?

He was right. It wasn't about whether she could forgive me. It was about whether I could face the truth long enough to forgive myself. Like, truly forgive myself.

"I'll go," I sighed. "Tomorrow."

Ethan nodded, his hand brushing my shoulder briefly before he stepped back. "That's all it takes. You start there."

I let out a breath before the moment settled between us, the ground under my feet becoming a little more solid.

Then, maybe to shake off the intensity or maybe because I needed to feel like myself again, I glanced at him and said, "All this motivational wisdom. I think it's time we find you a nice gal out here. Someone to distract you from fixing *my* life all the time."

He snorted. "You want me to date a Seattle woman? You really are trying to punish me."

I laughed, and it surprised me how natural it felt.

Maybe it was only a crack of light, but it was there.

Twenty-One

Even in Silence

CLARA

Ethan held my hand across the console as we drove to the hospital. My legs shook vigorously as I mentally prepared myself for this visit.

"I'll be right here. You can do this," he said, squeezing my hand before I got out of the car.

Checking in took seconds, and I faced my mother's room door like I had every time I came to visit.

The chill air licked at my skin when I finally walked in. The room was the same. Clean, quiet aside from the beeping machines, and too still. My stomach churned the closer I got to the seat by her bed.

She looked peaceful, still sunken into the hospital bed. I'd seen her like this for weeks, but what I hadn't done was *this*. Be this close.

I sat, and for a while, I didn't speak.

You can do this. You can do this.

"I didn't think I'd ever sit across from you again," I breathed, the words scraping their way out. I heaved a dry laugh. God, why was this so hard?

"I thought I had made peace with this. With you."

A long pause.

"But I didn't." A breath left my lungs with the admission.

My fingers interlocked on my lap, nails pressing into my bare thighs. I didn't look at her, just stared at the floor.

"I convinced myself that you shutting me out strengthened me. That I didn't need your approval. That I could build a life without you. Any of you."

I blinked away the stinging in my eyes.

"But that wasn't my strength. That was survival." I took a deep breath. "I stopped trying the moment you made it clear I wasn't the version of me you could accept."

My voice trembled. This was so hard.

"I thought I'd forgiven you," I said. "All this time, I've been telling myself that. I said it so many times that it sounded real. Being back here makes me realize I haven't. Not yet. I still carry it. The bitterness, the ache, the wondering if I was ever good enough for you to stay when I needed you the most."

My voice caught. I cleared my throat, trying again.

"I know now that you weren't evil. You were broken." *Had to be.* "And maybe that's what scares me the most. That I came from you. That I've spent my whole life trying not to become you, and yet here I am… lying to the one person I—"

I stopped, jaw clenching.

"I still love him," I whispered, closing my eyes to shut out the memory of the look on her face when I'd first told her that. "After everything, I told myself I wouldn't. I *couldn't.* I don't want to feel ashamed of it anymore. Because it's real, it always has been."

I wiped at the tears falling down my cheeks.

"I'm angry at you," I said through clenched teeth. "I'm angry that you weren't there. That you let me carry this alone, even though it seems like you've been doing the same. Angry that you looked at me like I didn't come from you, and angry that you didn't stay long enough to witness the woman I became."

I stared at her face, unmoving beneath my gaze.

"I still love you, and I want to believe deep down you love me, too. That, if you could hear me, maybe you'd tell me I'm not the villain in this story. That I never was"

I reached my trembling hand for hers again.

"This is my first step in trying to live in *my* truth. To stop running. For myself, my son, and even *him*."

The silence felt thicker now. My chest ached from holding too much for too long.

Then a sudden twitch.

Barely there. The faintest movement at the corner of her right eye.

I froze.

My heart leaped in my throat. I stood so fast that the chair scraped back loudly behind me.

"Mom?"

She didn't move again. The monitors just kept their steady rhythm.

I stumbled backward, chest rising too fast, panic crawling up my spine. I threw the door open, breath catching as I rushed out of the room.

I slammed straight into a hard chest.

"Shit—" Denver's voice caught in my hair. His hand steadied me just as my knees threatened to give. "I'll call you back, Jamie," he muttered into his phone before slipping it into his back pocket.

"Clara," he said. "Hey. Look at me."

I couldn't. My vision was swimming, fingers trembling at my sides, and my whole body felt too light. I felt like I was slipping out of myself.

I just confessed all of this, and she heard me.

"I think—I think her eyes moved," I managed. "I—I saw it."

His arms wrapped around me before I could pull away. "Okay. Okay. Just breathe."

But the hallway felt too bright, too loud, and exposed. He must've seen it on my face because he moved without another word, guiding me down the corridor and pushing open the door of a nearby supply closet.

It clicked shut, and suddenly it was just us. Dim light spilling from the bulb overhead, his hands still bracketing my arms.

"Hey, you're alright," he comforted.

"I'm not," I whispered. Hadn't been in a long time.

"Yes, you are," his sultry voice cooed as his hands slid up, gently pulling me against him. My head hit his chest, and I felt his steady heartbeat against my cheek. "Shh, baby… you're okay now."

The word slipped out so quietly I almost missed it. *Baby.*

Something within me broke, and I stopped fighting, surrendering to being held.

His fingers ran down my back. One hand curved protectively around the back of my head. The other pressed against my lower spine, grounding me. He said nothing else, just breathed with me until my own slowed, until the panic unknotted from my chest little by little.

In his arms, I remembered what stillness felt like.

He smelled of the usual cedarwood and spice. His jaw scraped against my forehead. I felt the line of his ribs beneath his T-shirt, the rise and fall of his chest.

It didn't feel like it was just yesterday that I was pushing him away, *again.*

We were too close. My skin itched with how familiar it felt. How right.

It scared me more than anything else today. Not my confession at my mother's bedside, and sadly not even the moment of life that twitched in her eye.

It terrified me how terrible that sounded. That there was a more pressing issue at hand.

Still, I didn't move from his embrace.

I tilted my head and looked up at Denver. Really looked.

His eyes were red-rimmed, like mine. His face was unshaven. His hair curled a little at the nape. His lips were parted slightly, and there was a line between his brows, like he was trying to process what had just happened.

He looked… devastatingly good.

More than that, he was here, holding me up with no need to be told.

I didn't know how long we stayed like that. It was enough for the storm inside me to quiet, replaced by something heavier. That impossible closeness I kept trying to run from.

He swallowed. I could feel the tension rising between us like a tide, and I think he was about to say something when I shifted.

"I should—" I started.

"Yeah," he said at the same time.

He reached behind me and opened the door.

The hallway came back in a rush of noise and light.

Standing just feet away was Tom.

His expression gave nothing as his eyes moved between us.

Denver dropped his arm from around me, but it was already too late.

Something passed over Tom's face, a narrowing of his brow that looked like suspicion.

My heart lurched in my throat.

"I think her eyes twitched," I blurted, too loudly. "I think she moved. Just now."

Tom's head moved swiftly to the closed door. "Really?" he asked in disbelief.

I nodded so fast I might've looked unstable.

"I'll go get the nurse." He wasted no more time trying to figure out what he just saw. He was around halfway down the other end of the hallway.

I still felt it. The weight of his glance lingered long after he was out of sight.

Denver looked at me. "Clara…"

"I know," I whispered.

I didn't know if I was talking about my mother, or Tom, or the way Denver's arms still felt like home.

We moved back into her room, Denver hovering over her, his expression unreadable as I retreated and stood far away.

Tom came back with the doctor and nurse minutes later.

Dr. Chambers stood at the foot of the bed, flipping through the chart while the nurse adjusted some of the monitoring wires. Tom took his place beside my mother, her small hands in his grip, as he smiled with hope.

"You said you saw her eyelid move?" Dr. Chambers asked, glancing up from his clipboard.

"Yes. Just once. Like a twitch," I explained, eyes shifting between him and my mother.

He offered one of those professional smiles. "That's promising. Especially if it was voluntary muscle movement and not reflexive. It's subtle, but for a patient who's been unresponsive as long as she has, it matters. We'll run a full neuro check and update her scans. But that kind of movement could show a change in her level of consciousness."

Tom exhaled. "That's good, right?"

Dr. Chambers didn't rush to answer. "It's… cautiously optimistic. Comas aren't a straight path. But we pay attention to every flicker, every change, no matter how small. A blink, a squeeze of a hand, those can be the first steps."

Tom looked at me, eyes glinting with something close to joy. "If you were talking to her, she heard you, Clara."

His words weighed heavily on my chest. I didn't know how to handle them. This is what I wanted, wasn't it? Yet all I could feel was the suffocating pressure bearing down on me.

I gave him a gentle smile, even though it felt completely fake.

"I'll have the nursing staff increase her responsiveness checks to every hour," Dr. Chambers added. "We'll keep a closer eye on any changes, and I'll be back once we've gone over the imaging."

"Thank you," Tom said, shaking his hand.

The doctor gave a nod and jotted a few notes on her chart. "This might be something. Let's hope it is." With that, she stepped out, leaving the quiet hum of the machines to fill the room.

Tom looked back at the bed, eyes misting. "She's fighting. She's still in there."

I stood near the door, barely breathing. Unsure whether to feel hope or panic.

Because if she was still in there… then maybe she had heard *everything*.

That's what I wanted. I reminded myself.

"I should go," I murmured, reaching for the door handle.

Tom looked my way, surprise flitting across his face. "You're not staying?"

"Ethan's waiting in the car."

At the sound of his name, I noticed it. Denver's head snapped in my direction, his gaze locking onto me, jaw tightening. It seemed like he'd swallowed whatever words he wanted to say, but I felt their weight.

Tom blinked, startled. "Ethan? He came down with you?"

"Yeah."

There was a pause, and something thoughtful flickered in his expression. He looked between Denver and me, then gave a gentle smile, like he was trying not to press too hard. "Well, since he's here, maybe you could come to dinner tomorrow night? Bring Ethan. If your little boy is here… I'd love to meet my grandson."

My heart sank straight through my chest.

I tried not to look at Denver. I didn't want to see his face; I feared what it might show.

I forced a small nod. "Sure. That sounds… good."

Tom smiled wider, relief lighting his features. "Good." He clapped a hand on Denver's shoulder, squeezing it. "We'll make it casual. Just the five of us."

The five of us.

The words echoed as I backed into the hallway, each step heavier than the last. My pulse pounded in my chest. Denver stayed silent, but his eyes never left me, boring into my spine. I glanced back once, just long enough to see him still standing there, frozen, as if any movement might break something fragile.

Neither of us said anything, not with Tom in the room, watching.

So, I said my goodbyes and left.

Twenty-Two

On a Loop

DENVER

I'd played the loop at least twenty times, but it still didn't sound right.

The layered guitars clashed with the vocal distortion, and I couldn't tell if it was the mix or if the song itself didn't want to cooperate. Mason's riff had started it. One he'd sent over, something raw and delicate. Now, it was this ambient, aching thing I couldn't stop adding pieces to. It was like I was trying to build something that might explain how I felt better than I ever could.

Clara's voice wasn't in the track, but somehow it still felt like every reverb line and downbeat featured her. That was the problem. She was everywhere, even when she wasn't.

I dragged my hand down my face and leaned back in the chair.

The studio dad built had always been the place I could breathe. It was small, but it was still mine. We'd started in Eli's living room, and bless his parents for putting up with all the noise. We'd moved to borrowed garages and midnight gigs. We weren't mainstream. Didn't want to be. Indie, weird, rough around the edges, and that was the point. I lived for the way we built something real out of nothing but noise.

Lately, everything felt off. I was chasing the sound, chasing the feeling, and coming up short.

The door creaked behind me.

Jamie slipped in like she owned the place, two iced coffees in hand, and sunglasses still perched on her forehead. She made a beeline for the cluttered desk, dropped one cup beside my keyboard, and flopped onto the couch.

"You live here now?" she asked, eyeing the screen. "You look like you haven't seen daylight in two days."

"Feels like longer," I muttered, reaching for the coffee.

She kicked off her boots and tucked her feet under her. "Let me guess, you're spiraling over that chorus again."

"Something like that."

I brought the cup to my lips as she studied me.

"You've been moody as hell since she came back."

I didn't look at her. "I've been working."

She hummed. "Right."

I didn't know what she was getting at, and I don't think I wanted to know.

I scrubbed at the keys, tapping the space bar again. The same echo loop played back. The same ache threaded through it. I hated how much of it was about Clara without ever naming her.

"You ever think maybe you're trying too hard?" Jamie asked.

I sighed. "That's kind of the whole point of producing."

"Yeah, but not the whole point of living." She arched her brow. "What's got you twisted up, Denny?"

I hated it when she called me that.

Jamie stood and crossed the studio, her fingers grazing the synth's edge like it was a stage prop. "I've known you a long time. Long enough to tell when something's got you in a chokehold."

"I'm fine," I blurted. I loved Jamie like a sister, but recently, the stuff that's been bothering me wasn't her business. I was taking a line out of Clara's book and pulling away a bit. I knew Jamie noticed, and she was just trying to be a friend.

She stood beside my chair and leaned a hip against the desk. "You could just say you missed her, you know. I get it, you two were close once, and she left."

I turned my chair slightly, jaw tight. "I didn't say this was about her."

Everything was about her.

"You didn't have to. You've been wound up since her return. Don't think I haven't noticed."

There she went again, pushing this Clara topic. We locked eyes for half a second too long; I was trying to read her expression. Then she smiled, small and calculated, and stepped back toward the couch.

"Why are you pushing? If anything, you're the one who's been off lately."

" I'm only looking out for you."

I said nothing to that, and we fell back into normal conversation until she left for her shift at the Vet clinic.

I didn't go back to working; I just sat and stared at the wall.

Dinner was the last thing on the list of things I wanted to do. It had me on edge since Dad asked Clara yesterday. It was the idea of seeing *him* with Clara. I still couldn't get over how comfortable she was lying across him when I went to her dad's house. He had a piece of her I didn't. It made me dislike the guy, and now I was supposed to sit through dinner and watch how close he was with Clara?

She said they weren't doing more than co-parenting their son, Eric, but the way she spoke about him made me think otherwise. Though I doubt she would've ended up in my bed if there was something more there. I haven't known Clara, who'd been gone for the last eight years, but I knew her better than to think otherwise.

Eventually, I shut everything down and headed inside. I hadn't even made it past the doorway when I heard small footsteps darting down the hall.

"Mommy, look! Guitars!" Eric's voice rang out, full of joy.

I stepped into the living room just in time to see him in front of the guitar wall. My pride and joy. Bare feet planted on the hardwood, one finger raised to a cherry-red Stratocaster like it was a spaceship.

"Mommy, can I have one?"

Before Clara could answer, I spoke. "Pick one, and it's yours."

He turned, wide-eyed. "Really?"

"Yeah," I smiled."That one there's a good place to start." I nodded toward a smaller-bodied acoustic I kept for guests. "We'll tune it up after dinner, if you'd like."

Clara appeared next, stepping into view. She wore a pale yellow sundress, thin straps slipping off one shoulder, her hair pulled into a loose knot. She looked like everything I wanted and everything I wasn't supposed to touch.

Her eyes flicked up and found mine, just for a second. Something passed between us, uncertainty. Like instinct, she reached for Eric and gently pulled him to her side, her hand curling around his shoulder in a gesture so fluid and familiar.

Something shifted in my chest. A pull I couldn't name. Not jealousy exactly, something deeper. A longing I'd buried beneath layers of restraint.

Ethan stepped behind her, then. He offered his hand.

"Denver," he said, like we were old friends.

I shook it. "Good to see you again."

Behind us, Dad emerged from the kitchen, tongs in hand, already smiling.

"You must be Eric," he said, crouching down in front of him. "You're bigger than I imagined."

Clara tensed, a subtle movement I noticed.

Eric grinned. "I grow fast."

Dad laughed, charmed. "Is that so? Well, we're glad you're here."

After shaking Ethan's hand, he turned, gesturing to us all. "Come on, dinner's ready."

* * *

Dinner flowed once Dad dished out the Italian takeout. Dad tried cracking a few jokes to make them feel welcome. Despite having his phone on his lap in case of a hospital call, he was still the warm and welcoming man I'd known all my life.

He'd been doing so much better since Clara saw Heleen's eyelids move yesterday. There was more hope in his eyes.

"So, how was Clara as a child?" Ethan asked Dad.

He leaned back in his chair, swirling the last sip of wine in his glass. "Clara? She came into this house like a hurricane. I mean that in the best way."

Clara smirked across the table, half amused, half warning. "Careful, old man."

Dad just chuckled. "I'm serious. Couldn't sit still. Always needed to be doing something. Organizing the fridge, dragging Denver into ridiculous adventures, and convincing me she could cook dinner alone at twelve. Which—" he glanced at me with a grin, "almost set the kitchen on fire."

I laughed under my breath. "She used cinnamon in spaghetti sauce."

"Don't knock it till you try it," she shot back, pointing a fork at me.

Ethan was grinning, completely charmed. "So, you've always been like this? Just… full-speed all the time?"

She shrugged, brushing a strand of hair behind her ear. "Still am, probably. I don't enjoy staying still too long. Life gets boring when you're standing in one place."

She said it like it's simple. Like she hadn't been running from something for years.

"She hated the quiet," I said, without meaning to. "Used to hum to herself just to fill the silence."

Clara paused, then glanced at me, just enough to acknowledge it, but not enough to linger. "Maybe the silence was too loud."

And there it was. The weight behind her chaos. The stillness she'd always feared.

Ethan looked between us, curious, and I felt Dad's stare on the side of my face. I averted my gaze from the prying eyes.

Eric tapped his spoon against his plate. "Mom sings in the kitchen," he chimed in on the conversation.

Clara smiled. "And I still suck."

You don't. Not when you're humming under your breath. Not when you didn't know anyone was listening.

Dad raised his glass. "To the girl who never stops moving."

"To Mom!" Eric chirped.

Ethan lifted his drink. "To chaos and cinnamon."

We all laughed.

After dinner, Eric's laughter drifted faintly from the living room. Dad and Ethan disappeared minutes before, when Dad pulled him to the side. Probably grilling the poor guy.

I followed Clara to the kitchen, where she rolled up her sleeves to wash the dishes.

Dinner wasn't as awkward as I'd thought it would be.

I leaned against the counter, watching her. "He's got a lot of energy," I nodded in the direction Eric was.

She chuckled. "Yeah, he never stops."

"He reminds me of you."

I saw the slightest hesitation on her shoulders. "Is that a compliment?"

"Always is."

That made her pause and turn to me, water dripping from her hands, eyes catching mine.

The kitchen instantly felt too small.

"Don't," she said, as if sensing where my mind was going.

I stepped closer anyway, not touching, just close enough to smell her perfume, to feel her breath fanning my face. The pull I had toward her was both suffocating and intoxicating, like poison I knew would ruin me but couldn't stop tasting.

"I'm not doing anything," I teased.

Her cheeks flushed, her gaze bouncing to the entrance and back to me. "That's the problem."

Her gaze fell to my lips, bringing back the memory of our nearness in the cramped hospital supply closet just yesterday. While my intention was solely to comfort her, I couldn't help but enjoy the feeling of such proximity to her. There was nothing, absolutely nothing, that could compare to the feeling of holding her in my arms, her golden eyes looking up at me, a simple yet overwhelmingly comforting experience.

God, I felt her everywhere.

Eric's loud laughter cut through the tension, and she blinked, taking a step back. She looked toward the hallway where his voice came from, where Dad could come in any second, and all this could come crashing down.

She wiped her hands on a dish towel. "I should go check on him."

When she turned to move, my hand moved before I could think, fingers wrapping gently around her wrist.

"Clara."

Her steps halted. Slowly, she looked over her shoulder at me.

"There's this place I've been working on music," I said, voice low. "Just me. It's quiet. Outside of town, no one really goes there."

Her eyes narrowed. "Why are you telling me that?"

"Because I want to take you."

She was silent for a second, lips parted. "It's not a good idea."

"No. It's probably the worst idea. But I still want to take you there."

She thought about it for what felt like minutes before she nodded. "Fine."

I nearly fist pumped, but nodded instead before releasing her arm.

This was good.

Twenty-Three

Played in Our Keys

DENVER

The drive out of town was thick with tension. My fingers drummed against the steering wheel to the song playing, as Clara sat silently in the passenger seat.

My heart raced. I didn't actually think she'd come. Well, yeah, she agreed, but I never know when it comes to her lately.

I was nervous. *Don't know why; it wasn't like this was a date. Wait, was it? Should I have worded it that way when I asked her? Shit.*

When we finally pulled up to our destination, the sky had dipped into the navy, stars blinking above the trees. The condo sat tucked behind a line of pines, low and modern, the lake just beyond it glowing like spilled silver.

"This is yours?" She asked as I unlocked the door.

"Yup." I pushed the door open and waited until she passed through. "Haven't told anyone about it yet."

I knew I couldn't stay at home forever. About a year ago, I started looking for a place of my own. Something simple, something cozy. The lakeview had been an unexpected bonus. I hadn't settled in much, though; between everything going on, the space still felt more like a stopover than home.

Clara turned toward me, eyebrows lifted. "Not even the guys?"

"Not even them."

I watched her eyes flicker over the place; open layout, hardwood floors, and a built-in studio, which was the main reason I knew this place was for me.

What caught Clara's eye was the wall of windows.

"God," she breathed, walking to them. "It's beautiful."

From here, the lake stretched out like a painting. It was still endless and reflected the last burn of the moonlight. She pressed a hand to the glass like she needed to feel it.

It was the same reaction I had when I first did a house tour.

I didn't know how to explain to her what this place did to me and how seeing her here just fit so fucking good.

I showed her around, then we wandered down by the lake and sat by the shore. We sat close enough that our shoulders almost touched, and watched ducks drifting across the water.

"Thanks for coming."

"You're welcome," she murmured.

I studied her profile, the way her jaw tightened just enough to betray that she was anything but calm.

I almost left it there. Almost.

Instead, I cleared my throat. "Why've you been dodging me?"

Her head tipped slightly, but her eyes stayed forward. "I haven't."

"Clara."

Finally, she turned, just enough to meet my gaze. For a second, it was there. The crack, the truth she didn't want to admit. She swallowed it down as soon as it came. "My mother could wake up any day now."

I heard what she was saying, clear as if she'd spelled it out for me. *What happened between us shouldn't have happened.*

"If she does," I said quietly, "you'll finally have her back. And I'll be glad for you." I paused. "Don't think for a minute it erases what's between us. Because it doesn't. Not for me."

I sat back, heat crawling under my skin, the echo of my own words heavy in my chest. Maybe I shouldn't have said it. Maybe I'd just tipped my hand too far. She was already running from this, and maybe I was just the idiot still standing in place, waiting for her to stop.

I dragged a hand over my face, forcing my voice lighter than I felt. "Are you hungry?"

Her lips twitched, the corner of her mouth softening. "Starved," she said. "But wait… as long as you're not cooking."

I pressed a hand to my chest, feigning hurt. "My gourmet breakfast the other morning wasn't good enough?"

"That was breakfast," she shot back, her tone playful now.

"Hmm," I pretended to think it over. "Grilled cheese it is."

Without giving her a chance to protest, I bent down, scooped her over my shoulder, and stood.

"Denver!" she squealed, pounding a fist against my back as I burst out laughing and carried her toward the house.

We threw it together like we'd done it a hundred times before. Bread, butter, cheese, and fruit on the side, as we laughed too loudly, like no one was around to hear. Because no one was.

No eyes. No weight. No pretending.

We ate on the studio couch as she asked about the song I was working on. I'd left out a sheet on the keyboard the last time I stopped by.

I picked up the guitar and strummed a few chords as she watched me.

"Play more," she hummed.

I did.

She didn't talk or interrupt, just listened like she always did.

After a while, she lay back on the couch, hands tucked behind her head as her eyes drifted to the ceiling.

I watched her instead.

There's a look she got when she forgot to guard herself. When the version of herself she shows the world slips, and the real one shines through.

She was that girl now. Barefoot, hair a slight mess, cheeks flushed, and eyes filled with life.

"You always look like that," I asked.

"Like what?"

"Like you belong in the moment. One no one else gets to see unless they look close enough."

I watched as she swallowed. "And you… Do you always say things like that?"

"Only to you."

I continued to play when she didn't respond, just laughed and turned her head toward the ceiling again.

I sat and watched her for a beat. The lake glimmered behind her, and my entire world quietly rearranged itself around the shape of her.

I guess that's why I wanted to bring her here. It was like I was giving her the key to the one corner of my life I'd kept untouched.

Once I cleaned up the little mess, I draped a blanket over her sleeping form, dimmed the lights, and climbed the stairs to my bedroom. I didn't know how she would've felt waking up beside me, and the last thing I wanted to do was push more than I'd already had.

Later that night, a shift in the bed woke me. I don't open my eyes. I waited, like maybe I dreamed it.

Then I felt the blanket lift, and her body slid beneath it. I turned over; the mattress dipped again as she stilled.

"Clara," I murmur, voice thick with sleep.

"I didn't mean to wake you."

"You didn't," I lied.

I blinked at her in the dark, her eyes meeting mine. I sat up, still halfway between dreaming and reality. "Couldn't sleep?"

She nodded, fingers twisting in the hem of her shirt. "I just… wanted to be next to you."

Music to my ears.

Without a word, I lifted the blanket, inviting her closer.

There was no hesitation as she moved closer, tucking herself against my bare chest. My hand slid instinctively to her waist, holding her there. Her leg tangled with a mine beneath the covers, and I swear, I could feel her heartbeat at every point we touched.

I pulled back enough to see her face, my hand brushing the hair from her cheek. "I don't think you realize what you do to me," I whispered.

She blinked.

"This," I said, my thumb dragging slowly along her jaw. "You. In my bed. Looking very much like mine."

Her breath hitched, chest rising.

"I'm not trying to ruin you." Her warm breath graced my lips.

"No?" My fingers slid down, trailing the slope of her neck, to the hollow of her collarbone. "Then why do I feel like I've already come undone?"

I don't get an answer. She just pressed her forehead to mine. I felt her exhale, her breath shaky.

"Say something."

"I don't know what to say. It's like… whenever I'm near you, I forget every reason we shouldn't be doing this."

I let that sink in. Let the weight of her honesty settle in the space between us.

My hand slid lower, finding the curve of her waist. Her skin was warm beneath her shirt. "I forget too," I murmured. "And when you're this close, I don't want to remember."

And because I was a glutton for punishment, I pressed my mouth to hers. It was slow and sure. There was nothing hungry about it. Her lips were soft against mine, and the way she kissed me back drove me crazy.

She shifted beneath me, arms slipping around my neck, and suddenly, I was above her. Caging her in, breathing in her lavender scent. Every inch of me was aching for her.

Her fingers threaded through my hair as we deepened the kiss. I tugged at the edge of the shirt, lifting it enough to touch bare skin.

I paused, forehead resting against hers.

"You can tell me no, angel. Right now. I'll stop."

She looked at me, eyes glassy and breathless. "No. I don't want you to stop."

That's all it took.

My mouth found her throat, her collarbone, earning me a moan.

I was so hard for her.

I pushed the shirt up and over her head, tossing it to the floor.

Her skin glowed in the low light, and for a second, I just stared.

"Jesus, angel."

She hid her face with one hand, but I caught her wrist gently and pulled it away.

"Don't hide from me. I want to see all of you." I hovered over her, kissing her once before moving to her neck, her chest. I reached under her and unclipped her bra, tossing it aside.

My eyes stayed on her as I blew over one of her nipples before taking it into my mouth.

"Oh-" She shuddered under me, her low moans getting louder the more I sucked.

I kissed my way down to her stomach, placing kisses right above her waist, and I pulled her shorts and underwear off in one swoop.

I felt her squirm as my breath lingered over her pussy. "Open up for me, baby. Let me see your pretty pussy."

Her legs shot open with a groan. I dove right in, giving her lips gentle kisses, her wetness dripping between her legs.

Her back arched off the bed. "Oh, God," she whimpered.

"You're soaked, angel," I said, taking in her scent. *So sweet. So mine.* I moved to the side of her, lying on the bed. "Come here. I want to drown in you."

I heard her loud intake of breath. I took her hand, pulling her toward me.

"Denver," she breathed, trying to protest.

I hummed while watching her move over me. "Sit on my face. I'm still hungry."

She moaned at my words as she took her seat right on my face. I held both her legs as I ate my new favorite meal. *So fucking sweet.* Her hips bucked above me, hands locked in my hair as she rode my face. Her moans filled the room, and it just made my cock jump in my pants.

"Den…ver…fuck…oh-"

She bucked, and I lifted her and sat her over me.

"Can't have you coming just yet, can we?"

She panted, chest heaving, as her lust-filled gaze locked on mine. My tongue ran over my lips, tasting her.

I flipped us and hovered over her as I pulled my pants down. I leaned over and got a condom from the nightstand, ripping it open with my knee, and rolling it over my hardness.

I kissed, then looked down at her. "You sure?"

Because god help me, if she flees when the sun rises.

"I need you, Denver. Need you in me," she whimpered.

A growl left my mouth as I captured her lips once more, guiding my cock into her wet pussy. I shuddered at her tightness around me.

She was a moaning mess as I pulled out and slammed back in; her back lifted with a moan. A beautiful mess was how I'd describe it as I looked down at her. Her eyes were loopy, but they didn't leave mine. I grunted, giving slow and deliberate strokes. Her hands grazed down my back, and I fucked her deeper.

I kissed her, slow and measured. We moved together like a perfect symphony. Panting, heartbeats beating as one, and sweat.

When she finally cums, it's my name she sings.

When I follow…When I lose myself in her completely, it's her hand in mine, our fingers locked, like even our bodies knew this was something we couldn't keep pretending wasn't real.

My forehead rested on hers as we tried to catch our breath. "Don't run away from me again, angel," I whispered. "I don't know if I could take it if I lose you again. You're the only thing that makes sense when everything else doesn't."

I kissed her before she could say anything.

We fell asleep, her legs and arms wrapped around me.

Right where she belonged.

Twenty-Four

Borrowed Light

CLARA

I woke up to an empty bed and sunlight slipping in through the gauzy curtains, dappling the rumpled white comforter and the naked skin beneath it.

Denver wasn't beside me.

I blinked up at the ceiling, letting the silence of the morning settle. The ache between my thighs was a faint throb now, more memory than sensation. I closed my eyes, remembering the way he looked at me and how his tentative touch lit me up. Just all of it.

God. Last night.

Don't run from me again.

Those words replayed like he'd just said them.

I pulled the sheet higher over my bare chest and turned to his side of the bed. *His side.* It was still warm and faintly indented. I dragged my fingers along the wrinkled fabric and wished I could pause time, just for a little longer.

The door creaked open a second later, and there Denver was.

Barefoot, curls damp like he'd just showered, a lazy grin tugging at his mouth as he carried a tray toward me.

"You brought me breakfast?" I asked, sitting up and clutching the sheet tighter.

"You looked too good to wake up starving."

"I think I'll have to get used to this." I raised an eyebrow.

He shrugged as he set the tray on my lap. "Well, it's reserved for women who completely ruin me and then pretend they didn't."

I laughed, despite the lump in my throat. "So just me, then."

He gave me that look, then one that said I knew exactly how much power I held and still had no idea. "Yeah. Just you."

I glanced down at the tray. Scrambled eggs, toast, and tea.

I ate as he stole bites off my plate and sipped from my tea like it belonged to him. Everything about him and this moment exuded warmth. I wanted to crawl into his lap and stay there forever.

When I leaned forward to grab a piece of toast, he reached up and brushed his thumb across the corner of my mouth.

"You had a crumb," he murmured.

I stilled as his hand lingered on my cheek.

We were close. Closer than I should've let us be. After last night, that thought was futile.

His thumb slid from the corner of my mouth to the edge of my jaw. Then he kissed me. Soft and slow. A kiss that shouldn't have hurt but did.

I let myself fall into it, then pulled away.

He didn't ask why, just looked at me the way he always did. Like I was something he didn't want to blink and miss.

"You okay?" he asked.

I nodded, swallowing. "Yeah."

"You sure? Because last night-"

"Was perfect," I said too quickly. "But it doesn't change anything."

Denver's eyes darkened, but he didn't push. That made it worse.

"I'm not running," I added.

"Good." He reached for my hand. "Because I meant it. What I said last night. I don't know what I'd do if I lost you again."

I looked away. My chest was so full it felt hollow.

He didn't know he already had.

My phone buzzed across the room, and I rose to grab it, wrapping the sheet around me. Three missed messages from Ethan. One of Eric grinning with cereal all over his mouth, and another that read: *Are we still going? He's counting down.*

I'd texted Ethan last night when I realized I'd be staying out here.

I stared at the screen as Denver shifted behind me.

"Time to go back?"

I turned. "I promised Eric I'd take him to the aquarium today."

He nodded. "We can head back after you shower."

I walked back to him, a smirk playing on my lips. "Will you join me?"

I could live in this moment a little longer.

"I already took a shower." He wrapped his hand around my waist and looked up at me from where he sat on the bed.

I hummed, dipping my finger into the tea and rubbing it on his face. "I think you missed a spot."

His smile was coaxing, that boyish grin I used to swoon over when we were younger.

The shower ran as I brushed my teeth with a fresh toothbrush he gave me.

He was already in the shower when I stepped in, head under the water as he held his hands on the wall. I took a breath and stepped toward him, running my hands down his back, then his tattooed arms.

He turned to me, water dripping down his body as he switched our positions. The water was hot, mist curling around us as he pressed me gently against the wall. His hands ran down my back, his mouth finding my neck, my shoulder, my collarbone.

My mouth fell open in a whimper. When his hands slid into my hair and tilted my face toward his, I didn't fight the kiss. I leaned in like I needed it to breathe. The kiss was needy as our tongues twisted together, little moans slipping from my lips, the more we fought for control.

I felt him hard against me, and I was already dripping. His arms came down and hiked my legs around his waist, and the water poured down on us. "You always look like art," he whispered as he used one hand to pump his shaft. Then he slid it in and held me against the wall. "Now let me hear those pretty moans, angel. Sing for me."

Afterward, I was dressed in his t-shirt that fit like a t-shirt dress, and boxers that couldn't stay up for dear life. It almost made me feel like I was doing a walk of shame as we headed out.

The drive back was quiet. His hand brushed mine on the gearshift once, and I let it stay there. Neither of us said much.

With every mile that brought us closer to the city, the spell faded. The lake house felt like another world. A soft, suspended place where maybe we could just exist. But the second I saw the first familiar street sign, I knew it was over.

Not the feelings for him. The lie. It was back in place, settling over me like a second skin.

I reached across the console and laced my fingers through his without looking.

Maybe if I held on tight enough, the truth wouldn't tear us all apart.

When we pulled up to my dad's, we sat for a second watching the house. He was probably thinking the same thing. Our night was just that, a night.

"Don't run again," he said without looking at me.

"I won't."

"Promise?" He turned his head, a soft smile on his face.

He lifted his pinky, and it brought back so many memories that I had to laugh.

"You remembered?" I laughed.

"Of course. Now, put it here."

I put mine up to his as we stared at each other for a second. "I promise."

I just hoped I'd be able to keep it.

Twenty-Five

Glass Walls

CLARA

The aquarium smelled like damp concrete and overpriced snack food. Sea salt and soft light bounced off the glass tanks, giving everything a blue glow that felt both surreal and too sharp for the mood sitting heavy in my chest.

Eric was darting ahead, all legs and excitement, yelling over his shoulder, "Mom! Dad! Come look! There's an octopus, and it's, like, moving!"

Ethan chuckled beside me. "You'd think he's never seen one before."

"Right."

He tilted his head toward me. "You okay?"

"Just tired."

It wasn't a lie. But it wasn't the truth either.

We followed Eric to the massive jellyfish tank where pink and purple tentacles swirled in slow motion, pulsing. The sound of kids murmuring and soft music echoing through the glass dome filled the room.

I let myself fall onto a nearby bench, watching my son practically press his face to the glass.

"I slept with him," I said suddenly as Ethan joined me.

His brow lifted, but he didn't look shocked.

"Thought you might've. I mean, you walked back into your father's house like you'd had a night." He grinned, leaning back, arms crossed loosely. "You okay though?"

"No," I admitted.

I felt like I'd peeled off one layer when I sat at my mother's side and got my feelings off my chest, just for another to take its place. I wasn't regretting Denver anymore, so that was good. If it were a few weeks ago, I'd probably already be on a flight back to New York.

Weren't my feelings justified? A relationship with Denver was taboo. I also couldn't get over the fact of my actions.

"At least you're honest about it," Ethan said.

"Honest?" I laughed, running my hand through my hair. "I keep telling myself it's not real. That I can't let it be real. It just feels like…like the more I try to pull back, the more I want to fall into it."

He nodded, watching the water. "It's okay to want something, Clara."

"Not if it breaks everything else."

"I don't think wanting someone has to break you. Not if they're the right person. Plus, he seems like a good guy."

My eyes snapped to him.

"Denver," he clarified. "He looks at you like you're gravity."

I laughed. "That's so dramatic. And you're so warming up to him," I teased.

"Eh," he shrugged. "But promise me one thing."

"What?"

"If you're not ready to tell the truth, Clara… then don't get in deeper. You don't get to reach for both. That's how people break."

His words lodged in my throat. I wanted to argue. I wanted to say I *wasn't* trying to have it both ways. But wasn't I?

Letting Denver hold me like I was his. Bringing Eric back here, where all my demons lie. Letting myself pretend I could balance this web of lies without hurting the people I loved the most.

"Come on," Ethan said, clapping his hands and standing. "Our boys ' on the move."

We followed behind Eric as he moved to the next exhibition.

"You know, I should start paying you by the hour for all this advice," I joked.

Ethan stopped in his tracks, not a smile on his face. "Never that," he held my face. "Not after all you've given me." He pressed a soft kiss to my forehead before pulling back. "Now come on, we have some dolphins to see."

We ended the afternoon with ice cream and greasy fries from a food truck just outside the aquarium. Eric sat cross-legged on the bench beside Ethan, happily dunking fries into a vanilla milkshake like it was a normal thing to do. I had no idea where he learned that. Probably Ethan. It had his chaos written all over it.

Seattle had been good to him. Better than I expected. He smiled more, slept more easily, and asked fewer questions about when we were going home.

"Can we stay longer?" he asked, his mouth full of chocolate drizzle. My sweet boy was too cute.

I smiled. "Longer than what?"

"Just longer." His small shoulders came up in a shrug. "Forever, maybe."

Ethan snorted into his water.

I brushed the hair off his forehead. "You like it here that much?"

He nodded, solemn. "There's a beach and cool fish and Denver has, like, a million guitars."

The way he said his name, like it belonged in his mouth, made something shift painfully inside me.

"He said I could play. Is he gonna let me play still?"

Ah, the conversation from dinner the other night.

"I'm sure he is, sweety. Finish up your food so we can head back, yeah?" I smiled, trying not to let my despair show.

He obliged, dipping more fries in his shake as Ethan and I looked at each other across the table.

The longer we stayed, the more my son was weaving Denver into his world. The more his little voice carried Denver's name like it belonged to him, too.

And if the truth ever came out, I wasn't sure which one of us it would break first, me, Denver, or Eric.

Twenty-Six

The Secrets We Keep

DENVER
16 Years Old

It's been a year since Clara and I sat on the rooftop as we stared up at the night sky, finally admitting what neither of us dared to say before. We had feelings for each other.

It was scary, but a part of me didn't care.

Since then? It's been moments to tuck in a box and keep forever.

A lingering glance that lasted a moment too long, subtle brushes in the hallway just to feel that fleeting contact, whispered late-night conversations when the house was silent. Even the weight of her head on my chest as we watched a movie we'd later pretend to forget.

Every time I thought we were going to cross the line, like really cross it, she'd pull back. Or I would. We'd both pretend we hadn't been about to fall.

We never talked about it again, but we also didn't stop either.

Mason's house was packed—music blasting, lights dimmed, and someone already passed out in the recliner. I wasn't really feeling it tonight, but Clara was coming. Besides, it was Mason's birthday, and I couldn't skip my boy's party.

I leaned against the kitchen counter, sipping from a solo cup that'd gone warm fast, trying not to scan the room like a loser waiting for her to walk in.

"Denver, right?" A girl with a high ponytail stepped up beside me. "You're the one playing in the school talent show, right?"

I gave a small nod. "Yeah. That's me."

The guys and I took every little chance we got to play. The talent show was one of them.

She smiled. "You're really good. I saw you play last year. The original song, that one kinda hit." She twirled the ends of her ponytail.

My mouth quirked up, half grateful, half distracted.

She was still talking over the music when I saw Clara.

With a few of her friends by her side, she walked in like she didn't belong, but everyone noticed her anyway. She'd pulled her hair back, had this little black tank top on, jeans that were just shy of dangerous. Her smile was tight, eyes scanning the room for me. Or maybe she didn't know she was looking.

Until her gaze landed on the girl beside me. Then me.

She looked away.

The girl said something else. I didn't hear.

"Hey, I gotta-uh-thanks for the compliment," I muttered, already stepping past her, my eyes locked on the back of Clara's head as she disappeared toward the back door.

I caught up to her outside. "You're leaving already?"

"Didn't feel like standing around and watching you flirt," she bit out.

"I wasn't."

"You never are."

"You want to talk about this?"

"No," she said, turning to me. "But I will anyway. You've been… we've been doing this thing for almost a year, and every time it feels like we're going to talk about what we are doing, we don't. I'm tired of pretending it's nothing."

I stepped toward her. Close. "I'm not pretending. But maybe I don't know what to do with it either."

Her arms crossed as she heaved a sigh. "We're not supposed to feel this way."

"Yeah?" My voice cracked. "Then why does it feel like the only thing that makes sense?"

She went quiet. It's stupid, but I want to reach for her. Press my forehead to hers and say screw it all.

The sky opened up without warning. Fat raindrops splashing down like the clouds just gave up on holding it in.

Clara let out a yelp, then laughed, and I caught her hand as we took off down the street. We're soaked in seconds, slipping on wet pavement and dodging puddles like kids again. Her laugh got louder, that wild and careless one that I loved.

I swear I could've lived in that sound.

We slowed just as we reached the porch, panting, drenched, faces flushed. She turned to me, pushing wet hair from her face. And I've never seen anything more stunning in my life.

"You're beautiful, you know that?" I said, breath caught.

"Even when I look like a drowned rat?" she teased, voice soft.

"Especially then."

It's all the invitation I needed.

I leaned in and kissed her. It wasn't like the first time, with two kids fumbling to get it right. No, this one was sure, and it made waiting this long worth it.

* * *

The storm still tapped against the window while she sat cross-legged on her bed, writing in that diary she hid under her pillow.

I sprawled out across from her, scribbling lines in my notebook; guitar chords, scraps of lyrics that might become something if I got the rhythm right. Every few minutes, she'd glance, and I did too. That pull was always there.

Our earlier conversation was just a distant thought. I knew it wasn't about the girl talking to me that made her upset. *It was us.*

The lamp cast a warm glow between us. The room smelled of lavender and shampoo, and a little rain that still clung to us even though we changed out of our wet clothes.

A creak from down the hall made us freeze.

These moments were always tricky. That Dad or Heleen might find us too close.

I watched her eyes widen as we glanced at the floor. She slowly set her pen down, and I leaned over just enough to whisper. "Think they heard us?"

She grinned. "Only if we start singing."

I laughed under my breath and went back to my notebook. A moment later, I felt her shift onto her side to face me.

I rolled to face her, just a few inches between us.

She opened her mouth to say something, then closed it.

I lifted a hand, reached up, and brushed a damp strand of hair off her cheek. She didn't move, just let me.

"You're mine, Clara," I said, the truth that'd always existed, even before we were old enough to name it.

Her breath hitched. "I know."

For a moment, it felt like the world went completely quiet. Even the storm outside seemed to pause. It was just the two of us under this roof, in a room we weren't meant to share this way. The silence lingered until reality shattered it apart.

"How's this going to work?" she finally asked. "What happens if someone finds out?"

I exhaled slowly, then reached for her hand between us. "I don't know."

"They'll freak out."

"Yeah. They will."

Her eyes fell to our hands. "We live in the same house. We eat at the same table every day. My mother shares a last name with your dad," she sighed.

"But we're not related," I tried to reason.

She shook her head. "That won't matter to them. It'll still be… wrong."

I hated how the word fit in her mouth. Like we're something dirty.

"It doesn't feel wrong. Not when it's just us."

She met my eyes again. "And when it's not just us?"

I stared back at her. At the girl I'd pick a thousand times over. "Then we keep it just us."

She swallowed. "Sneaking around?"

"If that's what it takes."

"And if someone finds out?" She asked the burning question again.

"I'll take the fall. Say it was me. That I started it."

"Denver…"

"I'll protect you. Always."

Her fingers tightened around mine, but I saw the thoughts working around in her head. "What if it doesn't last?"

The fear in her voice broke me. So I scooted closer, forehead brushing hers, my thumb running across hers. "Why wouldn't it?"

"People change. Things get hard. We're not… this isn't normal."

"I don't want normal."

Sighing, her fingers curled in the blanket between us. "What if our parents hate us for it? Because they will. It might even ruin their marriage."

"Then we leave," I shrugged.

Her eyes searched mine. "Leave?"

"When I graduate, I'll take a gap year until you graduate. We'll go somewhere new. Start over. Somewhere it's just us."

A spark flickered in her eyes. Like she was seeing it, too.

I had two more years of high school, and Clara would graduate the following year. What better way to live freely than to go to a college far away, where we could just be us?

She turned onto her back, staring at the ceiling, her voice barely above a whisper. "Florida."

"Florida?"

She smiled. "It's hot. It's always summer. We could be near the beach. Write. Make music. No snow. No rules."

The corners of my mouth tugged up. "You want to run away to Florida with me?"

She faced me again. "Only if you'd come with me."

"You really think I'd let you go without me?"

"What if someone else tries to date you?" She didn't miss a beat.

"They won't."

"Cocky."

"No," I murmured. "Certain."

"What if someone wants to date me?"

"Then you'll tell him you belong to someone else."

She lifted her pinky. I'd gotten accustomed to it by now. The pinky hold turned into fingers laced. We lay like that, barely touching, but closer than ever.

* * *

The following week, we stole seconds. Moments between moments. Like at dinner when our legs brushed beneath the table, and Clara's pinky hooked around mine under the cloth. She'd smile without looking at me, still carrying on a conversation like we weren't tethered in some invisible way. It was risky, with our parents just feet away, but somehow that made it worse. Or better. I wasn't sure anymore.

The week after that, we almost got busted. A group of us hit the night fair downtown. The crowd was thick and chaotic, but in the best way. Lights blinking, kids screaming, the smell of funnel cakes and burnt sugar in the air.

Clara stuck close to me, our shoulders brushing now and then, but never too long. Never too obvious.

When we reached the Ferris wheel, everyone started picking who they wanted to ride with.

"I'm calling Clara," Mason shouted before anyone could move, but she laughed and shook her head.

Over my dead body.

"We're not twelve, Mason," I said, trying not to grit my teeth.

Jamie lingered by my side, getting on her tiptoes to put her elbow on my shoulder. "Are you riding with anyone?"

Clara stood a few feet away, pretending to study the ride's safety instructions, like she wasn't listening but definitely was.

I stepped back slightly, letting Jamie's arm fall off my shoulder. On any day, I wouldn't mind. Especially with Jamie. She was one of my best friends. "Clara and I'll ride together."

She paused, then a small smile crossed her face. "Cool. I'll go with Mason." She sauntered off to find him.

Clara didn't look at me as we climbed into the cart, but once we were tucked inside and the wheel started lifting us into the sky, her hand found mine. Her fingers laced through mine like it was second nature.

"Nice save," she murmured, a smirk playing on her lips.

"Wasn't saving anything. Just wanted to be next to you."

She laughed quietly and leaned back, her hair catching the breeze. The town spread below us in the blur of color and soft sound, and I couldn't stop looking at her.

By the time the cart stopped at the top, I couldn't hold it in anymore. I leaned in and kissed her. It was quick and hidden in the shadows.

It was just ours, that kiss. Until we started descending.

My eyes scanned the crowd, and I caught Jamie glancing up, a look in her eyes I couldn't quite read. She turned away just as quickly, saying something to Eli and laughing.

I sighed. *Close call.*

* * *

A few nights later, we escaped in my car, driving until the town lights were a distant glow. Clara brought snacks we didn't touch, picking the music while I parked on a hill. We climbed onto the hood, backs against the windshield, watching the town blink below.

The cicadas hummed around us. The night was wide, endless. Clara tilted her head toward me. "Do you ever think about the future?"

"Sometimes."

"You want kids?"

The question caught me off guard, but with her, it didn't feel crazy. "Yeah. One day. You?"

She nodded. "I think so."

"How many?"

She smiled. "Two. Maybe three. What would you name them?"

"John." The answer came easily.

She turned, laughing softly. "Of course you'd say John."

"What?"

"You and your John Mayer obsession."

I grinned. "You asked."

She shook her head, still smiling. "It fits, though."

We went quiet, hands brushing on the cool metal. It was reckless, maybe even stupid, dreaming like this. But out here, under the dark sky, it felt safe to imagine a future that could never really exist.

And still, I wanted it anyway.

Twenty-Seven

Thread by Thread

Present Day

The smell of fried dough and hot pavement clung to the summer air as we waited backstage. Kids screamed from the spinning tilt-a-whirl behind us, and the speakers buzzed with the leftover feedback of soundcheck. Mason sprawled on a folding chair, while Eli paced as he always did before shows, tapping drumsticks against his thighs. Sadie leaned against a post, sipping something neon green from the fair cup.

Me? I was glancing at the back entrance every thirty seconds like a guy who'd just lost his mind.

"Are you expecting someone?" Eli's voice came from behind me, sharp with amusement.

Ever since he told me about seeing Clara and me kiss the night of our show, he hadn't mentioned it since.

I kept my face neutral. "Just checking the crowd."

He snorted. "You've been checking the same corner since we got here."

I didn't respond. Because there, finally, Clara rounded the corner.

She looked effortless. Hair catching in the breeze, soft curls framing her face, sunglasses perched on her head. Her dress fluttered just a little, and

151

beside her was Ethan, holding a water bottle.

My jaw tightening seemed like a reflex. I felt it slackening the moment I saw Eric.

"Denver!" His little voice rang out before I saw him sprint.

I'd taken a liking to the little guy. He was full of energy.

I crouched without thinking, catching him mid-leap. The smell of cotton candy and sunscreen wafted off him. His cheeks were flushed, and a bright smile shone.

"You made it," I said, heart kicking in a way I hadn't prepped for.

"You said I could help backstage," he grinned. "And that you'd show me how to slide the strings!"

I think I liked him even more when he took a liking to my guitars.

Footsteps slowed behind us. Clara. Ethan. I stood, Eric still clutching my hand, and for a second, just one, I forgot everyone else existed.

From the slight flush of her cheek, her eyes honing in on me, I was a goner. Her tongue came out and swiped over her bottom lip. The act was quick, but it made my mouth water.

The simple act transported me back to the lake house. Her smile, how comfortable we fell into step.

"Hey," Clara said.

I met her gaze and felt everything I couldn't say rise like heat in my chest. *I want to touch you. I want to hold you. I want to be something I can't.*

"Hey," I replied, keeping my voice steady. I couldn't reach for her. Not here. Not with this many eyes. But God, it took everything in me not to.

A new voice chimed in. "And who's this little guy?"

Jamie.

"This is Eric," Clara said simply, her posture shifting.

"Well, aren't you handsome?" Her eyes flicked from Eric to Clara, then back. "Definitely got your mommy's genes."

Eric giggled behind me as Jamie approached Ethan. "I don't think we've met. I'm Jamie." She extended her hand.

"Ethan," he replied, shaking her hand with a polite nod. "Nice to meet you."

"Likewise." Her smile lingered too long while his brows furrowed. She was between the two of them, and my jaw almost ground to dust when she said, "You two look cute together," before hugging Clara and murmuring something about it being good to see her again.

Sadie slid in next, all sass and hip sway, flipping her braid off one shoulder.

"Well, hey there, future roadie," she said to Eric. Then to me, with a smirk. "You didn't tell me you had such a cute competition."

"Competition's stiff these days," I said flatly, stepping away as Eric jumped up and down in my hold. She didn't miss it, but she let it roll off with a wink.

I felt Clara's eyes on me, but Eric pulling my sleeve brought my attention back to him.

"Can I stay back here during the show? I won't get in the way."

I ruffled his hair, watching Clara's eyes soften at the sight. "Of course. Just don't start heckling Eli."

"I might," he whispered, grinning.

Eli, behind us, called out, "I heard that!"

We all laughed, and I realized how normal it felt. When Eric ran back to Clara and Ethan's side, Eli leaned over my shoulder.

"Cute kid," he muttered. "He's yours?"

The question hit like a dart. "What? No. Clara's, and that's his dad, Ethan. You've known me long enough. I think I'd tell you if I had a kid running around the world." I watched Eric with both of them as they smiled down at whatever he was saying.

It stung.

"Ah." He didn't push.

The set was about to begin, the crew motioning for us to head toward the stage. The crowd's buzz grew louder, lights shifting as the sun sank lower behind the trees. But I lingered for a moment, watching Clara kneel beside Eric, brushing something off his cheek. Ethan leaned in to say something, and she smiled. They looked like a family.

And I?

I felt like a ghost hovering just outside the frame.

The lights hit hard when we stepped on stage. My guitar hung from my shoulder like a second skin, but I felt everything under it. I ran through the soundcheck, my fingers moving out of instinct, muscle memory keeping me afloat.

Mason cracked a joke into the Mic. Sadie blew a kiss toward the crowd, and Eli gave a low thumbs-up behind the drum. The crowd pushed closer.

My eyes kept sliding back to the side of the stage.

Clara was there, tucked just behind the curtain, her arms crossed, while Ethan stood behind her, one hand resting on Eric's shoulder, whispering something to make him laugh.

I turned back toward the mic and leaned in. "We're Fever Light," I said, voice raspier than I meant. "Let's make this one count.

The music started. The first note echoed across the fairground, catching the breeze and rolling through the trees. I let it swallow me. Let it fill the space where the ache sat deepest.

Halfway through the third song, one I'd written months ago, back when Clara wasn't even a possibility—I rewrote the lyrics in my head. Every line twisted toward her. Toward what we were and weren't. What we'd lost and hadn't touched yet.

When I looked back toward the side of the stage, Eric was sitting on a small amp, legs swinging. His eyes were glued to my hands. Watching every chord.

And Clara was smiling. It wasn't the kind you gave to a stranger. It wasn't the one she gave Ethan, or even Eric. It was filled with pride and awe.

It was mine.

It hurt more than I could explain.

Because I couldn't have it.

Not fully. Not yet.

We finished the set to loud cheers, and Sadie soaked it in like she always did, blowing kisses and high-fiving the fans as we left the stage. I handed my guitar off to a tech and stepped toward the edge.

Eric was the first to greet me. "That was awesome!" he said, bouncing on the balls of his feet. "You were so fast with the strings!"

I knelt at his level. "Think you're ready for a solo next time?"

He nodded hard. "Can we still play together like you said?"

Clara froze a second too long, listening.

"If your mom and dad say yes, then yes."

He squealed, looking up at Clara.

"We'll see," she smiled down at him.

Not a yes. Not a no. *I'll take it.*

Ethan came up behind them. "You killed it out there, man."

"Thanks," I said, standing. "Appreciate it."

We stood like that for a beat. The band around us was packing up, and Sadie was still chatting with fans. Some time during the show, Jamie had disappeared. She was in the corner taking a phone call.

"You looked good out there," Clara said.

I smiled, taking her in. "Thanks."

We stood in front of each other, not saying anything. What could we say with prying eyes?

The crowd was dispersing from the fairground as the sun dipped low.

In the middle of it all, I stood, watching Clara buckle Eric in his seat in Ethan's SUV.

When she was done and turned to me, I asked, "You guys taking off?"

"Yeah," Ethan answered first, walking to a trash bin to toss an empty juice pouch. "Long day."

Clara nodded. "He's wiped. I should get him back."

I took a step closer. "It was good to see you." I had to get that out of the way, with the few seconds we had alone.

"It was good to see you, too."

My chest lit up. "Uh, so I'll see you," she said, taking a step back.

I closed the distance, and because I couldn't help myself, I wrapped her in a hug. She clung to the back of my shirt as I breathed her in. I didn't let the hug linger, although I didn't want to let her go.

"Yeah, I'll see you." I took a step back as her face was flushed on the way to the passenger side of the car.

"Bye, Denver!" Eric shouted from the back seat. I shot him a wave.

Ethan stepped in front of my view, an unreadable expression on his face, but he held his hand out before I gave him a firm shake.

"Just so you know," he began, looking over his shoulder at the car, "nothing is going on between me and Clara. Not like that. So you can stop giving me the death glare every time I'm standing in her vicinity."

I blinked. "I wasn't—"

What the fuck? This guy knew?

He lifted a brow. "You were. And I get it. If things were flipped, I'd probably be doing the same thing."

"You know her," I said. "In ways I don't think I ever will. I think I'll always envy you for that."

I wasn't afraid to admit that. I also didn't care if he knew. I never cared. But Clara always did. This thing between us might be taboo in others' eyes since our parents are married, but so what?

Ethan gave an understanding nod. He turned, but paused, looking over his shoulder. "She's a good person."

I frowned. "I know."

"No." His gaze was head-on. "I mean, when the time comes, and you feel like questioning her, just remember that. She's a good person."

He didn't wait for my reaction and headed back to the car, opening the door and sliding in beside Clara.

I stood there, watching the SUV pull away, trying to figure out what the hell he meant.

And why it suddenly felt like something in me was unraveling, thread by thread.

"There he is," Eli said, walking up with a lazy grin and a soda in one hand. "Was thinking you'd ditched us for the mini groupies."

Eric's cooler than any of you," I muttered, rubbing the back of my neck.

"Fair," Mason chimed in.

Sadie caught up a beat later, looping her arm through Eli's and sipping from a lemonade. "We're hitting that bar Sadie picked. You in?"

I hesitated. I wasn't exactly in a drinking mood. Not with Ethan's words replaying in my head.

But I also didn't want to go home and be alone with it.

"Yeah. I'm in."

Mason clapped my shoulder. "That's the spirit. You need to loosen up. "You've been too tense recently."

Eli snorted next to us.

As they started heading toward the back lot, I hung back a little and turned to Sadie.

"Hey. Can I talk to you for a sec?"

I still didn't understand her flirting earlier.

She arched a brow but didn't protest, peeling away from the group as the guys kept walking. "What's up?"

I glanced away for a second before looking back at her. "What was that earlier?"

Her mouth twitched. "Oh. That."

"Yeah. That."

She shrugged. "Was testing a theory."

I frowned. "What does that even mean?"

"Something's been off for a few weeks. I was trying to see if I was imagining it."

"Off how?"

Oh, I knew how.

"You know, I always wondered why you didn't want to take things further with me. Or why I've never seen you with a girlfriend."

"We play together. That would be unprofessional." I ignored her second comment, already knowing where this was going.

She laughed. "I know, and I'm not harboring any feelings toward it. I respect it."

I looked at her in confusion. "So why the flirting?"

"To see if my theory about you and your stepsister was correct." Her voice didn't hold anger or disgust. More like amusement.

I swallowed.

"The way you look at her does not go unnoticed. You're not subtle at all. And the way her face turned beet red when I touched you gave me my answer." She took a sip of her drink, smiling like she'd just solved a mystery.

"You're crazy." I walked off. "And knock it off. This isn't a joke."

I didn't have to turn to see that she was smiling at her brief victory.

And now I have to work on being subtle.

***

O'Malley's was crowded. It was loud, but not loud enough that you couldn't hear yourself think. Unfortunately, loud enough that Mason's laugh cut through the hum of background conversations and Eli's half-hearted groans over losing at darts for the third round in a row.

I sat at the edge of the booth, fingers wrapped around a sweating glass of beer, barely sipping it. Across from me, Sadie leaned back with her boots propped on a bench, eye fucking some dude in the booth across from us. Eli was mid-complaint about Mason's cheating, and Mason, of course, was doubling down like a true menace.

"Swear on your bass I didn't cheat," Mason said, grinning as he threw a handful of peanuts into his mouth. "You're just bad at math. And darts."

Eli flipped him off without even looking up.

I laughed. They were like children.

I had just tuned them out when a shadow fell across us both.

"Mind if I sit?"

The voice was smooth, a little coy. I looked up.

She was… pretty. Tall, long blond hair that framed her face, red lipstick that matched her top, and confidence. She had that kind of presence that turned heads, and judging by Mason's not-so-subtle glance, I wasn't the only one who noticed.

"Sure." I nodded vaguely to the seat next to me as I took a drink of beer.

She slid in without hesitation, hips brushing against mine. "Saw your set earlier. You've got something."

O'Malley's wasn't that far from the fairground, so it wasn't a surprise that she'd been in the crowd when we played.

I smiled. "Thanks."

"I mean it." She leaned in a little, her perfume catching in the air. *It wasn't lavender.* Her knee brushed mine under the table. "You were electric. The whole band's good, but I couldn't take my eyes off you."

I knew what this was.

I'd been here before. After gigs. After bars. After every decent show, when the stage lights faded, people clamored for a piece of what they thought they had seen.

She was good on the eyes, no doubt. A while ago, I wouldn't have thought twice.

But tonight?

All I could think about was her.

Clara stretched out on my couch at the Lake house. Clara, laughing as we shared breakfast in bed. Clara, tracing her fingers along the foggy glass of my shower door. Clara, whose eyes seem to see right through me when she looks at me.

Fuck.

The woman said something, but I didn't catch it. My eyes drifted to my phone on the table. I wondered if she'd answer if I texted or called her.

"Sorry, what?"

The woman smiled, teasing. "I asked if you were always this quiet or if I'm just intimidating you."

I forced a half-laugh. "No, I'm just… tired. Long night."

Her smile faltered, like she could sense the wall building up.

Eli raised an eyebrow at me from across the table. Mason looked amused, and Sadie was lost in the guy who'd finally had the balls to approach her.

The woman's arms slid on my forearm, and I jumped. It felt wrong. It wasn't as delicate. "Maybe I could buy you a drink? Or something stronger?"

She was still smiling. Still trying.

It did nothing for me or my dick, which seemed to deflate more than it already was.

All I saw was Clara. Her eyes. Her laugh. The little crease between her brows when she was overthinking. The way she looked at her son was like the entire world existed in him.

I pulled back. "I appreciate it," I hissed. "Really. But I'm—"

"Taken?" she guessed.

I paused.

"No. Just not looking."

She held my gaze, something understanding flickering behind her expression. She nodded, smiled at me, then slid out of the booth without another word.

Mason let out a low whistle. "Man. You really are off your game."

Sadie snorted. "That wasn't game. That was… restraint."

They laughed, and I tried to laugh with them.

Not taken. Not exactly free, either.

"Heading to the bathroom," I told them before sliding out of the booth.

The bar noise swallowed me, and I pushed through the crowd to the men's room. I leaned against the cool tile wall, took in a deep breath.

I pulled my phone from my pocket, thumb over the screen. *Fuck it.*

I typed, **When can we get away again?**

I sent it before I could second-guess myself.

The screen glowed softly in the dim light. I ran a hand through my hair, letting the muffled music fill the agony I felt inside.

Twenty-Eight

Cautiously Optimistic

CLARA

The benches outside the hospital were cold. I sat with my arms wrapped around myself, staring at a patch of weeds breaking through the concrete, while Denver paced just a few feet away.

He had said little since we walked out here. I hadn't answered his text the other night, and it hung between us.

"I don't get it," he finally said, voice tight. "I don't get how we can be like that at the lake house, how you can look at me like that, and then come back and pretend like it didn't happen."

I didn't look at him.

He laughed under his breath, bitter. "You promised."

"I'm trying," I murmured.

His steps stopped. "You promised not to run."

When I got his text, I stared at it until my eyes drifted shut. I wasn't running, but I knew what getting closer to him meant. I might have also ignored his messages in the following days.

I closed my eyes, hating how fast my throat tightened. "I didn't run."

"That's not what it feels like. You're shutting me out. Again. After everything I—after everything we—" He cursed under his breath. "What am I supposed to think?"

"That we don't live in a fantasy," I snapped. "That I have a son to worry about in all of this. That your dad is watching our every move. That my mother might die there."

"And that makes me what? An inconvenience?" His voice broke on the last word. "Because that's what it feels like, Clara."

"That's not fair. You don't have a child to worry about. I do."

Upending Eric's life is the last thing I want to do. But that was inevitable. I knew it.

"Don't use Eric as an excuse to push me away."

"He's not an excuse. He's my entire life, Denver."

He stepped closer. "What's not fair is you giving me just enough to feel this, and then taking it away."

I pressed my lips together, nails biting into my palms.

"I'm not running." I don't know who I was trying to convince, me or him. "I'm thinking about Eric." Everything was about him. "About the fact that everything we do ripples into his life, whether or not we mean for it to."

I'd seen firsthand what a broken home does to a person. I spent Eric's entire life shielding him from the wounds that faded but didn't disappear. Now, he was back in the same world, and he was loving it. He was innocent. What kind of mother would I be if I messed all of that up? I certainly didn't want to be like *her.*

"I think about him too."

"You think this is just about feelings?" I stood, finally facing him. "What about when she wakes up? Your dad doesn't even know. You think this will go over well with him?"

His expression twisted, but he didn't back down. "I don't care what they think, Clara. I *never* have! Because if loving you is wrong, then I've never been right a single day in my life. And I don't regret a moment of it."

My breath caught as his chest heaved.

"What the hell is going on here?" Tom was walking toward us, eyes flicking between us.

I stepped back, putting space between Denver and me. "Nothing," I breathed.

Tom's voice was like ice. "Didn't sound like anything."

I've never seen him like this.

"We were just talking, Dad," Denver muttered.

Tom looked straight at me. "Clara. You've been avoiding my calls. And now I find you two out here arguing like teenagers? What's going on?"

My stomach twisted. "It's complicated."

"Try me," he said, voice flat.

"Dad." Denver stepped in front of me, hands crossed in front of his chest.

"Tell me," Tom demanded. "From where I'm standing, this looks like the kind of mess we've all been trying to avoid."

I looked down at the cracked concrete. Eric's face flashed in my mind.

Was this how it was going to crumble?

"Fine." There wasn't any hesitation in his voice, as I was mentally freaking out. "We…"

"Mr. Stone!"

We all twisted as a nurse ran up to him.

"Your wife. She's awake."

The intake of our breaths was loud. Tom didn't hesitate. He bolted through the doors like his heart had jump-started. I stood frozen in place, the sound of his footsteps still echoing in my ears.

Denver twisted around, our wide eyes staring at each other without a word.

My legs felt like they didn't belong to me when I finally moved toward the entrance, pushing through the doors and into the hallway. My palms were cold. My fingers felt numb. The fluorescent lights above me buzzed as if the world hadn't shifted under my feet.

She was awake.

Tom was already in the room when we got there, clinging to my mother's hand like it was the only thing anchoring him to earth. He was speaking low, his voice cracking as he called her name repeatedly.

And then I saw her.

My mother's eyes were open. Barely, but open.

I stopped in the doorway. It hit me hard, not all at once, but in waves. The shock of it. The quiet after waiting for so long. She blinked again, and something in me crumpled.

Her eyes are the same shade as mine. I hadn't thought about that in years. The way they used to match when she'd watch me across the dinner table, sizing me up. How they'd gone cold the day everything broke.

But now?

They looked soft. Cloudy. Human.

The nurse's voice floated beside me. "She's responsive, still in a post-coma state. She may drift in and out, but this is good. This is the first step." Her voice held hope as she smiled at us.

Tom nodded at her side, not taking his eyes off of her. I nodded, following along with the information the nurse provided.

"She'll need neuro ovals," the nurse continued, checking the monitors. "Speech. Memory. Motor function. But we're cautiously optimistic."

Cautiously.

I took a step forward as my hands trembled at my sides, and tears blurred my vision. This isn't how I'd expected to see her again, but here we were. Some semblance of grace flowed through me for stepping in here, for being here despite how I felt about my mother.

"Hi, Mom," I whispered, the word feeling foreign to my tongue.

Her head turned a little. It wasn't swift or clear. But it was toward me.

Her lips parted.

Not a word. Just the intention of one.

I didn't move any closer. I couldn't.

I felt Denver behind me, still near the door, just watching.

He hadn't come in. That was me when I first started visiting my mother.

As I tried to keep my eyes on the woman who'd given me life, I remembered how he used to talk about her like she was his world. He'd believed in her before I stopped believing in anything.

But he hadn't said a word. Maybe now he was seeing what I'd known for a long time. That she was just a woman. That she made mistakes, too.

Tom was crying softly beside her. Whispering words I couldn't hear.

I didn't touch her. I stood next to the bed, fingers barely grazing the blanket. Not her skin. I wasn't ready for that yet.

She was breathing on her own. She was alive.

Her dazed eyes looked at me like she was trying to remember something she'd lost.

I blinked fast, forcing the tears back.

I'd waited weeks—years—for this. But the minute it happened, I wasn't sure how to feel. Hope. Fear. Grief. I couldn't sort any of it out.

Behind me, I felt Denver shift. He still said nothing. And I didn't turn around. This moment belonged to her. I didn't want the first thing she saw when she woke up to be our closeness. The shame she made me feel for loving him was still there.

I stayed a little longer. I watched the nurses and doctors try to ask her questions, but she still wasn't speaking. When I did finally leave, it was when she fell asleep. I said goodbye to Tom, whose question about what was going on between Denver and me was long forgotten. I only stopped in front of Denver, but his eyes weren't on me. They were on her.

* * *

Back at dad's, I slumped on the couch, eyes closed, as I ran over what had happened today. Eric's laugh was the first thing I heard. Then Ethan's voice and footsteps rushed to the door. Dad had taken them out. He wanted to show them around.

"Mom!"

His arms flew around me as he jumped into my lap. His energy rushed into me, full of color and speed. I wasn't ready for it, but I let it hold me upright.

"You're back!" he grinned. "Guess what? Grandpa and Aunt Claire took me out. We went to the museum and I got something. Wanna see?"

I smiled, kissing his forehead. "Of course."

He darted down the hall, already narrating the entire outing.

165

Ethan walked up and pulled me into a hug. His chin rested on my head as his hand rubbed my back, easing my tension. I didn't need words right now, and he knew that.

"Want me to make some tea or something stronger?"

I gave a tired smile. "Tea's fine."

"You okay?"

I didn't answer right away. "She woke up."

"Damn. Seriously?"

"She looked at me," I said. "Didn't speak. But her eyes were open."

"That's big. Jesus, that's good news, Clara."

It was.

Eric returned holding a box with a picture of a cartoon rocker on it. "It's a puzzle! A really hard one. Grandpa said I could pick anything, and I picked this. Aunt Claire said she'll help me build it."

"Wow." I took the box. "This is so cool."

He flopped onto the carpet when I gave the box back and dumped out the pieces. I sat with him. Helped him sort edge pieces, nodding along as he kept talking. My mind wandered back to the ICU. To Denver, standing at the door. To the weight in my chest, I hadn't been able to shake.

Eventually, Ethan scooped Eric up and carried him to the bathroom. I stayed behind, staring at one stubborn puzzle piece in my palm. The color didn't match. It didn't fit anywhere.

I didn't realize how long I stared at the piece until Eric was back, dressed in pajamas, hair still damp as he crawled into my lap without asking.

His sleepy green eyes looked up at me. "Are you going to tuck me in, mommy?"

"Of course." I kissed his hair. "I'm not going anywhere."

His breathing slowed against me as my hand ran through his hair. I looked at him, soft, tired, and trusting. I realized I didn't have the luxury of falling apart. Not while he still believed I'm the one holding it all together.

"Planning on dropping that puzzle piece anytime soon?" Ethan whispered as he sat next to me on the floor.

I was still gripping that one puzzle piece like it mattered more than anything else in the world. I let out a breath as I dropped the piece with the others.

My head rested on Ethan's shoulder as I closed my eyes.

My mother had opened her eyes. I'd felt the shape of something like hope press against the inside of my chest. I didn't know what to do with it. I didn't know if I could trust it or what it would cost.

And Denver…

He seemed so sure about all of this until he was standing like a shadow in her room, like I used to.

I don't care what they think, Clara.

I wish I didn't care. It just wasn't that simple. I wanted to go back to his house by the lake, where everything was quiet. Where thoughts of judgment didn't exist, because it was just us.

"Everything's going to be okay," Ethan said.

I held onto his words as I drifted to sleep. Back against the couch with two of the three most important people to me.

Twenty-Nine

Love

D**ENVER**

Boxes were stacked in the living room, half of them taped, most of them still gaping open. My closet was a mess. Shirts hanging by one sleeve, drawers half-emptied, guitars leaning like they knew they were next.

Mason stood on the coffee table, balancing a lamp. "Hey! If I bring this to the van, do I automatically win the title of Strongest and Sexiest?"

Sadie passed him with a roll of her eyes, a half-empty box of mugs in her hands. "Sure, Mason. You can be the Strongest and Sexiest, as long as Jamie gets the Most Delusional."

Jamie, behind me, didn't budge. "I'll take it. Comes with main character energy," she shrugged.

I rubbed my face, palms gritty with dust and regret. "Can we just not break anything? Please?"

"You mean besides your spirit?" Eli didn't miss a beat, lifting a box labeled vinyl and giving me a look. "Because that's been cracked since Tuesday."

"Eli," I warned.

He held up a hand in surrender. "Hey, I'm here for moral support and bubble wrap. I know my place."

Mason carefully jumped down from the coffee table with the lamp raised above his head. "You gonna tell us what this is about, or are we pretending this is a spontaneous life reboot?"

I didn't answer.

The truth was, after seeing Heleen wake up, I had conflicting feelings about her. I was happy she was awake, finally. We've been waiting for this moment for over a month now, and it was good to see my dad's worry vanish.

There's just been something gnawing at me, and I hated how I couldn't figure it out just yet. So, after leaving the hospital that night, I told my father about my house and my plans to move. He didn't press; he was just shocked. I got the good old 'proud of you son' with a shoulder clap.

When I told the guys about Heleen finally waking up, they've been by my side since. That's why we've been tearing up the house all morning, getting all my stuff packed and loaded to take to my house.

They're a great support system, no matter how annoying they might come off sometimes. Then again, that was family for you. I wasn't complaining. Until they pried.

Mason leaned in front of the doorway. "So what's the plan, bro? You're gonna disappear into the woods and write love songs?"

"Wouldn't be the worst idea," Eli added. "You've been brooding like a man with a secret Spotify playlist titled *She Said Nothing*, and *That Hurt Worse*." He gave me a knowing look.

"Shut up," I muttered, tugging another half-full bin from under the bed.

Sadie knelt and opened it without warning, then froze. "Oh, my God."

"What?" I looked over.

Eli leaned in to see. Then he burst out laughing.

Sadie held up a t-shirt with *Mayer is My Spirit Guide* printed across the chest.

"Is this…" she began.

"It's a collector's box," I said quickly, grabbing it back. "It's sentimental."

"It's *John Mayer* merch," Jamie deadpanned.

"Signed," I added.

"Oh my God," Mason said. "You're not moving out, you're moving into your Soft Rock era."

"He's not writing breakup songs," Eli added, grinning. "He's becoming one."

"You guys done?" I asked, stuffing the t-shirt back in the box like they hadn't just exposed my most emotional treasure trove.

Mason mock-sobbed. "Bro, I just—' Slow Dancing in a Burning Room'? That song is Denver."

"Shut up," I laughed when they burst out in laughter.

Jamie smirked but didn't pile on. She just looked at me a little too long. Like she saw what the others were laughing at.

And I hated how much she might've been right.

We made a trip out to the house—mine, the one no one knew about until recently.

It was just a few boxes. Gear. Clothes. Mason claimed my kitchen was haunted, and Jamie reorganized records without asking. Eli left a six-pack in the fridge for "emergencies." I didn't tell them to leave, but eventually they did. Sadie lingered a little but said nothing, just bumped my shoulder with hers on the way out.

The drive back was quiet.

I still had a lot of things to pack, but I needed a few things right now, mostly toiletries.

Halfway up the stairs, I heard footsteps and stopped.

Dad stood in the hallway, towel slung over his shoulder, hair damp from a quick shower. He froze a little when he saw me.

"Didn't know you were back," he said.

"Just grabbing a few more things."

"Right."

He didn't move. Neither did I.

Ever since the scene outside the hospital, things have been weird. I was ready to tell him about Clara and me. Ready for it to be in the open, so she could stop feeling like something was holding her back. Holding her back from the happiness we both knew we could have together.

That would also entail mentioning how Heleen knew this entire time. I still couldn't wrap my head around that. That was the million-dollar question, and Clara said herself, she didn't know how she found out.

My hands clenched at my sides at the thought. Everything I thought I knew was a lie. *She* was a lie. I'd accepted her into my life as a second mother, and she'd been lying to my face for eight years. Lying to dad, too.

Dad looked tired. The hospital had hollowed him out. I doubt dumping all of this on him would do him any good.

Watching Heleen wake up and trying to figure out what came next… he was carrying more than he'd ever admit. I didn't want to add to that weight. Not right now.

"You got some of the things out of the house okay?"

"Yeah. It's quiet out there."

"That's good." A pause. "Are you settling in alright?"

I shrugged. "Still feels weird."

He nodded. "Yeah. First place always does."

He was watching me differently now. Closer. Like something had shifted. *He knew.*

"I didn't mean to push the other day," he said. "Outside the hospital."

"It's no worries, Dad." I made a move to walk up the stairs.

"Denver."

I froze.

"I love you, son. Always will."

I swallowed. "Love you too, Dad."

There was silence before his footsteps retreated.

Upstairs, I scanned for the last few things I came to get. Some notebooks, a hoodie, my broken capo, but as I reached under the desk, my fingers brushed something soft.

Tucked under a box, I pulled it out, and my stomach tightened before I flipped it over.

A photo book. The one I made for Clara for her fourteenth birthday. I brushed some of the dust off it before opening it.

We were just kids, both a little bruised by the world but trying to make something of every moment. I spent hours pulling photos I'd taken with that camera. I laughed at the thought. There were so many memories in those pages: lake days, fire pits, her laughing with her hair in her face. I printed each one, wrote stupid captions, and taped the last page with a note that said: *You're the best part of it.*

I found it under my bed a few days after she left. I'd never asked why she didn't take it with her.

Now, holding it again, I felt the same tight knot in my chest. Like, I really didn't let go all this time. Like, part of me had been waiting for her to come back for it. *For me.*

She was here, but she wasn't here for me.

I flipped to the back, tracing the smudged ink of my handwriting. It felt like someone else had written it. A boy who believed that the right people always found their way back.

When I flipped back the pages, I stopped on a family photo. My dad's hand was on my shoulder, Heleen's bright laugh was frozen in time, and Clara's head was tucked under my chin like it belonged there.

We were happy. All of us.

I didn't know what hurt more. That it fell apart or that she never looked back until now.

I snapped the book shut, heart pounding. The surrounding silence was buzzing at the edges of my thoughts.

Then something in me cracked.

I stood and flung the book across the room, hard enough to hear it snap against the wall and hit the floor with a dull thud.

My breath was jagged, hands shaking.

Why?

Why was I always the one still standing with arms outstretched, waiting for someone who couldn't care less?

I sat down hard on the edge of the bed, burying my face in my palms. Let the heat flush out. Let the ache settle.

I got up, shaking my head as I crossed the room. I picked the damn book off the floor. The corner was bent. One sleeve had slipped loose.

I fixed it and tucked it under my arm. Because no matter how much it hurt… You don't throw away the things that shaped you. You carry them. You learn where to set them down..

I didn't put it in a box this time. I held it and grabbed my bag and the rest of my things. On my way out, I stopped at the liquor cabinet and took the bottle of scotch Dad always kept tucked behind the boring stuff. Something about that felt fitting.

A parting gift. God knows I was going to need it.

The drive to my house was a blur of empty streets and too much thinking. By the time I got there, it was already dark out, crickets chirping in the grass. I threw my keys on the counter, dumped the book and my bag on the kitchen table, and poured a glass of scotch.

One turned into two.

I leaned back in a chair by the window, staring out at the lake. The moon shone down on it just right.

Three sharp knocks sounded at my door. I froze, the glass held mid-air before another drink.

If it were Mason and Eli, I wasn't ready for their foolishness.

I got up when there was another knock, cursing under my breath.

"If you guys are here to—"

When I opened the door, it wasn't the guys.

No.

It was Clara.

Thirty

The Softest Lies

C LARA
I didn't know what I was doing here. Well, I did, but…

As if he were expecting someone else, Denver's mouth clamped shut when he saw me. Drink in hand, he brought the glass to his lips and finished the drink without taking his eyes off me.

For a second, we just stared at each other before he stepped aside to let me in.

Boxes lay scattered in the living room and kitchen. It wasn't a total mess; it was clear someone was moving in.

"Wow," I said as I looked around. "You're really doing this-"

The door shut behind me.

"Why are you here?" Denver cut in with an edge to his tone.

"Uh… your dad called. Said my mother's doing okay."

"So you finally stopped ignoring *him*?"

I didn't answer.

"Why are you here, Clara?"

My hands rubbed together as he moved to the kitchen to drop the class on the counter. He turned, leaned against the island, and watched me, waiting.

"He mentioned you moved. I guess I wanted to see it for myself."

After Tom confronted Denver and me outside the hospital, I had no idea what to expect when he called earlier. He was completely innocent in all of this, and it wasn't fair. I'd worried he might bring up where we left off, but he didn't. Instead, he asked if I was okay and even apologized when he didn't have to. Somewhere in the conversation, I think he accidentally mentioned Denver moving. Mentioned he might need someone.

"Not good enough." Denver pushed off the counter. "Why are you here?"

He was on my trail, fire in his eyes, and I backed up, my back hitting the wall.

"I don't know!"

"Bullshit!" His hands caged me in, palms pressed to the wall on either side of my head, his face lowering until we were at eye level. "Why. Are. You. Here."

I smelled the alcohol on his breath and how close he was. I couldn't answer. Not with his breath this close to my mouth, and his eyes locked on mine like he was daring me to lie.

"Say it," he whispered.

"I wanted to see you."

His hand came up slowly, fingers skimming the side of my jaw, barely there, but I felt it everywhere.

"You're going to be the death of me, angel," he said, voice thick with something between ache and anger.

His fingers dragged slowly across my mouth, and I parted my lips without thinking.

"Why do you keep twisting the knife, knowing I'd take the blade every damn time, if it meant staying close to you?"

I swallowed, not knowing what to say.

His breath tangled with mine, hot and uneven. I shivered. He felt it. His eyes dropped to my throat, then back up, catching something in me I didn't mean to show.

I shouldn't have come here. I shouldn't want a lot of things. Somehow, I just kept punishing myself. Punishing him.

Being away from him left me feeling hollow. Even when all it would take was my mother to finally speak again, I just wanted to see him.

His hand drifted down, fingertips skimming my jaw, sliding along the curve of my throat. Not possessive, but careful.

Even so, he didn't kiss me yet.

His forehead tipped to mine, his nose brushing gently against the bridge of mine, too intimate. Too much.

"This is a mistake…" he murmured, almost to himself. "And I'm a goddamn fool for walking straight into it." His green eyes bore into mine, the smell of scotch fanning my lips.

My chest rose and fell with anticipation.

His lips crashed down on mine. A groan broke free the second our mouths met. His hands caught my waist, pulled me flush against him. Our kiss deepened, hot and desperate. My back hit the wall, and he pressed in like he couldn't bear the space between us. His mouth moved over mine with too much hunger, and mine followed right after it.

I kissed him like I'd never get to again.

His hands slipped under my shirt and ran along my waist, making me shiver at every spot he touched. He broke the kiss to pull my shirt over my head. His lips were back on mine as I worked to get his shirt off. He knelt in front of me, looking up at me. Need filled his eyes as he worked my pants button.

I bit down on my bottom lip as he placed kisses on my bare thighs, hands sliding my panties down in one swoop. An appreciative hum rolled through him at what he saw. I didn't hide away.

My chest was heaving as he hooked one arm around my leg and placed it on his shoulder. My hand came down to brace myself. He licked his lips before diving into my wetness.

I moaned, back arching off the wall as his warm mouth teased me. My head hit the wall when his tongue played with my clit. My other leg was suddenly on his other shoulder, and I was being lifted in the air against the wall, as he stayed buried inside of me.

"Denver! Fuck," I whimpered, hands gripping his hair for dear life. He hummed and groaned, picking up his pace, almost driving me over the edge.

"Shit. I'm close," I breathed, tugging on his hair to stop him.

I needed to savor this.

He pulled back, mouth wet with my juices, eyes filled with lust as he carefully placed me down on my legs. On shaky legs, I dropped to the floor, pulling his pants down.

I faced his beautiful cock. It was big, veiny, and just… beautiful. I wrapped my hands around him.

"Angel," he groaned, hands falling to the wall as he looked down at me.

I wrapped my lips around him, taking him as deep as I could, as my other hand stroked him at the base. His groans made me pick up my pace. Every curse under his breath fueled me as I closed my eyes and sucked him, his musky scent filling my nose. I loved it.

"Oh-Oh-" He pulled me back. "Not so fast." He pulled me up in one swift movement, my legs wrapping around his waist.

He shook his head, gaze locked on mine like he knew how this was going to end.

Please, let's just have this one moment.

Holding me against the wall, he used one hand to slide himself into me, the other to hold my hips up.

"Angel," he breathed against my forehead as he thrust in and out of me. "Fuck."

"Yes," I whimpered as he fucked me.

It was just us. The view behind me brought me closer to the edge. The way he grunted and pace jerked, I knew he was close, too.

I came with a loud whimper, sweat trickling down my body, out of breath, and sated. Denver pulled out, his cum landing on the wall and floor.

I needed this. I needed him. Right here. Right now.

I blinked into the quiet, disoriented, when I woke up the next morning.

Then I remembered where I was.

Denver's house.

His bed.

His body, warm beside mine.

The morning light spilled through the window in slow streaks.

Denver was still asleep, lying on his stomach, one arm bent under the pillow, the other stretched out, hand resting near my leg. The blanket barely covered his hips. His back was smooth and bare, muscles relaxed in sleep.

When we'd caught our breath, he'd picked me up on shaking legs and carried me to bed.

My hand moved to trace the tattoo on his arm, just below his shoulder. It was one with fading lines, the ink a little older than the rest. A compass, half-wrapped in lyrics he never explained.

He shivered at my touch, but didn't wake.

I followed the line of another, something newer, near his wrist. My fingers hovered there, pressing it gently.

He sighed in his sleep, and I felt something ache in my chest.

I closed my eyes, breathing him in. His skin. The lingering scent of sweat, scotch, and sex.

I wanted this.

I wanted this so badly it hurt.

I also wanted to protect everything I'd built. I wanted to hold my son in my arms and not feel like I was living on borrowed time. I wanted to believe I could give Denver all of me without everything else falling apart.

But the truth…

The truth lived in my bones.

And once it came out, everyone would see the broken person I was. They'd see why no one ever stuck around long enough. They'd see the ugliness I carried, and I couldn't stick around for Denver to see that. *Not him.*

I came here last night because I wanted to live in the quiet for one more moment. See him look at me like I was everything, one more time.

My fingers stopped moving, and I rested my forehead against his arm.

You don't lie to someone you love, unless you're trying to protect them from a truth you know will break them.

Even then, you don't lie. I was filled with lies.

I stayed there a little longer, letting the warmth soak in, holding the quiet a little longer.

Eventually, I pulled the blanket up to his shoulders. Moved slowly, as if I made too much noise, I'd undo the entire night.

I stood there for thirty more seconds, just watching him.

Then I slipped out, closing the door softly behind me. My clothes were where I left them, cold on the floor.

I didn't look back.

Thirty-One

The Shape of Us

CLARA
16 Years Old

I found Denver in the nonfiction aisle, slouched against the end of a bookshelf with his hoodie pulled halfway over his head and a stack of books scattered at his feet. One sneaker tapping against the baseboard.

Denver looked up when he saw me, smiled, and held up a paperback. "Did you know Florida has more alligator farms than anywhere else in the country?"

I smiled and sat cross-legged in front of him. "We're not majoring in swamp life."

He grinned and tossed the book back on the pile. He scooted closer, our knees brushing. "Shame. I was hoping to impress our future biology professors."

"Did you even get your paper done?"

It was the beginning of eleventh grade for him, which meant college essays were due this year.

"Almost," he said, leaning over towards me. "I got distracted by the thought of the future."

I mirrored his movement, then backed until my back hit the shelf behind me. Sometimes we forgot where we were, forgetting we couldn't be so close to avoid causing any suspicion. "The alligator-infested one?"

"Exactly."

The library was quiet in that soft, hum-dampened way I loved. The smell of books was always a welcoming greeting.

I pulled my knees up and opened my notebook. "I've been looking at my course load. If I talk to Ms. Henderson, I think I can double up next semester. Maybe take a couple of online electives, too."

I felt him watching me as I flipped through the pages. "You don't have to do that. I said I'll take a gap year, it's not an issue."

"I know what you said, but still."

I peered over the book.

"You've got that determined look. You're not going to change your mind, are you?"

I smiled. "Nope."

He ran his hand through his curls, lips in a thin line, before he leaned over, just inches from my lips.

I looked around cautiously to see if anyone was nearby.

"Anything you want, then. But if it gets to be too much, we go back to the original plan." He leaned in to kiss me, but I stopped him.

"Not here," I whispered, feeling heat rising to my cheeks.

"Oh…yeah." He looked around, catching himself.

"Your dad's going to freak out when you tell him," I coughed out, changing the conversation.

"He'll be alright," he shrugged.

I prayed that he would be. And my mom, too.

* * *

We told our parents over dinner a few days later.

It was casual, just the four of us, a casserole in the middle. Mom was drinking wine while Tom dug into his food. Denver kept nudging my foot under the table, giving me the little push I needed to broach the subject.

I'd been rehearsing it all week.

"So," I started, pretending to stab my green beans with a little too much concentration. "I was talking to my guidance counselor this week."

Mom's head tilted up, already carrying a bored expression. "About what?"

"Graduation," I said. "She thinks I could finish early. If I take two night classes this summer and do dual enrollment in the fall, I could graduate in December instead of May."

Mom's brows furrowed as they both stared at me like I was speaking a foreign language.

Denver's hand landed on my lap under the table, out of view.

My shoulders released some tension as I waited for their reaction.

Tom set down his fork. "That's... fast."

"Yeah, but it's doable. I already have most of my credits. I just need to double up on English and take one more math class."

"Why the rush?" Mom asked, eyeing me over the rim of her wineglass.

Like she cared.

Denver jumped in like we planned. "She wants to get a head start. We've been talking about college stuff lately."

"Together?" Tom's eyes flicked between us, and my heart pounded at the thought of him knowing why we were planning this together. I held my breath as he proceeded. "As in... the two of you?"

Denver shrugged, trying to play it cool. "We've both been looking at schools in Florida. Thought it'd be cool to be close. Familiar faces and all."

I didn't dare look at Denver. I could feel his hand squeeze my thigh, and it took everything in me not to squirm. I felt a little relief when I felt his knee bouncing. It meant he was just as scared as I was.

"We've been talking about the University of Florida," I added. "They've got excellent programs in what we're both interested in. And, I mean... it just makes sense. We already study well together."

Tom leaned back, processing what I'd just said. Mom glanced between us as if trying to catch something in the space between our words.

"You're sixteen," she finally said. "You'd be moving out a year earlier."

"I'd be seventeen turning eighteen," I corrected. "It's just a semester early. It's not that wild."

"Some of your ideas are always wild, Clara."

"Not this one," I challenged.

"Why so far?" Tom cut in as Mom and I glared at each other.

"We want to spread our wings."

He cleared his throat. "Well… we'd need to look into it. Talk to your school counselor. Make sure it's actually viable. If it is and your mom agrees," he said, looking over at her. "Money isn't an issue, so we'll work on it."

"It is. I already got the forms. I just didn't want to bring it until I was sure."

They both went quiet. For a moment, I thought the plan was falling apart right in front of us, but then Mom sighed and reached for her wineglass again.

"You'll have our support, even though it seems like you're trying to get far away from us," Tom said with a smile.

I waited for Mom to chime in, but she didn't.

Denver let out a breath next to me. I felt his knee bump against mine under the table. This time, it didn't feel like nerves. It felt like a victory.

By the time we cleared the table and Mom disappeared into the laundry, and Tom retreated to his den, Denver grabbed my hand. He didn't say a word, just tugged me toward the front door.

We slipped outside into the dark. The porch light cast a gold glow across the grass and caught in the steam of our breath as we took off for the roof.

"Well," he said after we had sat down. "That could've gone worse."

I laughed, a quiet, breathy kind of sound. "I thought your dad was going to ask if we were joining a cult."

"He still might."

I nudged his shoulder. "You were perfect, by the way. Smooth, just the way we practiced."

"I blacked out halfway through. Did I sound convincing?"

"You sounded like you meant it."

He turned to look at me then, and something in his face softened. That slow, rare melt I only ever got when we were alone like this.

I leaned in, and so did he. His mouth brushed mine. I breathed him in, the warmth of his skin, the faint taste of mint and dinner.

When we pulled apart, my forehead rested against his.

"I did," he said quietly, answering the question I hadn't realized I'd asked.

I felt the words in my chest before I understood them. He meant what he said at dinner. He meant all of it. I felt something else in my chest, but I didn't name it. I felt it every time I was around Denver. He just made everything better.

I leaned my head on his shoulder. He shifted, just enough to press his cheek to the top of mine.

"We really did it," I whispered. "We got them to say yes."

"Well, we got a 'maybe'. But still… It's a 'maybe' we didn't have this morning."

I closed my eyes and smiled.

I reached for his hands, fingers lacing with his. "Do you think they'll figure it out?"

"Eventually. But not yet."

"Not until we're already gone," I said, and he nodded like that was the only outcome that ever made sense.

We sat like that until we felt like we couldn't keep our eyes open any longer.

When we went back inside, the house was quiet, and the hallway lights were already turned off. We kept our distance as we made our way upstairs.

I couldn't wait for the days when we didn't have to pretend anymore. Where we didn't have to keep our relationship a secret.

Denver caught my hand, pressing a kiss to the back of it. "Come tomorrow?"

I gave him a look. "Have I ever missed one?"

He grinned. "Didn't think so."

* * *

By morning, I couldn't sit still. Like if I stopped writing things down, lists, schedules, and credits I still needed, I'd lose it all.

I grabbed my diary and a pen, and by early afternoon, I was in the back seat of Eli's truck, Denver beside me, tapping out a rhythm on his knee.

They'd graduated from practicing in Eli's living room to his garage. I guess his parents were tired of the noise and the messy living room by the end of their rehearsals.

I perched on the couch, pushed against the wall, notebook open in my lap, pen tapping. Denver was tuning his guitar, squinting at one string.

I loved watching him. I'd name everything I loved about watching him, but somehow that felt like I'd be incriminating myself. I confined all those thoughts to my diary.

Mason marched in late with Jamie in tow. We've been suspicious lately. About the two of them. But they swore there wasn't anything going on.

Jamie was already smiling, sunglasses covering her eyes as she took the seat next to me while the guys lay into Mason about being late.

They'd snagged a gig at the town's fundraising event, and they wanted to make sure they perfected everything. They were already great, but I wasn't a musician, so what did I know?

"Any juicy secrets?" She wiggled her brows as she leaned over, trying to read what I was writing.

I shut it. "N-no. Just boring stuff."

She reared back, eyeing me. "Oh?"

"Yeah," I laughed.

"Oh… Wait, are you writing about a boy?" She whispered, smiling.

"Something like that." Red crept to my cheeks. I didn't need her digging into this.

"Tell."

"It's nothing, really."

"Liar."

Her nagging stopped the moment Denver's guitar played its first note, and she let it go as we stood there, watching them like we always did.

As I rolled over how I'd almost let her into my deepest secret, I vowed to keep that diary to myself. Carrying it around like it didn't have stuff in there that didn't need to be seen wasn't a good idea.

Later that night, doubt settled in. If someone were to find out before we followed through with our plans, everything would fall apart.

It scared me.

I was lying on my side when I heard the door open, then shut with the click of the knob. The mattress dipped gently behind me a moment later. Denver slid his arm around my waist and pulled me back against him. I let him.

Nights like this were risky.

His chest rose and fell, warm at my back, grounding. But my mind didn't settle.

I turned over, facing him. I stared at him for a long moment, then rose onto my elbow, hovering over him. I reached out, fingers trembling slightly, and traced the familiar map of his face.

I started at his brow, memorizing the way it creased, the way it always did when he was overthinking, even if he didn't say a word.

Then came his lashes, unfairly long and thick, the kind I'd once envied in secret before I ever dared to call him mine.

I moved lower, to the slope of his nose, the soft curve of his cheek. His skin was warm, a little flushed as I kept going. My thumb hovered over his mouth. His lips were parted. *Always soft. Always.* The way they pressed into my forehead when no one was looking, or brushed my lips every time he stole a kiss.

I let my hand rest there, my eyes memorizing every inch of him.

"You're so sure about this," I whispered. "Why is that?"

"Because I've never felt this way about anyone, not even close," he said, his voice low but steady. "I know what this is."

My hands lingered, stilling over his heart, right where it beat the hardest.

He caught my wrist and kissed the inside.

"I love you, Clara."

The words knocked the air out of me. For a while, I had been afraid to say that four-letter word.

Heart fluttering, I leaned down and kissed him. I didn't rush it when his mouth welcomed mine. It was a kiss I wanted to savor at the moment. It was slow, deep, and did things to my insides I couldn't explain. Like something blooming in my chest had been waiting for this moment to finally unfold.

"I love you too," I said, breathless. He closed his eyes before opening them and kissing me again.

We didn't stop. At some point, the covers slipped back, and my leg hooked over his hip. His hands found the small of my back, fingers splayed wide, anchoring me.

My hands slid beneath the hem of his t-shirt, fingers skating over skin I already knew by heart. He made a sound, and I felt it in me. His mouth moved from mine to my jaw, down the side of my neck, each kiss slower than the last.

I'd never been touched before. Not like this.

My shirt lifted with his. The warmth between us burned hotter, the space narrower.

He rolled over, enough to look me in the eye, his breath uneven, his voice hoarse.

"Are you sure?"

I was. I knew nothing about sex, but I knew I wanted it with him. But the thought of being exposed, of the world finding us before we were even ready, still lingered like smoke in my lungs.

He kissed my forehead, then my cheek, then the corner of my mouth. "There's no rush," he whispered, brushing my hair back behind my ear. "We'll wait. When you're ready, I'll still be here."

It was the most romantic thing anyone had ever said to me. There was no bargain or disappointment. Just love. Because Denver loved me, and I loved him.

He pulled me again, and this time, we settled. My head found the curve of his shoulder, his arm wrapped firmly around my waist.

"You asked me why I'm sure," he said after a stretch of silence. "It's because when I think about the future… It's always you in it, angel."

"I don't know where we'll be or how hard it'll get," he continued. "But that part never changes. It'll always be you. You're the only thing I don't second-guess."

He pressed a kiss to the top of my head, then whispered it again, softer this time, like a promise.

"I love you."

I smiled into his chest. "I love you."

We lay like that for a while, tangled in each other until sleep found us.

Thirty-Two

The Moment Between

DENVER
Present Day

When I got to the hospital, Clara stepped out of the car at the same time I did. It was as if the universe thought it would be a great idea to torment me first thing in the morning.

It wasn't a surprise that Clara had left yesterday morning. I expected it. Did it make me feel any better? No.

Her eyes locked on mine for half a second before she looked away. Like nothing had happened.

I laughed under my breath, bitter. "Here we go again," I said loud enough so she could hear.

"It was late. You were sleeping," she said, as if that's supposed to make it better.

It was, in fact, around nine in the morning when I woke up.

"That's what you're going with?"

We came face to face as we stepped away from the rows of cars.

"What do you want me to say, Denver?" Her voice was flat, like she'd rather be doing anything than having this conversation. It contradicted the Clara I'd seen last night. Hungry and wanting, as we fought for pleasure together. As I carried her delicate form to bed with me.

"I don't want anything from you, Clara." I stepped closer. Not close enough to touch her, just close enough that she couldn't pretend this was casual. "That's the point."

Her mouth parted, then closed. "Then why are you here?"

"I wanted to get this over with," I said, matching her bored tone.

I'd come to an epiphany. This, whatever it was, had to end. I was losing it, and if I didn't stop it, I'd continue letting her walk in and out like a rotating door.

Something flickered across her face—panic, guilt, something so quick it barely had time to register before her walls slammed back up.

As if she read what I was thinking, she said, "If you're done, then go." Her arms crossed over her chest, holding her ground.

I laughed again. "That's your move, right? Push people until they give up. Then act surprised when they finally do?"

"I didn't ask you to stay."

"No, but you never asked me to leave either. You just keep making it impossible to stay. Was that your goal?"

"You're being dramatic."

"No," I said. "I'm being honest. Asking the right questions here since you give me nothing to work with. So, no, I'm not being dramatic. You don't get to walk away every other day and pretend it's not cutting you deep… Or maybe… maybe you're not pretending."

That realization stung.

"Don't do that," she snapped. " I've been here, so don't make me into the bad guy."

She was still giving me nothing. The constant hot-and-cold was draining.

"You do that all on your own, Clara."

Nothing.

"Don't you see the problem here?" I asked. "I'm tired. Tired of the push and pull. Tired of guessing which version of you I'm going to get. I can't do it anymore."

"Then don't!"

I stared at her, throat tight. "Why do I feel like that's the first honest thing you've said this entire fucking time."

For a second, she looked like she might break. Like she might finally let me in.

Of course, she didn't.

I felt that final thread snap somewhere in me. I turned around without another word.

* * *

Fresh pink and white flowers filled Heleen's room. Dad sat at her side, leg crossed over his knee, as he laughed at whatever he was telling her. He'd been in a better place.

Heleen was alert but tired. Doctors said that was expected. When we explained how she ended up in the hospital, it'd all been a blur to her. Especially learning she'd been in a coma for over a month. But she was alive and well. Had a good amount of recovery ahead, but everything was looking good.

"Hey," Dad smiled when I stepped in. "She's been responding more today. Not much, but enough."

A small smile touched my lips. I nodded and crossed the room, but I didn't feel present. My body moved on autopilot while my brain burned through everything that happened over the past month.

Heleen's eyes found mine when I sat next to Dad. "You look tired," she whispered.

I forced a breath through my nose. "You're not wrong."

She gave me a look. Familiar, almost maternal, as if she were trying to read me without asking questions.

I didn't give her anything to work with. I stayed quiet, watching her watch me. I didn't recognize the woman who'd raised me, who I thought of as a mother. She lied. To me, to Dad.

I tried to keep my face neutral and stop my jaw from clenching.

Was I an asshole for wondering how she could lie there knowing she'd been holding something back all these years?

My eyes broke her gaze when the door opened. We turned as Clara walked in.

She hesitated by the door, then gave the softest greeting. "Hi."

Heleen turned toward her. "Clara." There wasn't any smile, just an acknowledgment.

Clara moved to the foot of the bed but didn't reach out. She just stood there with her arms at her sides, fingers twitching like she wasn't sure what to do with them.

This couldn't have been more awkward.

Heleen didn't bother attempting either. Didn't ask how she was or seemed pleased to see her daughter after eight years. Her expression didn't change at all. I told myself it probably had to do with her not being fully recovered.

I watched the exchange like a bystander, watching two people meet for the first time. The tension was too loud, almost insufferable.

I couldn't make sense of it. Clara said she left because her mom found out. She said it like it explained everything. But Heleen wasn't angry, not cautious, just… I don't even know.

Dad must've noticed the tension, because he stood and smoothed a hand over his pants. "Hey, how about we let these two have a moment? Could use a coffee anyway."

He was trying to be gentle, but I heard the subtext. He could feel the weight in the room, too.

I didn't move right away.

My eyes stayed on Clara, but she didn't look my way.

I waited for her to show some kind of sign that she didn't want that 'moment' Dad was referring to. But it was like I wasn't there.

So I exhaled and followed Dad out.

I stopped just outside after shutting the door. I leaned my head against the wall and let the back of my head fall against it. The ceiling above was white. Unmoving. Easier to look at than anything else.

Dad stood next to me. I could feel him watching.

"You okay?" he asked.

"I'm good."

He waited, like maybe I'd say more.

I didn't.

I pushed off the wall and glanced toward the far end of the corridor. "I'm gonna get some air."

"Don't go too far. It'll be good to spend more time with your stepmom. She needs it."

I almost scoffed. *Stepmom.*

"I'll be back, Dad."

What I needed was my guitar. I needed to feel the strings under my fingers. I needed the stage. I needed to do what I love to calm the storm I felt was brewing.

I needed an outlet.

Thirty-Three

Awaken

CLARA

I watched as the door closed behind Denver and Tom, my throat feeling too tight, the walls seeming like they were closing in around my mother and me.

She sat upright, eyes moving from the window to me.

We hadn't been alone in years. Not since the day I left.

It was hard keeping my eyes on her. Those eyes that resemble mine tormented me in my sleep for years.

Her voice came out hoarse and strained. "Why are you here, Clara?"

Not an *'I'm glad to see you'* or *'I missed you'.*

It should've been a welcome. A whisper of relief. Instead, she sounded like the past never ended.

That cut deep.

"I got the call about your accident," I murmured, feeling small under her scrutiny.

I heard her exhale a breath, eyes boring into me. "He doesn't know, does he?"

"No." My stomach twisted.

Her pale skin grew color, her head shaking. Disappointment oozed off of her.

Neither of us said anything for a beat. It was just the rhythmic beep of monitors, the soft hum of oxygen machines, and the lies between us, filling the room.

"You shouldn't have come back here."

Eyes widening, I couldn't believe what she was saying.

It was the last match I've been trying to contain, just thrown into the flame.

I stepped forward, my hips bumping against the bed. "Then why did I?

Her eyes opened, tracking me, but she didn't answer.

"Why come back to the town that buried me?" My voice was cracking too tightly in my throat. "Why walk into this hospital when I knew I'd have to look at you, remember what you did?" I pointed a finger at her, tears stinging my eyes. "Knowing neither of us came back from that day?"

Her expression didn't change, but something in her face tensed.

I knew she knew what day I was referring to. It was etched in my memory. I couldn't forget it, no matter how much I tried.

"You think I wanted to come back and see you like this? You think I didn't hear your voice in my head every day I spent away from this place? Every time I tucked my son— my son into bed and had to wonder if I'd ever be strong enough to face you?"

The monitor beeped steadily beside her.

"You didn't just let me leave," I said. "You pushed me out. You made sure I couldn't stay. I was seventeen. And you…" I couldn't even finish it. She knew what she did.

Still, she appeared indifferent to me.

I shook my head. "Still, I came back. For me. For them. Because I'm tired of carrying all of this. Because even though you fucked me up, I was scared you might not survive. So, yes, mother, I fucking came back when I found out you were in a coma."

The monitors beside her spiked. A shrill, piercing tone cut the room like a knife.

I stopped breathing.

"Mom?"

Her head slumped slightly. Her face went pale, even paler than before.

"Mom!"

The door swung open hard. A nurse burst in, followed by two more. I backed away as they moved toward the bed, barking numbers and instructions I couldn't process fast enough.

"Get her on oxygen! BP's dropping!"

Tom appeared in the hallway, eyes wide. "What's happening?"

"Step outside, please," one of them said firmly, her hands already on Heleen's chest.

"Miss, we need space. Now!"

Her voice didn't register as she repeated herself. I stumbled into the hallway, numb. Tom was saying something beside me. It didn't register.

Everything was buzzing and moving too fast.

I came back to fight, but forgot how it felt to lose control.

I don't remember how I got to the bathroom. Maybe Tom or a nurse may have pointed. I heard nothing after they shut the door in my face.

My hands gripped the sink, the cold porcelain under my trembling fingers. When I looked up, I hated what I saw.

Her.

Me.

Both.

The woman staring back at me had my mother's eyes. The same sharp cheekbones, the same tired eyes, and the same way my mouth pulled tight when I was trying not to cry.

You don't get to look like her, I thought. *You don't get to carry her face after what she did.*

But I did.

I had her blood, her anger, her cruelty, buried deep under restraint and politeness.

The same restraint I used to protect everyone but myself.

I pressed my hands to my face like I could block it out. To unsee what was always there.

"God, I hate you."

I wasn't sure if I was talking to her or myself.

She let me leave without stopping me. She watched me break and reveled in it.

The moment I heard about her accident, I came running. Like an idiot. Like a child who still wanted something from a mother who never once looked back.

The tears flowed, burning down my cheeks. I slid to the floor, pressing my hack to the wall, and dug my nails into the denim stretched over my knees.

There's nothing to fix here, nothing to rebuild. There's just damage, and history, and blood I never asked to be born from.

Inside that damage, I could feel myself cracking. *Maybe I wasn't lovable. Maybe she saw it before I did.*

I cried until I didn't recognize the sound coming out of me.

I came back here because I thought healing meant facing her. But healing might just be leaving her behind, and any ideas of rekindling a relationship.

When the tears slowed, I didn't wipe them away.

I stood, looking at myself in the mirror.

Still her. Still me.

Still broken.

But no longer pretending to be whole.

The chaos in the hallway had dwindled when I left the bathroom. I didn't bother going back. I just needed to leave.

By the time the sliding doors opened, I was already fumbling with my keys.

"Clara!"

Of course, he was there.

I didn't turn, just kept walking toward my car.

"Clara, stop."

"Don't," I said when he caught up to me. "Please don't."

"You can't drive like this."

I looked at myself, noticing how he winced at seeing my face. Why couldn't he just leave like everyone else? I'd pushed him enough earlier when he said he was done.

"I'm fine."

"You're not."

"Just go back in there. I already caused more damage. They might need you."

"I'm out here, Clara. Your mother will be fine, it was just a scare. I'm here for you, regardless, so let me help you."

I reached my door and dropped my keys, trying to unlock it. I pounded my hand on the hood in a scream as if it caused all of this.

"Stop. Stop. I'll take you." Denver's hands grabbed mine, placing them at my sides. He knelt and picked up my keys. "We'll worry about the car later."

"Fine," I breathed. "But Denver…"

"Yes?"

"I don't wanna talk."

"You won't even know I'm here, angel."

Angel.

A small laugh slipped out despite myself.

He jerked his head toward his car, and I followed.

I didn't deserve this—his patience, his kindness, his presence.

The drive was, as expected, quiet.

Seattle flickered by in the late afternoon light. I barely registered any of it. When I noticed we weren't heading the way to my dad's house, I didn't have it in me to ask where he was taking me. I didn't care. Plus, I didn't want to see Eric while I was in this condition.

When Denver finally turned off the main road, I realized where we were headed.

I knew this place.

The car crept up the long gravel hill until we reached the top. We used to come here to be alone. The view stretched far beyond the city lights, mountains rising just past the skyline.

He parked, and neither of us moved for a long time. We let the needed quiet sit between us.

When I finally got out, I felt like I could breathe again. I took two steps forward. Then three. I screamed from the gut. The sound tore through the wind and vanished into the horizon. It still didn't take the pain with it. So I screamed again and again.

I felt him before he touched me. The heat of him, the steady rhythm of his breath cutting through the chill air. Then his arms were around my waist, firm and grounding, and I broke all over again.

I turned into him, my fingers fisting his shirt, forehead pressed to his chest. He didn't speak, didn't try to quiet me. He just held me tight enough that I could feel his heart beating through the cotton.

I let myself fall apart in his arms, my tears soaking through his shirt. His thumb brushed slow circles over my back, and every breath I took shuddered against him.

When I finally stopped shaking, when there was nothing left to cry out, I drew a breath that almost hurt. Another followed. I looked up at him and said softly, "You could take me back."

He pulled away just enough to look at me, pain flickering in his eyes. He didn't speak, just nodded once, lifting his hand in that quiet reminder of our *no-talking* deal.

My head rested against the window on the way back, the glass cool on my skin. I kept my eyes on the blur of trees and concrete, too drained to speak, too full to cry again.

When he parked, and I made a move to get out, he grabbed my hand. He didn't say anything. His eyes did it for him. *"I'm here. Always here."*

I sat in the car as I watched him walk back into the hospital.

I couldn't bring myself to go back. So, I pulled myself together and took the drive back to my dad's house.

Thirty-Four

What Was Stolen

D**ENVER**
Clara hadn't been back to the hospital since Heleen's scare. I didn't know what the hell happened, but whatever it was, it kept her away.

What I couldn't stop thinking about was the way Clara looked after, how badly I wanted to hold her. I wasn't going to fight for her if she didn't want me to, but it didn't mean I cared for her any less. That would never change.

So I did what I could. Just… be there. Let her break where no one else could see.

It was only a few days, but we still kept in contact. I called the day after to make sure she was doing okay.

The last time, she surprised me.

"Eric still wants that guitar lesson if you're up for it."

She'd sounded hesitant, like she expected me to say no. I shouted *yes* before she finished, then cursed when I heard her laugh through the line.

It was small, but it was real. And I'd take anything real from her. I was looking forward to giving Eric a lesson or two, so it worked out.

My house was still a mess, with boxes still scattered with anything I hadn't unpacked yet, but I'd cut my unpacking short on Saturday. I had reserved it for spending some time at the hospital, and the afternoon for Eric.

I don't remember the last time I taught a guitar lesson, so in a way, I needed this. It was a little refreshing. Plus, I loved the kid's enthusiasm, and I had no problem sitting with him all day if he wanted to. I was just waiting for the okay from Ethan and Clara.

I was setting up the studio when the doorbell rang. My hands were clammy, nervousness rushing through me at the thought of seeing Clara again.

I hoped like hell my disappointment didn't show when I opened the door and didn't see her. Eric stood in front of me with a little backpack and enough excitement to power a stadium. Ethan stood behind him with that usual calm that made him seem like he never rushed through anything in his life.

"Denver!" Eric wrapped his tiny arms around my legs, almost toppling me over with a grin.

"Thanks for doing this," Ethan said.

I wanted to ask him where Clara was. Instead, I said, "Of course," before leading them inside.

"You sure you're up for this?"

"Are you?"

Ethan smirked.

I gave a quick tour, even though my place looked trashed. Every one of Eric's 'wow' fed my ego.

Ethan took a seat on the couch, watching my every move. I handed the kid one of my smaller acoustics and adjusted the strap until it sat just right across his chest.

"Have you ever held a guitar before?"

"No, but I've watched a lot of videos," he said confidently. "Like, ten." He held up all ten fingers,

"Alright, let's make it eleven." I ruffled his hair.

He focused more than I expected. I went through the basics: fingers, strings, posture. He didn't get frustrated when he messed up. His eyes lit up as if they were made of gold.

He's got Clara's fire and his father's calm. But everything about him was completely his own.

We played until he complained his hands ached. I handed him a bottle of water and let him sprawl out across the couch while I sat back, telling him how well he did for the first session. I meant it, too. I watched Ethan take out a few snacks and handed them to him before he joined me.

"You thinking about getting him some lessons?"

The kid was a natural.

"He's got school, but yeah. This is the first thing he's wanted enough to keep asking."

I smiled. Maybe that's why Clara finally said something.

We sat in silence until I turned to him. "Can I ask you something without it being weird?"

Something was itching at me.

He arched his brow. "That's usually how something weird starts."

The smirk that followed relaxed my nerves for what I wanted to ask.

"How much do you know?"

"Everything," he said.

I figured that. By the way, he seemed cool with everything; it was interesting.

"Why didn't it ever work out? You and Clara?"

He turned back toward Eric, who was dipping crackers in some melted cheese.

"Because we didn't need to happen. We just… needed each other. She was broken. So was I. We filled the cracks for a while. When Eric came, we realized what mattered was him."

"That's rare," I said. I didn't understand it, and maybe it wasn't for me to understand.

That kind of bond? I couldn't hate it. How could I? He'd been there when she had no one else.

"She's still in love with you," Ethan added quietly.

I snorted. Never in a million years would I have thought I'd be sitting next to Clara's ex and discussing how she felt about me.

"She doesn't act like it."

"She's been protecting him for her whole life. You don't understand what that does to someone."

The way he said it—like he did know—stuck with me.

There was more I wanted to ask about Clara, about all the cryptic shit he was dropping like eggs on an Easter Sunday. Before I got the chance, his phone rang, and he held up a finger before stepping out of the studio.

I sighed, joining Eric on the couch as he dipped another cracker in the cheese.

"When did you start playing?" he asked with a mouthful.

I leaned back. I enjoy telling this story. My friends would give me shit if I admitted this out loud, but John Mayer will have a tiny space in my heart for that. "I was a little older than you."

He nodded, curious. "Why?"

I thought for a second. "My dad took me to a concert. A musician named John Mayer was playing this song, just him and a guitar, and it was like the entire world stopped."

Eric perked up. "Hey! That's my name."

I blinked. "What?"

"My name," he said, like it was obvious. "John. John Eric. Everyone just calls me Eric, my middle name." He smiled, going right back to finishing his snack, completely unaware of the way my breath just left my lungs.

I stared down at him. *John.* The kid with Clara's eyes and this wide-open way of looking at the world. The kid who shouldn't matter this much to me, but somehow does.

I cleared my throat. "How old are you again?"

He grinned. "Seven and a half. Turning eight in…" he used his little fingers to count, "2 months."

Before I could say another word, the door opened behind us.

Ethan stepped in, phone in hand. "Hey, bud. Time to wrap it up."

"Okay," Eric chirped, carefully gathering his things.

I stood up, still trying to find my footing. Ethan didn't seem to notice my face, or maybe he did and just didn't say anything.

I followed them to the door in silence, Eric asking Ethan a million and one questions.

"Thanks again," Ethan said as Eric wrapped his arms around me.

I held him a little tighter than usual. I only managed a nod before shutting the door.

I wasn't some self-centered idiot, but *John*? She named him *John*.

The kid isn't turning six. He's turning eight. *Eight*.

My stomach felt like it was folding in on itself. I sat down on the arm of the living room couch.

I reached for my phone. Scrolled to Eli's name and hit call.

Voicemail.

Called again. Voicemail.

Come on, man. I need someone to tell me I'm losing it.

I scrolled further, hesitated, then tapped on Jamie's contact.

She answered on the second ring.

"Hey," she said. "Everything good?"

"I don't know. Can you come over?"

"On my way."

She showed up within thirty minutes, carrying two bottles; one wine, one something stronger, and kicked off her shoes the second she walked in. She took off a rain jacket. Apparently, it'd just started pouring down.

"Alright," she began, planting herself on my couch. "What's going on? You look like shit."

I huffed a laugh and sank into the chair across from her.

"You ever thought you've been in the wrong version of your life?"

Jamie tilted her head. "Are we talking existential dread, quarter-life crisis, or Clara?"

I didn't answer.

She set the wine aside. "Talk to me."

"I can't even say it." I ran a hand across my face, trying to make sense of this.

"Try."

"I don't know what it is yet," I said. "But I think…" I cut myself off, pressing the heels of my hands into my eyes. "I think I know something I shouldn't. Something big."

"Do you need a friend or a fix-it?"

"Friend," I huffed.

"Okay."

She slid off the couch, sitting cross-legged in front of me. Her hand rested on my knee. Her face tilted closer, too close.

She leaned in as I moved my hands from my eyes. Her fingers curled around my jeans, her face tilting just a little too close.

"Jamie—"

She kissed me.

I pulled her away, holding her at arm's length. "What the hell, Jamie!"

She blinked, startled, then stood quickly.

Her eyes narrowed, voice tight. "This is about her, isn't it?"

"Jamie." I didn't recognize her. This wasn't Jamie.

She laughed, but it wasn't funny. It was almost scary. "God, you don't even see it." She threw her hands up. "You've been spinning in circles since she came back."

"Why do you sound jealous? Jesus, Jamie, you're my best friend."

Another laugh. "She's been feeding you half-truths for years, and you're still waiting for her to love you back. Aren't you tired of it yet?"

I stood, too. "You don't know what the hell you're talking about."

"Don't I? He's yours."

Silence.

She blinked. "Did you know that?"

I took a step back and swallowed.

She stared at me, wild and breathless. "Her son. You didn't figure it out?"

Everything stopped.

"Your precious little Clara isn't innocent, Denver. She has you wrapped around her fingers all while lying to you and everyone else."

John. She named him John. I wasn't going crazy.

I stood there, staring at her, and the floor beneath my feet felt like it could crumble. "How…how do you know that?"

Her arms crossed her chest.

"Jamie!"

Her eyes dropped to the floor.

My voice rose, demanding this time. "How the hell do you know that?"

She flinched.

"I—" Her voice was small, not the loud mouth she'd been seconds ago. "I saw something. The day she left."

I watched her, waiting. My chest burned.

She let out a shaky breath. "If you remember the day you told me she was gone, I was there earlier in the day. When I was leaving…"

"Jamie, what did you do?"

"I went into her room to look for her diary, okay? We used to read it together, remember? Dumb secrets. Stupid poems. But then she stopped letting me in. So I—" she broke off. "It was just supposed to be a joke."

I couldn't see straight, but I needed to hear this. "Keep going."

Her hand ran through her hair, breath coming out shallow. "I found it. It was just supposed to be a joke, but she wrote about you. About how scared she was. How much she loved you. How she didn't know what to do. But mainly about your relationship. About her finding out she was pregnant with your baby"

It felt like she ripped open my chest and pulled my heart out.

"She never told me any of that," Jamie added. "She stopped telling me anything."

I clenched my fist. "So, what did you do?"

"I left it open."

"You what?"

"I pretended I forgot my necklace on my way out. Asked her mom if she could go check her room again." Her eyes filled with tears. But I wasn't buying it. "I didn't think she'd actually read it. I didn't think she'd—"

"That's how Heleen found out," I whispered to myself.

Jamie didn't deny it.

"You're the reason Clara left."

"I didn't mean—"

"You're partly the reason I lost everything."

"I didn't know it would get that bad," she whispered.

I shook my head. "You didn't care."

"I was your best friend," she snapped, then softened. "I've always been yours." She took a step closer. "You've never noticed it, have you?"

There's only one person I've ever noticed.

I didn't move.

"I've loved you for years, Denver. Even when you didn't look at me like that. Even when you were too busy, being in love with someone who'd already left you heartbroken."

Maybe I wasn't hearing her right. Jamie. My best friend. The one I thought I could trust.

This?

This was never supposed to be in the story.

She reached for my hand. I pulled back.

"I trusted you. She trusted you. Why would you do this?"

"I was just a kid," she tried defending.

"So was she."

Silence.

"I did it because I loved you, Denver. I still love you."

"Get out."

"Denver, please!"

"If you think Clara was the issue, you're dumber than you look," I spat. "You want to know why I didn't see you in that way? It's because all I could see was her! Nothing was going to change that, Jamie. Not you, not her mother, not anyone."

She was crying now, but I continued. "You hurt her, which means you hurt me, too. Now. Get. Out."

She didn't move, just sniffled as she wiped her tears with the sleeve of her shirt.

When she noticed I wasn't budging, she turned to leave.

"And, Jamie."

She turned back.

"You went behind her back, played a game with something sacred, and cost me years I'll never get back. You don't get to call that love. You don't get to call yourself a friend. Not after this."

"I'm sorry. I didn't think it would cause her to leave. I didn't mean for any of it to happen."

"You're dead to me."

I didn't give her another second. I walked over and opened the door, not sparing her another glance as she got her stuff.

I let her walk out of my life.

The door slammed shut behind her.

But the damage stayed.

I stood in the middle of the living room, breathing like I'd run a mile, my hands shaking, jaw clenched so tight it hurt.

I have a son.

She knew.

They all knew.

Except me.

I flipped the nearest table in my path, and then another.

"Fuck!"

The only thing louder than the blood rushing in my ears was the storm hammering down outside. Thunder cracked and rain hit the windows like fists..

She lied.

Jamie lied. Clara ran and has been lying this entire time. Heleen lied. My dad's still in the dark.

I needed to see her. Now.

I grabbed my keys, threw on a hoodie, and stormed out. The rain was heavy, but I got in my car and drove.

The street lights blurred with tears. I couldn't stop. I screamed into the storm, into the empty car, into the pain of it all.

"You should've told me!"

The tires hit a slick patch.

I barely saw the turn.

The wheel jerked.
Everything tilted.
Metal screamed.
Glass shattered.
And then… darkness and a bell ringing.

Thirty-Five

Paper Cuts and Bruises

CLARA
<u>**17 Years Old**</u>

The restaurant buzzed with weekend noise that clung to your skin. Laughter, the clatter of dishes, and someone singing *Happy Birthday* two tables over. Denver leaned back into the booth, flanked by Mason and Eli, one arm over the edge like he owned the place. He didn't, but tonight was his anyway.

Eighteen.

The past year has been a busy one. Back in May, Denver graduated, but he kept his promise to wait until I finished my last year. He spent the months either planning or booking gigs with the guys. I also kept up my end of the bargain. I was officially getting my diploma next month, in January.

It was a lot of late nights and early mornings, but I did it.

"Tomorrow's the big day," Mason said, nudging Denver with his shoulder. "You're gonna finally do something reckless with your life? Get a tattoo? Join a group of rebels?"

"Already in a band. Close enough," Denver muttered, grinning as he stole a fry from Eli's plate.

Denver didn't want to do anything big, but Tom insisted. This was the last birthday he'd get to share if Denver decided not to come home for the holidays. The idea of us crossing state lines still shook him, but he supported our decision. Even though he didn't know the reason behind it.

We settled into an Italian restaurant. The lights dimmed to exude a relaxing atmosphere, and the smell of delicious pasta and seafood filled the air. The snow and winter weather kept the restaurant from being packed.

Denver was turning eighteen tomorrow, but Tom and my mom had plans to go to the Poconos tonight for the weekend.

It worked with the plans I had for Denver and me. I could barely eat when they brought our food out, just thinking about it. I tried to add to the laughter going on around the table to ease my nerves. It wasn't any help.

When dessert came around, some of the staff came out to sing with us, followed by a one-tier Vanilla frosting cake with birthday candles. I laughed as Denver's cheeks grew red, having the attention on him.

After dinner, we all walked out together, huddling in a group, trying to shy away from the wind.

The guys and Jamie had gone their way, the guys gifting Denver another guitar to add to his collection. Tom and my mom had their things packed in their car. I watched as Tom held Denver to him before placing the keys in his hands.

"Your first apartment, when you get to Florida. Happy birthday, son."

Denver beamed up at him before saying his goodbyes and listening to all the rules of the dos and don'ts while they were gone.

* * *

Back at the house, we were alone. We went our separate ways to change. I'd be spending the night in Denver's room. I took a while staring at myself in the mirror, trying to calm my racing heart.

Denver sat on his bed, the last glow of sunset stretching through his window as he mindlessly scrolled on his phone. I stood in the doorway, holding his gift behind my back.

"What are you hiding?" he smirked.

I stepped forward and pulled it out. It was a guitar, worn but perfect, with a John Mayer signature etched across the pale wood. I'd gone through so many loopholes, but I got it. Just for him.

His eyes went wide. "No fucking way."

I smiled. "Happy birthday, babe."

He took it like it was sacred, running his fingers over the strings, reverent. "How did you—?"

"You don't even wanna know," I laughed. I'd like to say I'd sent over twenty emails, but that would be silly.

He set it down gently before pulling me into him. "You really didn't have to."

"I wanted to." My heart was pounding. "I wanted this to be special."

He leaned in and kissed me. When he pulled back to look at me, there was nothing uncertain about my plan.

"I'm ready," I whispered against his lips when he leaned in for another kiss.

We didn't have anyone to worry about for the entire weekend. I've been thinking about this for a while now. I wanted tonight to be our first time.

His head pulled back, brows knitted as he searched my face for certainty.

"Wait. Are you sure? We don't—"

"I'm sure. I want this. With you."

When he didn't say anything, I kissed him and walked us back to his bed.

His legs hit the bed. He fell back and sat up on his elbows to watch me.

His eyes were hooded as I pulled each strap of my tank top off with trembling fingers. My dress came next, and I stood before him in a Victoria's Secret lingerie set I bought just for this.

"Wow, you look… just wow."

I bit down on my bottom lip and straddled him.

"Are you sure? I could wait, there's no rush."

"I'm sure." I kissed him, rocking my hips into his.

He gripped my hips, his fingers digging into my thighs. When I thought he'd resist, he flipped us, so I was under him. He rocked into me, and I felt his bulge, hard as ever.

Denver and I never passed first base, so I was nervous. He'd be my first.

"Wait," he said, pulling back and walking to his dresser.

My eyes widened when he pulled out a box of condoms.

"Dad bought it for me when I grew my first chin hair," he said, answering my unasked question. "Something about the birds and the bees. But I haven't used them. Didn't need to."

My chest warmed with his admission. I leaned back onto the bed when he walked back to me, hovering before kissing my lips, cheeks, and then my neck.

He pulled back, tucking my hair behind my ear. His eyes locked on mine as he unclipped my bra. His hand trailed down my stomach, leaving goosebumps everywhere he touched. He stopped right above the lace of my panties, brows raised for permission.

"Yes," I breathed.

He moved just as unsure as I felt. Not unsure of doing this, but unsure of what to do. When he slid my panties down my legs, I squirmed.

"Fuck," he whispered. "Is this your first time being touched, angel?"

I nodded.

An appreciative hum rolled through him. "I won't promise this will be perfect because this is my… first time, too. But I'll make it perfect for the first time."

What followed wasn't perfect. It wasn't supposed to be. It was soft, a little clumsy, filled with nerves and wonder and vulnerability that only existed when two people were in love.

Afterward, we lay tangled beneath the covers, breath slowing. I curled into his side and whispered into his chest, "Happy birthday."

He kissed my forehead and held me close.

* * *

The test blinked up at me from the sink. Two pink lines.

I sat on the bathroom floor, arms tight around my knees. We'd been careful. I remembered the click of the wrapper, remembered his hands steady even while mine shook. But the lines didn't lie. Four tests later, the truth stayed the same.

Seventeen. Graduated less than a week ago. And pregnant.

My stomach rolled. I wrapped the evidence in a paper towel, shoved it deep in the trash, and reached for my diary. Writing always made things clearer, but this time it didn't.

Denver and I were good. Better than ever after losing my virginity to him. It wasn't until a few weeks later that my body started to feel off. I'd get lightheaded out of nowhere. Foods I loved made me nauseous. I ignored it at first because we used protection, and the possibility of getting pregnant was still slim.

The symptoms didn't go away. I wasn't coming down with the flu. No, I was freaking pregnant. When I did my research and learned that eighteen out of one hundred women get pregnant while using a condom, I knew I couldn't ignore it.

My mother was going to kill me. Kill us. We'd planned everything so perfectly so we could be together, and now this.

I felt sick, lightheaded. I crawled to the toilet and threw up, making this more real.

I walked into my room, shoved the diary back under my pillow, and threw on a hoodie.

I needed to get out of here to think, to breathe. Writing it down didn't help. Not one bit.

I was halfway down the stairs when Denver called my name.

"Where are you going? Jamie's coming over, remember?"

"I'll be back."

"Hey." I heard his footsteps on the stairs before his hand wrapped around my arm.

I couldn't even look at him.

"I-is something wrong?"

"No."

I met his eyes.

"You'd tell me if something was wrong, right?"

I paused, then nodded. "Of course."

"Do you want me to come with you? I could tell Jamie to come back later."

I shook my head, holding on to the railing. "No. It's fine."

He eyed me skeptically before letting out a sigh. He looked around, but our parents were nowhere in sight.

"I love you," he whispered before kissing my forehead.

"I love you too."

I hated lying to him. We didn't keep secrets from each other. I just needed time to think this through first.

I needed to do that anywhere but here.

* * *

I spent hours at the library, researching everything about teen pregnancy. Who knew there was so much to learn? Not the girl who thought she knew what she was doing almost a month ago.

I got a few text messages from Denver that made me realize I shouldn't be scared to confide in him. This was an 'us' situation, not just mine.

Thirty-Six

He Knows

CLARA
Present Day
I woke up to stillness.

Stillness that felt like it was waiting for something to happen.

For a second, I forgot I'd turned my phone off the night before. I told myself it was to sleep better. That wasn't true. I couldn't trust myself not to call him, not after everything. I'd just be confusing him even more.

There was so much I needed to tell him, so much I needed to come clean about. I needed to do that before it was too late. I was still in love with Denver, and despite my push and pull, he still made sure I was okay. Still made it his mission to show up when he didn't have to.

I pushed the covers off and looked at Eric's peaceful form next to me. I kissed his forehead before making my way down to the kitchen. Ethan was already there, coffee in hand, as he stared at nothing.

"Morning," he said when he spotted me.

"Morning." I walked around to where he sat and hugged him.

I started making tea. Something to do with my hands. I pulled out a pan for eggs. Claire and Eric went feral if they didn't have breakfast. It was funny to see how similar they were despite their age difference.

"Thanks again for taking him yesterday."

When Eric wanted to do something, he made it his mission to get it. He wanted to play guitar with Denver, so I gave in. I couldn't bring myself to take him over there myself.

"Of course."

I worked in the kitchen, and by the time I finished, Claire and Eric were already seated. It was like they could smell breakfast cooking in their sleep. Ethan and I stood side by side, watching them eat and talk. It was going to be hard to get him to leave when the time came. And the time was coming soon.

My mother was awake, and the guilt I'd felt about not speaking to her for eight years no longer lingered. After the way she treated me at the hospital, I still didn't regret coming back. It was long overdue, and I'll be thankful to her because of it.

I heard footsteps and looked up to see Dad walking in. Although sleep filled his eyes, he had a grim expression.

"Clara." He jerked his head toward the hallway, and I took the cue.

He held up his phone. "Tom's been trying to reach you," he said. "Been calling all night."

My stomach dipped. "Is it… her?"

He shook his head. "No. It's Denver."

My heart thudded. "What happened?"

So many thoughts were running through my mind.

He looked at me with that quiet worry I used to ignore when I was younger. "He's been in a car accident."

"Ethan!" Everything inside me dropped. I didn't wait for his response before running upstairs, fumbling into clothes with shaking hands.

Ethan was on my heel. "What's going on?"

"Denver's been in an accident. I need you to take me to the hospital."

I brushed past him and met Dad downstairs, a knowing look in his eyes.

"I'll stay with Eric," he said. "Go."

I walked over to Eric, put on a smile to make sure he didn't detect my frazzled state, and kissed his head. "Mommy's going to be right back. Be good for your grandfather and Aunt Claire, okay?"

He shoved eggs in his mouth and nodded around them.

The rain had stopped, but the sky looked like it could still rain any moment now.

My legs shook, hands trembled as I worked to turn my phone on. The ride felt too long. My thoughts came like waves, each one louder and more accusing than the last. I should've kept my phone on last night. I should've gone with Eric over there. I should've faced him sooner.

Eight missed calls and text messages.

If I hadn't been so caught up in my head, I wouldn't have missed this. If anything happened to Denver, I wouldn't forgive myself.

He needed to know how I felt. He needed to know the truth.

Ethan barely parked the car before I was out.

"Clara, wait—"

Something was wrong. The guys and Sadie were outside. They stood in a loose huddle at the edge of the entryway.

I didn't spot her at first, but Jamie was crying in Sadie's arms, face blotchy.

"You!" she shrieked, voice slicing through my turmoil. I didn't register she meant me until her tear-soaked face twisted with rage.

I stopped short. "What?" The words landed like a slap. I staggered a step back, unsure if it was from the force of her voice or the guilt I hadn't dared acknowledge.

She was shaking. "You did this!" She cried. "You're the reason he crashed his car."

My mouth dropped as I listened to the words spewing from her mouth.

Mason moved in to pull her back, but she wasn't done.

"Clara, let's just see him," Ethan bit out, hand on my arm.

I was unable to move. The ground beneath me felt like it had tilted, and I was the only one sliding. I could feel the eyes on me. The truth was coming, and some part of me already knew it. I had no armor for this. No way to stop it as Ethan tried to move me.

"He knows." Her voice dropped to something almost triumphant, a cruel whisper that screamed louder than any shout.

Every pair of eyes swung to me. Mason's, Sadie's, Eli's. All my fears had come true. *Denver knows.*

"What did you say?" I asked, but already knew. My blood ran cold.

She stepped out of Mason's embrace. "He knows, Clara. Eric's his."

The world shrank. My heart collapsed into itself. There it was, everything I ran from, everything I hid. Exposed. I couldn't breathe.

She turned to Ethan, a smirk on her lips. "Did you know she lied to you? I bet she has you wrapped around her fingers, too."

"Jamie, that's enough," Eli's firm voice cut in as he stepped in to pull her back.

"You're out of line," I heard Ethan say next to me. His voice sounded muffled as blood rushed to my head.

No one said anything else. I looked at the girl in front of me as Mason held her back. I knew something had been off with us, but why was she doing this? If she knew the entire time, then why do this now? Why pretend? That morning, when she came over and pretended she knew because of some bullshit excuse. It was just that, an excuse.

She had a smirk on her face like she'd won something, and that enraged me. My cheeks flushed red, not from embarrassment, but from a desire to attack her and punch her in the nose. Out of everyone I'd left behind, I'd stayed in contact with her.

"You're pathetic, you know that?" she spat out.

"Me? Look at you, Jamie." She wasn't worth it. Not right now. I brushed past her.

"I told you there was something off with that girl," Ethan said when we walked away.

I ignored him.

I spotted Tom near the front desk, speaking with a nurse. He turned, and the moment he saw me, his face softened. I wrapped my arms around him as he hugged me back.

"Is he—?" I choked out, eyes closed shut in fear of hearing the answer.

"He's okay," Tom said, gently. "Banged up a bit. Scared the hell out of all of us, but he's okay."

"I want to see him."

Tom stepped back and gave me a soft, knowing look, but heavy with something else.

"Go ahead. Room 312."

The receptionist behind the desk couldn't move fast enough as she checked my ID and printed out a visitor's badge. My fingers drummed on the desk, just thinking about what the hell I was going to say when I saw Denver.

He was fine. That's all that mattered.

"I'll be right here." I hugged Ethan before walking away. Jamie thought she did something when she brought up that Eric wasn't his. What she didn't know was that there wasn't a secret between Ethan and me.

Every step to his room was a countdown to heartbreak. I stared at the room number, hoping it would change, hoping this wasn't real. It was real. I had no idea which version of Denver I'd find on the other side of that door: the boy who once loved me endlessly, or the man now piecing together the truth I never let him have.

I pushed the door open. He was awake, sitting up with a bandage above his right eyebrow and his arm in a soft sling. Bruises marked his jaw and cheekbone.

But his eyes… his eyes were clear, and when they landed on me, the room felt too small. I took slow, measured steps to his bed, waiting for him to yell or scream at me for my lies. He just looked at me, anger, disappointment, and judgment showing on his handsome features.

That was worse than anything that would've come out of his mouth.

"You're okay," I whispered.

He just lay there, jaw tight, gaze locked on mine. It was as if he were trying to decide which version of me he was looking at right now.

I took a few more steps forward, my hands itching to reach out for him. "I'm glad you're okay."

He rested his head back on the bed with a long sigh as he closed his eyes. "Leave, Clara."

"I didn't want you to find out like this. Can I just explain?"

"Leave. Please," he pleaded.

"Not until you hear what I've got to say." I stood firm.

He winced as he tried to sit upright. I rushed to his side to help, but he pulled away.

"You've been lying to me. You have enough time, Clara. How many times have I asked you to let me in? To give me something? Just go. I can't do this right now."

"I've been meaning to—"

"Just go."

The finality of his voice was sharp. My mouth opened to protest, but no words came out.. I had no right to beg, no right to stay. So I nodded, even though he didn't see it. I turned, my knees buckling with every step.

Tears pricked my eyes as I took measured steps back toward the door, hoping he'd just look at me.

He didn't.

As if he knew how this was going to go, Ethan was outside the door, leaning against the wall. He looked at me, and that was enough. He didn't have to ask. I didn't say anything, just kept walking with his arm wrapped over my shoulder. Tom wasn't in the lobby when I walked back out, and I was glad for it. Sadie, Mason, and Eli were tough. I paid them no attention as Ethan and I headed back to the car. Jamie was nowhere in sight, and it was a surprise since she reacted that way.

When we reached the car, Ethan opened the passenger door for me. "What do you want to do?"

"Is there an option to run away?"

"No."

"He's angry. Rightfully so. I'll come back. I can't lose him, Ethan."

He nodded, rounded the car, and drove us back.

I couldn't be mad at Denver. This was too big. I just needed him to hear me out, that's all.

Ethan didn't get out of the car when we got back, just kissed my forehead and promised everything was going to be okay. When I went in, I cuddled my son on the couch as he played a game on his tablet. He was my greatest joy in all the mistakes I'd made, and I'd do it all over again if it meant protecting him.

I used to think the truth would destroy me. But watching my son, whole and happy, despite everything, I realized the worst part wasn't losing Denver. I was losing myself. Every lie I told protected someone. Eric, Denver, Tom, and even my mother. Maybe for a while, I believed that made them noble.

But noble lies were still lies. Because when it came down to it, some lies protect you. Others destroy you.

Thirty-Seven

Aches

DENVER

I opened my eyes when I heard the door click behind Clara. I hissed when I tried to sit up again. The drugs they'd given me for the pain were wearing off.

The last thing I remembered was everything going black when I was driving to her dad's house last night. Then I woke up in the hospital. Why did it feel like I'd become injury-prone since she came back to Seattle?

I slid off the road into a ditch and hit a tree. Luckily, I didn't take anyone with me. Everything hurt. My arm was in a fucking sling, and I had a few cuts and bruises on my face. None of it hurt more than finding out Eric was my son.

I was a father.

I couldn't look at Clara. Not right now.

On my second failed attempt to sit up without wincing, Mason popped his head in the door, followed by Sadie and Eli. Eli held up a paper bag as Mason grinned in that sideways way that always meant he didn't know what to say, but showed up anyway.

They all filed in slowly.

No Jamie. Thank God.

Mason took one step and whistled. "Well, shit, man. You look like someone picked you up, shook you, then threw you off a bridge."

Sadie rolled her eyes. "He means he's glad you're alive."

I tried to crack a smile. Even that was painful.

Eli set the bag down beside me. "Hospital food's garbage. I brought Thai."

"Appreciate it," I said.

They hovered, moving around as if not sure if I wanted them to stay. I didn't know either. But I was glad they came.

"Jamie lost it out front," Eli said.

Sadie made a face. "Yeah. It was…loud."

Mason gave a half-laugh. "She said some shit, man."

I groaned. How was she causing trouble in such a short time? I was still trying to piece together yesterday's events.

"Stuff we probably shouldn't have found out that way," Eli added carefully.

I looked down at my arm in the sling. They clearly knew, so I stayed quiet while they glanced at each other, deciding who would disclose the bomb that had been dropped on me. Sadie, out of all people, added, "We don't care."

I looked up.

"I mean, love is love, right?" She shrugged.

Even though I never cared what anyone thought about our relationship, not hearing judgment or concerns from those closest to me meant something.

"Yeah. Even if it's your hot step sister," Mason laughed.

I shot him a stare. I was going to make him eat those words later.

Eli covered his laugh. "It's taboo as fuck, though."

"I love taboo," Sadie wiggled her brows.

I groaned again.

They made movements, digging out the food from the bag, going back and forth over the definition of taboo. My friends, everyone.

"And a son, huh?" Mason asked.

Yeah. I had a son. A whole life I didn't know was mine.

I swallowed over the lump in my throat. "I keep trying to wrap my head around it. Every time I think I've got a grip, it slips."

"That's what happens when your life changes overnight," Eli said. "Don't mean you're not allowed to feel it. Or figure it out."

For the first time since I woke up, I breathed a little easier.

They weren't trying to fix it. They were just here.

They filed around, taking a seat wherever they could as they dug in. I took an egg roll that tasted like a gourmet meal.

Shit. When was the last time I ate?

"You gonna start wearing white New Balance and tucking your t-shirt into your jeans now?" Mason smirked.

Eli snorted. "He's halfway there."

Sadie leaned up. "We should get him a 'World's Okayest Dad' mug."

"Can we please not?" I muttered, but my mouth twitched.

"Oh, come on," Mason grinned, "you're not curious about Dad jokes now that it's officially your lane?"

He cleared his throat dramatically.

"Why did the scarecrow win an award?"

I gave him a flat look.

"Because he was outstanding in his field."

Eli groaned. "God, that one hurt."

"It was more painful than the pain I'm in now," I added.

"You should've heard the one he told the EMT he was trying to get a number out of. Something about needing a crash course in fatherhood," Eli added.

I buried my face in my hands. "Please. Stop." I was still smiling.

Mason nudged my leg. "We're still here for you, man. All the way. Even if you suddenly start showing up at rehearsals with juice boxes and apple slices."

Sadie added, "Just no matching dad-and-son flannels. I have limits."

I sat back and looked at the three of them; goofballs, smart asses, my people.

Ethan's entrance interrupted their bickering as he walked in.

Jaw clenched, I sat up despite the pain. "The fuck are you doing here?"

"I need a moment." He stepped into the room, hands clasped in front of him like he owned the room.

"Uh, we'll give you a moment."

They picked up whatever food was left and left the room, looking back every so often. But I couldn't take my eyes off the man who'd been acting like my son was his for his entire fucking life.

"You've got some fucking nerve."

"I figured you'd say that," he said evenly. His calm demeanor pissed me off even more. "Listen, I didn't come here to pick a fight."

"No?" Then what? See the damage she's caused?"

His jaw tightened. It was the first time I'd seen anything but the 'cool guy' demeanor.

"This isn't my story to tell, so I won't. What I said yesterday about Clara and me meeting at a time where we needed each other, that was the truth."

I listened as the calm fell apart, fire flaring in his eyes. In almost anger, hurt?

He looked me straight in the eye. "When she came to New York, left everything behind, she almost lost herself. She was pregnant and felt like she had no one. I was there for it all. I'm not here to stop you from knowing Eric or anything like that. But if you're going to be mad at somebody, you're pointing that anger in the wrong direction."

My heart twisted. Oh, my anger was pointed in the right direction.

His chest was heaving by the time he was done. He'd come here to defend Clara. For the second time within these twenty-four hours, I'd had another bomb dropped on my doorstep.

"You love her."

He didn't deny it. "Yeah. But not the way you think."

I stared, not sure if I could get any angrier than I already was.

"I never asked for anything from her," he said. "Never crossed that line. Never tried something she didn't offer. I just… stayed. Part of me needed to. She saved me, in a way. That alone was and still is enough for me. It always will be, no matter what."

I let him continue.

"I knew she was in love with you. Even when she couldn't say your name without choking. I knew the second I walked into that hospital room and saw her holding that boy like the world would take him if she let go."

My jaw clenched, rage buried under grief.

"I knew the truth, and yeah, I helped her keep it. I told myself it wasn't my place to break it open. I'd do it again."

He let that hang for a moment, then looked down.

"I'm sorry for that. For my part in all of it."

My throat burned, the bandage on my arms itching. None of this made sense. Yet, all of it did.

Ethan took a breath and met my eyes again.

"But I told you, if there's ever a time you ever question her…"

He paused.

"This is that time."

Shit. The guy made it impossible to dislike him. This was far from over, but being angry at him in all of this was pointless.

"I need a favor," I said after a beat.

"I'm listening."

He left me with information and confusion all in one. I don't know if it was adrenaline, but all the pain came rushing back all at once.

I remembered Dad coming back in, the nurses giving me more drugs for the pain.

I closed my eyes to the vision of Clara and Eric.

Thirty-Eight

The Hate You Give

CLARA
17 Years Old

I drove home with determination and an upset stomach. My insides were churning, but I knew what I needed to do.

It was too quiet for my liking when I got back home. As I climbed the stairs, my stomach turned. Not from nausea, but nerves. *This was it.*

I'd tell Denver. I'd say the words. We'd figure it out together.

My bedroom door stood cracked open, spilling light into the hallway. *Probably Denver.*

I pushed open the door, my mind racing with rehearsed words. Would he freak out? Be mad?

The second I looked up, I saw my mom sitting on my bed, silent, upright, holding my diary in both hands.

I felt the color drain from my face. "W-what are you doing?" I was shaking, holding onto the doorknob.

In front of me, my mother saw everything I'd hidden. *Everything.*

She didn't move. Her eyes stayed glued to the pages, reading as if trying to burn the words into memory. When she finally looked up, her face was rigid, angry.

"I thought it was fiction," she said.

"That's private," I gritted out.

"You wrote about him. About that night." She flipped a page. "You wrote about being in love. You wrote about being pregnant."

Her face twisted in disgust. "You've been sleeping with him? With Denver?"

I couldn't move. Couldn't talk.

She rose to her feet, tossing the diary across the room. Fury bled off of her. "He's your stepbrother!"

I flinched. "It's not like that." My voice came out weak. *It was, in fact, like that.* Tears pricked my eyes.

"We share a home. I married his father. You two live under the same roof, for God's sake, Clara." Her eyes gleamed with something feral. "It's disgusting," she spat.

"I didn't plan for this. We were careful, I swear—"

"Oh, don't," her voice cut through me. "You opened your legs for your stepbrother. You two have been walking around here under our noses doing God knows what."

"I love him."

That did it.

The first hit landed with the flat of my mother's palm, loud and blistering. I staggered back, hand flying to my cheek.

"You love him?" she spat. "You've ruined both your lives. What are people going to think?"

"I didn't ruin anything—"

The second strike came quicker. Backhanded this time. My head snapped sideways. I gasped and blinked stars from my eyes.

My gasp and her heaving filled the room as I looked at her in shock. *She hit me.*

"You don't get to speak." She was seething now, like she didn't just assault me, knowing I was pregnant. "You don't get to justify this. You're a child. And you've shamed this family."

"I'm not ashamed," I choked out, eyes wet, face stinging.

"You should be."

My lip trembled. "You don't understand—"

"I know enough. He'll be taking off with his career, and you'll what? Drop out of school to take care of a baby? Your father trapped me, and you'll be trapped just like that.

Denver wasn't like that. Dad wasn't even like that.

Here it was, the truth of how my mother viewed me. The lack of affection, no interest in my likes and dislikes, came down to her feeling trapped.

I don't know which hurt more.

"You think this pregnancy makes you special? Like it's some kind of miracle? No, Clara. It makes you a statistic." Her voice sounded like venom to my ears.

Her hands clenched at her side, making me stagger back. For the first time in my life, I feared my mother.

"You'll fix this. You'll go to the clinic this week."

"No. I'm telling him." I turned to go, but her demonic laughter stopped me.

By the time I turned around, her fingers were digging into my cheek. "He's not here, Clara. I told Tom to take him out for a bite because we needed to talk."

Nausea crawled up my throat.

No.

She let me go with a push. "Pack your things."

"What?"

"You heard me. You think you're grown? Then be grown. You want to throw your future away? Do it somewhere else. You are not staying here and playing house with your stepbrother."

"Mom…"

"You walk out that door with that thing inside of you, and you are not my daughter anymore."

I was full-blown crying, cheeks stinging from where she slapped me.

"I gave you every opportunity." Tears of fury welled in her eyes. "You had college ahead of you. You had a future, and you ruined it, and you'll ruin this family too."

She just kept digging the knife deeper.

"If you were wiser, you would dispose of it. Everyone will recognize the shame you bring. People will gossip, and I won't intervene. If you choose to destroy this family and his career, you will face it. I will not support you. Therefore, pack your belongings and leave Clara. No one will stand by you in this matter, least of all Denver."

I fell to my knees, clutching my stomach, the room spinning as her words kept coming. I couldn't understand how they belonged to her. To my mother. Maybe she was right. Maybe I was a disgrace. Would Denver even be happy if he knew?

If you choose to destroy this family and his career.

She didn't care or flinch at the sight of me folding into myself, shaking. Breath caught somewhere between nausea and grief. Her voice didn't soften, face didn't change. She stood there with fire in her eyes and no love left in her chest. I realized that where she was concerned, I had always been alone.

My mother wasn't a mother. She was just the woman who gave birth to me.

I was just a fuck-up who spread her legs for her stepbrother. *Disgusting. A freak. If I stayed here, everyone would know it too.*

She left me there. Walked out of my room like I was something rotting.

Florida felt like another life now. A fantasy. All the plans, all the whispers, all the 'almosts,' they were gone. We did all of this for nothing.

I hated myself. I hated him for being so easy to fall in love with. I hated her most of all for leaving me like this.

I didn't know it then, but this moment would follow me. It would bleed into every decision I made after. Every silence I held, every truth I swallowed.

This was the moment I stopped being someone's daughter, someone's mistake, waiting for the world to point and laugh at me.

It was the moment I started being someone's mother.

Thirty-Nine

Back to You

~~~~~~~~~~

C LARA
Present Day

The rain had passed days ago, but the air still felt heavy. Like the storm had settled inside me instead of the sky.

I sat in the living room, curled into the corner of the couch while Eric played on the rug with his tablet. His little hums of concentration should've been enough to settle me, but all they did was remind me of Denver.

The look on Denver's face when he told me to leave was etched in my mind. It hadn't been anger alone; it had been grief. Betrayal. And I had put it there.

I told myself for years I'd done the right thing, keeping him from the truth. That protecting Eric meant burying everything else. But watching Denver look at me like a stranger, watching him look at Eric and not know, had shattered every reason I ever clung to.

Eric was his. *Ours..*

I thought I could live without Denver knowing the truth. Without him in our lives. But seeing him, broken and bruised in that hospital bed, proved how wrong I'd been. The thought of losing him forever, of Eric growing up never knowing him, felt unbearable.
~~~~~~~~~~

My chest tightened as I glanced at my son, sprawled across the floor, legs kicking lazily while he laughed at something on the screen. He was my joy. My strength.

I couldn't ignore the pieces lining up now. Jamie was screaming outside the hospital, and the smirk she wore when she thought she was taking a dig at me in front of everyone.

Jamie.

I used to tell her everything. She'd been the friend I leaned on. And now I could see it clearly, the cracks in every smile she'd given me. She'd known. All this time, she'd known. And she let it fester like poison, waiting for the right moment to use it against me.

The betrayal stung worse than I wanted to admit.

"You're quiet," Ethan's voice broke through my spiraling thoughts. He leaned against the door frame, arms crossed, watching me with that steady calm that never failed to ground me.

I forced a small smile. "Just… thinking."

"Dangerous habit," he said lightly, moving closer.

I laughed, though it came out brittle. "It feels like all I've been doing since we got back here."

He lowered himself into the chair beside the couch, eyes never leaving mine. He didn't push.

"I thought I was protecting him," I whispered. "Both of them. Eric didn't deserve to grow up with chaos, and Denver…" I swallowed hard. "He had his whole life ahead of him. Music. Freedom. I thought I was sparing him. But maybe I was just being… selfish."

"You weren't selfish. You were seventeen. You were scared. And you did the best you could."

"What if the best I could do wasn't good enough? Then what?"

"Then at least the weight of carrying all of this will be lifted. That's got to be worth something."

I closed my eyes, letting the weight of it sink in.

When I opened my eyes, Ethan was still watching me, quiet, steady. The hum of Eric's game filled the pause between us.

"What about you? How do you feel about all of this?"

"I really don't get a say."

"You do." I clasped my hand over his.

"What I mean is, I never took a spot in Eric's life to erase his father. I love him like my own, but he does have a father, and I'm in whatever way you'll continue to allow."

"You're too good to me."

"You say that like you don't deserve it, " he teased. "You know what, come on."

I frowned. "Where are we going?"

He only gave me a small, knowing smile. "You'll see."

* * *

"Tell me," I said for the fifth time since we got on the road.

"So impatient."

"No. Just hate surprises."

I leaned back into the seat, clutching the hem of my sweater. My mind wouldn't stop circling back to Denver.

When we turned off the main road, my stomach dipped when recognition bloomed.

The car slowed over the graveled path. When Ethan pulled to a stop, I didn't need him to explain. My heart already knew.

The lake house.

Denver's house.

"Ethan, what are we doing here?"

"Go," he said, no explanation.

"Ethan."

"Clara," he said pointedly. "Go. You wanted a chance to explain, now this is it."

I hesitated at first, but eventually shot him a death stare before stepping out into the cool air. I watched as his car backed out and then turned out of view.

I turned, noticing fireflies flickering near the edge of the trees, and soft golden lights in mason jars marked the path toward the water. My heart pounded with every step.

And then I saw him.

Denver stood at the end of the dock, one hand braced against the table, the other hanging in his sling. The fading sky painted him in streaks of amber and mauve, the lake reflecting it all.

He did all of this. It had been a week since he kicked me out of his hospital room, so I didn't know what to expect. But it definitely wasn't this.

Forty

Nothing But the Truth

CLARA

When Denver looked up and saw me, neither of us spoke at first. He clenched his jaw; some scars from the accident on his face had faded. Hesitation and regret flickered in his eyes, and I understood it.

I kept his son a secret, and he found out from someone else.

He motioned gently toward the chair across from him.

I held my breath as I took a seat.

The setup was simple. Two plates, candles in mismatched holders. The lake lapped softly behind us.

"How are you?" I swallowed around the words.

"Thanks for coming," he said instead, eyes pinning me.

"Yeah, sure."

"I need to hear it from you. Everything this time."

My fingers dug into my thighs as the words clung to the inside of my throat. I didn't even know where to start.

I shifted my eyes to the lake, following the calm lapping of the water. I couldn't bear seeing any hints of judgment when I told him.

"When I told you my mother found out, that was true."

I looked down at my hands.

"You could thank Jamie for that," his voice cut in like a knife.

"What do you mean? I know at the hospital she said she knew, but I didn't know how.

"She told Heleen something about leaving something in your room. Asked her to go check, knowing she went in there and found your diary. She… read everything."

Jamie? My pulse roared in my ears. I knew there was something off between us since I'd come back here, but I couldn't believe she'd do something like that.

"No. She wouldn't—"

"She did."

"But, why?"

He didn't answer, and I mentally locked it away for later.

"When I found out I was pregnant, I wrote it all down…" I began.

I was still staring at the water when I finished telling him everything that went down that day. So I flinched when he stood suddenly, the chair falling with a thud on the deck.

Red-rimmed eyes and a tightly clenched jaw marred his wrecked face. "I'm going to kill her!"

I shot to my feet, wiping my wet cheeks. "Denver."

"She hit you?" His voice cracked, and he walked over to me. He raised a trembling hand, then pulled it back, fearing to touch me.

He stepped toward the edge of the dock, like he needed space to contain what was rising in him. "I should've been there," he growled. "She would've had to go through me first."

His whole body shook, not with rage alone, but with the helplessness of knowing what happened.

I took measured steps toward him. "You didn't know."

He turned back, chest rising and falling.

"No. But she did."

"I'm sorry," I murmured, knowing it was insufficient. When I met his green eyes, they held no judgment for me. Instead, I saw anger.

That alone illustrated the man Denver was. I was unworthy of his pity, unworthy of him.

He looked at me, eyes steeled with something different now. "I'm going to the hospital."

"What?"

"I'm going to see her."

He took a step forward, close but not touching. "You can stay, Clara. Or you can come with me. But one way or another…"

He held my gaze.

"I'm going to the hospital to see your mother."

I saw the fury in his eyes that didn't need shouting to be lethal. I swallowed around this dryness in my throat, nodded, and followed him.

Denver's knuckles whitened around the wheel the further he drove.

***

Each step to her room felt like newfound determination. We stopped right outside her door. "Denver…"

His hand found mine. "You've been running from this for too long," he said. "It's time to face it. My dad deserves the truth. You deserve to tell it. Your mother deserves to pay for what she did."

He was right.

He squeezed my hand once, then opened the door.

Tom was standing by the window, arms crossed, a coffee untouched in his hand. He looked up with a small smile until he saw our hands.

My mother turned her head at the sound of the door, and I almost reveled as I watched all the color drain from her face.

"Clara," she said, voice hoarse as she tried to sit up.

That alone almost made me stop.

Almost.

Denver gave my hand another squeeze. It reminded me of the times we'd sit and have dinner with our parents. Whenever a tough conversation arose, we'd squeeze a hand or a leg to remind each other of our support. To let each other know we were there.

I pinned my mother with my gaze, her head shaking. She knew what was coming.

I cut my eyes at Tom. "I didn't leave because we had a falling out. I didn't leave because I was dramatic, confused, or rebellious."

Tom's face shifted, confusion blooming into something heavier.

"I-I left… because she found out that I was pregnant…" I felt Denver's hand squeeze mine harder, "with Denver's child."

I felt a wind knock out of me, and the truth slipped from my lips for everyone to hear. Denver's heaving was the only sound in the room. Mom's lips formed a tight line, and I could see the anger rising. She did a good job keeping it at bay. Tom's gaze was burning fire at the side of her head.

"You told me I was disgusting. That I'd ruined everything. You assaulted me, threatened me. Your seventeen-year-old daughter, who you were supposed to protect." I turned to Tom. "You knew none of it because she made sure you didn't. She made sure no one did."

"Heleen, what is she talking about?"

She kept her mouth shut.

"Jump in any time you feel the time's right, Heleen," Denver stepped in.

"I thought I was protecting everyone," she finally spoke up.

A sadistic laugh roared from Denver. "Protecting? You destroyed her. Made her feel like she couldn't stay. You made me think she left all these years!"

"Watch it, son," Tom warned.

Head held high, I let go of Denver's hand and stepped toward her bed.

"I've run from this way too long."

My voice didn't crack, not this time. I stopped at her side, fingers trembling as they reached for hers. I hadn't touched her since I'd been back and been visiting her here. Not after the slap. Not after the words that felt like she buried into my skin.

She tried to pull away. I didn't let her.

My hands closed around hers, firm enough to say *I'm not afraid of you anymore.*

I looked her in the eyes. The longer I held her gaze, the more the resemblance between us faded.

"I'm tired," I breathed, "of dragging around the guilt you helped me bury.

Of pretending what you did was out of love. It wasn't."

Her eyes glistened, but I didn't stop.

"You made me feel like I was something to be hidden. Like love, real love, was a crime."

I leaned in.

"Well, I'm done hiding. I don't care what anyone thinks. I don't care what you think."

Her lips trembled.

"Can I just ask you why?"

She owed me that much.

I watched as a single tear fell from her eyes. She couldn't even give me an answer.

"I forgive you. But I'll never forget the way you tried to erase me. Tried to erase my son."

When I let her hand go, it dropped limply onto the blanket. I took a step back, one I never thought I'd be strong enough to take.

I took a breath like I'd just taken one for the first time. I didn't feel peace or victory; I felt relieved. Heavy aching relief that bloomed somewhere in the center of my chest and cracked open everything that had been closed off for years.

This wasn't about shame anymore or about a forbidden relationship or the weight of carrying my stepbrother's child. It was about survival. About love that had never stopped being love, even when everything around it turned cold.

I'd buried it for so long. Buried myself.

But now?

I was standing. Breathing. Speaking.

I had been a girl once, terrified, pregnant, in love, and told that all of those things couldn't exist together.

I wasn't that girl anymore.

I was a mother. I was in love. I was still *here.*

I turned to Tom. He hadn't said a word. My heart broke for him.

"I'm sorry," I mumbled. "For not telling you sooner. For all of this."

His mouth opened, but no sound came out. His eyes flicked between me and her, and I could see the betrayal setting in. Not just in her, but in everything he hadn't known to look for.

Denver stepped forward. "We'll uh… give you two a minute."

He reached for my hand, his fingers lacing through mine, and I let him lead me out of the room.

I let out a breath. Denver looked at me from the corner of his eye, a hint of something soft pulling at his mouth.

"How'd that feel?"

I leaned back against the cool wall of the hallway. "Better. It felt better."

He stepped closer, his gaze dipping to my lips. I felt the pull, the ache. But he exhaled and stepped back.

I could see it. The pain that hadn't been addressed, the betrayal I hadn't answered for. He ran a hand down his face, then nodded toward the hallway.

"Come on. Let's go."

It really hit me then. Denver was too good. Too good for me. Even after everything, he'd stayed by my side.

The guilt lingered as we got back into his car. I should've been happy that I didn't have to carry the burden of the truth. I should've been happy that I was finally letting go of my mother and the trauma she'd left me with eight years ago.

Forty-One

One Last Time

D ENVER

The dock creaked under my boots, the old wood groaning with every step I took. Out on the lake, the moonlight caught the water in shimmers, ripples breaking against the pilings. I'd meant to take her home, drop her at her dad's, and be done with it. But when the highway split, my hands turned the wheel without asking me first.

I couldn't let her go. Not tonight. Not with everything clawing at me.

Clara walked behind me, quiet, arms wrapped tight like she was holding herself together. I heard the soft pad of her sandals against the wood, the faint catch of her breath. She didn't ask why I brought her back here. Maybe she already knew.

I stopped at the edge of the dock and stared out at the black stretch of water. It smelled like summer—like damp wood, lake weeds, and the faint tang of gasoline from boats long gone. All I could see was her mother's face in that hospital bed. All I could hear was Jamie's scream echoing in my house. And behind it all, the thought that wouldn't leave me—the girl I'd loved since I was thirteen, being seventeen and pregnant, standing alone because of me.

She came up beside me, close but not touching. When she finally spoke, her voice was soft, steady in a way that made me ache.

"I met Ethan when I first moved to New York," she said. Her eyes were on the lake. "I went to my dad's first, but I couldn't tell him everything. I felt like… like I didn't belong anywhere. I couldn't go to Florida like we'd planned, I couldn't stay, and I didn't know what I was supposed to do with myself."

Her words were quiet, but they sank into me like stones.

"There were days I thought about giving up on everything," she whispered. "Ethan saw it. He knew. He lost his mom when he was ten—she was pregnant when it happened. I think he carried that grief with him everywhere, and when we met, it was like… like two broken pieces recognizing each other. He was safe. He never judged me. And when Eric was born, he stepped in. Not to replace anyone. Just… because I didn't have anyone else."

She kept her eyes on the water. "He was safe, she said again."

"Safe," I repeated, the word tasting wrong. I wanted to tell her she didn't have to explain. I wanted to tell her I understood. But the look on her face stopped me. She was shaking, and every instinct in me wanted to pull her in.

I started to move closer.

"Stop," she said suddenly.

My hands froze halfway to her shoulders. "Clara—"

"Don't." She finally looked at me, eyes wet and wild. "You don't have to do that."

"Do what?"

"Act like I'm breakable. Like if you hold me long enough, it'll fix something." Her voice cracked. "You should be mad. You should hate me."

I took a few steps back, confused about how we got here.

"I don't hate you."

"Then maybe you should!" She stepped closer, tears trembling on her lashes, and it squeezed something in my chest seeing her like this. "You were upset for maybe a week—one fucking week—and the next you're holding my hand to face my mother like nothing happened. You don't get to be calm about this."

My jaw locked so tight it hurt. "You think I'm calm?"

"You're standing there like you're not drowning inside!"

"You don't know what you're talking about."

She stepped so close, there was barely any room to breathe. "Then tell me, Denver. Tell me what's going on in your head, because you can't even look at me for more than a second without looking away. Tell me."

I let out a breath that sounded much like a laugh, humorless and broken right down the middle. My chest ached with it. The sound scared me a little, mostly because it felt like the last bit of control I had left.

"You want me to tell you? Fine," I snapped, voice cracking under the weight of it. "You screwed up, Clara. You wrecked everything we could've had. You lied. You ran. You let another man raise my son. Is that what you wanna hear?"

"Yes." Her breath stuttered, but I couldn't stop. The words had been waiting too long. "I missed his first. His first step. His first everything. Do you get that? Do you know what it's like knowing someone else was there for every moment I should've had?"

"I know—"

"No, you don't!"

I was understanding. Always giving everyone the benefit of the doubt. How could I not when it came to her? Clearly, I was doing a piss poor job because everything that's been simmering beneath the surface was coming to light.

I ran my hands through my hair, eyes burning. Every word I spewed felt like another dagger to my chest. "You decided for me. You did!"

She flinched, but she didn't shy away. This was what she wanted. She let every word hit, tears sliding down her face, silent and endless. Through it all, I still wanted to reach for her and wipe it away. Wipe away her pain, even if it meant I was stuck feeling it all.

"So yeah," I heaved, feeling like a weight had lifted off my chest. "You screwed up, Clara. You broke my trust, and it might take some time to get that back."

She blinked hard, like she was holding herself together by a thread. "Then why are you still here?"

I looked at her as her question lingered between us. I realized what this was. She wasn't done hating herself. She wasn't done blaming herself for everything she'd been through. The sudden urge to get back in my car and pay Heleen another visit came to the surface.

"Because I love you," I bit out. "That's what makes this unbearable."

I reached between us, and my fingers wiped her tears. Her lashes fell closed before she looked up at me. "And no matter how screwed up things are right now, we have an amazing son."

A smile tugged her lips. Gone was the Clara who was riling me up just a second ago.

God, I loved her. I still loved her so much it felt like it was killing me. Every part of me screamed to pull her in, to wipe her smile away with my lips on hers. To tell her none of it mattered, that I'd forgive her for everything if it meant she was mine again. But the wound was too raw. I didn't know if love was enough to stitch it shut.

"I don't know how to be a dad," I admitted, the words tearing out of me as I stared at her. "I don't even know how to try."

Her hand didn't hesitate this time. She pressed it flat against my chest, right over the spot where my heart fought against my ribs. "You don't have to know. You just have to show up. He already looks at you like you're everything."

"I'm trying," I whispered. "It just hurts so fucking bad, angel."

Her breath hitched at the name. She leaned her forehead against mine, and suddenly we were both crying, both of us breaking on the edge of something too big to hold.

"Don't walk away from me," she whispered.

My hands shook as I gripped her waist. "I want to stay more than I want to breathe. Wanting that doesn't erase what you did. I don't know how to trust you after this."

"You can trust me. I screwed up, but I never meant to hurt you. I hope you know that"

I nodded. I knew she didn't intentionally hurt me. It didn't change the fact that she did.

"Tell me how to fix it. Please. Tell me what I need to do, and I'll do it. Anything. I'll tear myself apart to make it right."

God, she meant it. I could feel it in the way she held onto me, the way every word came out with conviction.

I should've pushed her away. I should've let the rage carry me out of her arms and off this dock.

I couldn't bring myself to do it.

Her lips trembled, and then she kissed me. Hard, reckless, like it was the only language left between us. For one dizzy, shattering moment, I let her.

Because as much as I wanted to hate her, I couldn't. I only knew how to love her.

I lifted her, dropped to my knees on the dock, pulling her against me like I'd die if I let go. Clothes tore away piece by piece, scattered like they had no meaning. Our breaths came harsh, ragged, the night air cool against overheated skin.

When I slid inside her, it wasn't the frantic hunger I'd expected. It was grief and love and every missed moment crashing together. She clung to me, nails dragging across my back, and I held her like I was memorizing her.

Her voice broke into soft cries against my neck, each one cutting me open.

"I'm so sorry," she moaned. "I'm so sorry."

"I know," I breathed, kissing her hard, because words weren't enough.

We moved like people who knew this could be the last time. Every kiss was a bruise, every touch a plea. I tried to memorize the arch of her back, the warmth of her skin, the way her breath caught when I thrust deep. She kissed me like I was the only thing keeping her alive.

And maybe I was.

When it was over, I didn't let go. I kept her pressed against my chest, our skin sticky with sweat and saltwater air, her hair tangled across my cheek. I didn't speak. Anything I said would've sounded like a promise.

Tonight wasn't that.

Forty-Two

Still

DENVER

I sat at the kitchen table, scrolling through photos on my phone. Eric, with my guitar balanced awkwardly in his lap. Eric was laughing so hard he'd fallen back in the grass. Eric was concentrating, tongue sticking out, when I showed him the chords to "Wonderwall."

Every picture hit harder than the last. My son. My son and I hadn't known.

The screen blurred, and I dragged a hand down my face before shoving the phone flat on the table.

The floor creaked behind me, and I didn't need to look up to know it was her. Bare feet, my T-shirt brushing her thighs, hair tangled from sleep. The image should've been everything I ever wanted. Instead, it gutted me.

"Morning," she said softly.

I managed a grunt. Coffee was safer than words.

She moved toward the counter, filling the kettle with water, pretending she didn't notice the space between us was heavier than the silence.

I picked up my phone again, thumb hovering over the screen. Missed calls. My dad, three times. Jamie, five. I hadn't answered either.

"Denver," she started, hesitant.

I set the phone down. "He looks like me."

Her breath caught.

"In the pictures," I clarified. My chest tightened, the words scraping out. "The way he holds the guitar. The way he grins when he figures something out. He's mine, Clara. And you let me miss everything."

Her back stiffened as she turned, tea bag dangling from her fingers. "I know. And I know sorry isn't enough. I don't know what else to say."

I looked at her then, really looked, bare legs, my shirt, eyes rimmed red from crying, lips swollen from what we did last night.

"You don't have to say anything. But you should probably talk to your dad."

Her eyes flicked to mine.

"He deserves the truth. I hate how dad found out, and I'd hate for a wedge to come between the two of you because... of this."

I was ignoring my dad. I knew I'd have to face him soon.

"I'll go with you," I continued.

She blinked. "After everything?"

I leaned back in the chair, rubbing my temple. "I might not know what we are right now. All I know is—whatever comes, you won't face it alone. You've never had to earn that from me, Clara. You never will."

"Thank you, Den."

Looking at her hurt in ways I couldn't explain. I turned away, shutting off the whistling kettle. I poured hot water into two mugs, dropped in tea bags, and slid one in front of her.

"I'll drive when we're done."

Her fingers curled around the mug, but my eyes lingered on her—barefoot, hair tangled from sleep, drowning in my clothes. It all did something to me, despite everything. Too familiar. Too much like the way I'd always imagined mornings could've been if nothing had come between us.

I tore my gaze away. "I'll go get dressed," I said, leaving her at the table.

Forty-Three

Confessions

CLARA

The house was still quiet when we pulled into the driveway. Morning hadn't fully broken, the sky pale and low.

I slipped upstairs before anything else. Eric was curled on his side, tangled in his blankets, his small guitar propped against the nightstand. I leaned down and kissed his forehead. He stirred but didn't wake. My chest ached at how peaceful he looked, untouched by the storm I was about to bring downstairs.

Denver was waiting in the kitchen, leaning against the counter, sling tucked close to his side. He didn't speak when I came down, just gave the smallest nod, like he was bracing himself too.

Dad shuffled in a few minutes later, still in his pajama shirt, rubbing a hand over his face. His eyes sharpened when he saw the two of us together.

"Clara?" His voice was rough. "What's going on?"

I gestured toward the table. "Sit with me. Please."

We sat across from him, Denver close enough that I could feel the heat of him beside me. My hands shook when I folded them on the table.

"I should've told you years ago," I began. "I didn't. But you deserve the truth. All of it."

So I started. From the beginning. From seventeen. From the night I lost my mother and myself. Denver held my hand the entire time.

When the words finally emptied from me, silence filled the kitchen.

Dad leaned back, staring at me like he didn't recognize the girl sitting across from him. His throat worked, but no sound came out. Then, slowly, his eyes glistened.

"She did that to you?" His voice broke. "Your own mother?"

I nodded.

"And Eric…" His eyes flicked to Denver, then back to me. "He's his?"

"Yes." The word felt like it cost me something, even though it was the truth.

He covered his mouth with his hand, his shoulders caving forward. For a long time, he just sat there, shaking his head, trying to take it all in.

Finally, he dragged his hand down his face and looked at me. "And Ethan? Where does he–" His voice faltered. "Where does he fit into this?"

I swallowed. "He helped me. He knew, and he stayed. But he never replaced Denver."

Dad let out a sound somewhere between a sigh and a sob. He blinked hard, swiping at the corner of his eye. "I should've seen it. I should've known something wasn't right. I'm so sorry, Clara. For everything she put you through."

The weight I'd been carrying shifted, not gone, but lighter. Because his words weren't like hers. They didn't condemn me. They grieved.

I wiped my tears as I watched my father fall apart.

I squeezed Denver's hand under the table. He didn't let go.

Dad's eyes shifted to Denver. "And you?"

My chest tightened, but I spoke before Denver could. "He didn't know, Dad. None of this was because of him."

Denver's jaw flexed, but his voice stayed steady. "If I did, it wouldn't have come to this."

The silence stretched until Dad pushed back his chair. The scrape made me flinch, but then he was walking around the table. He stopped in front of me, and before I could brace myself, he pulled me into his arms.

I broke. My tears spilled hot against his shirt, and I clung to him with every bit of strength I'd spent years holding back.

His hand cradled the back of my head. "Don't ever think you have to hide anything from me, Clara. Don't ever think you'll find judgment here. You're my daughter. That means I take the weight with you. All of it. Always."

Something in my chest cracked wide open, and for once, it didn't close back up.

Maybe *she* gave me life, but she was never the one who taught me how to live it. For too long, I let her voice be louder than my own, and it nearly broke me. *Nearly.* Eric wasn't a mistake. He was the one thing in my life that had always been right.

I sank into Dad's embrace, the kind that didn't demand excuses or conditions, and for the first time in years, I felt like I wasn't something to be ashamed of. I was his daughter, and I was enough. I was always enough.

When I finally lifted my head, Denver was still there. He hadn't spoken, hadn't tried to fix it, but he stayed. Even knowing everything I'd hidden, he stayed.

And that, more than anything, told me I hadn't lost him. Not yet.

Forty-Four

Fair Grounds

DENVER

A week had passed since Clara and I sat her dad down. I thought anger would burn holes in me every time I saw Clara, but mostly, it was Eric who kept me grounded. The kid had this way of tugging me into his orbit until I forgot everything else.

I'd taken more pictures in the past week than in the last ten years combined. Half of them, Clara was in too. She didn't know it.

Eric was already halfway through his pancakes, sticky syrup across his cheeks, when I slid into the seat across from him. Clara handed me a mug of coffee without looking up, her hair still damp from a shower.

Ethan sat at the far end of the table, quiet but present, the kind of steady weight you didn't notice until it was gone. He didn't hover, didn't insert himself, but his eyes never strayed far from Eric. Years of habit.

Eric kicked his feet under the chair. "Can we do something today?"

Clara glanced at me. "What'd you have in mind?"

I let my eyes flicker between the two of them before I spoke. "What about the fair?"

Eric's face lit up, his grin wide and immediate. "Can we go on the Ferris wheel this time?"

Clara laughed, brushing her hand over his hair. "You swore it was too high last time."

"I wasn't scared," he muttered, puffing out his chest. Then, quieter, "Maybe a little."

Her smile softened, but her gaze lingered on me. We both remembered the first time we'd ridden it together. Different lives. Different versions of ourselves.

"Ferris wheel, huh?" I said, more to her than to him.

She nodded once. "Ferris wheel."

Eric didn't catch the weight of it. But we did.

The scrape of a chair pulled my attention. Ethan stood, gathering his plate and mug. "Sounds like a good day," he said, his voice even. "I'll stay back, let you three go."

He didn't owe me that, but he was giving me room anyway. Summer was dwindling, and I wanted to spend as much time with my son before they took off for New York. So, that meant breakfast at the Monroes and whatever activity Eric had in mind for the day.

As he brushed past, I caught his eye and gave a small nod. A silent thank you. For stepping back. For knowing when to let me in.

He returned it without words . A sign of respect that I appreciated.

* * *

Eric's laughter carried over the midway, sharp and bright. He tugged us from booth to booth, convinced he'd win every stuffed animal. I let him win one—okay, two—and carried the oversized bear when it got too heavy for him. Clara teased me for being a pushover. She wasn't wrong.

" Denver, look!" Eric pointed at the Ferris wheel towering above us, lit in red and gold against the sky. "Can we?"

"Of course," I said before Clara could answer.

By the time we squeezed into the seat, Eric was wedged between us, his little hands gripping each of ours. The ride jolted, and his eyes went wide, but he was smiling.

"Don't let go," he said.

"Never," I promised.

The higher we climbed, the quieter it got. The lights below blurred, the air cooler. Eric leaned forward, eyes wide at the view. Clara's shoulder brushed mine, light but steady.

She whispered, "He's braver than I thought."

"So are you," I said before I could stop myself.

Her eyes flicked to mine, holding. For a moment, with the night stretching around us, it felt like nothing stood in the way. My hand itched to reach across Eric, to tilt her face up and kiss her like I used to. She must've felt it too because her breath caught, lips parting slightly.

But then Eric turned, grinning, his small voice cutting through. "This is the best day ever!"

Clara laughed, shaky, brushing his hair back. I leaned away, dragging in the air. Hope and ache twisted in my chest, impossible to separate.

* * *

Eric was out cold by the time I carried him to the car, the giant bear slumped over my shoulder. Clara buckled him in, her hand lingering on his cheek.

On the drive back, the road stretched quietly. She looked at me in the reflection of the window, her voice soft. "Thank you, Denver. For today. For him."

"You don't need to thank me," I said. "He's mine too, whether he knows it or not. I'm not rushing that truth, but I'm here."

Her lips trembled, relief in her eyes. "That means more than you know."

I kept my focus on the road, but I felt her watching me, the air between us tight with everything unspoken.

"You wore him out," she whispered.

"Good," I said, a small laugh following.

She smiled, soft and tired, and I let myself look at her longer than I should've. Long enough to know that no matter how bad it hurt that she hid him from me, I'd never stop loving her. She made it impossible.

How do you stop loving someone you've loved all your life? Somehow, I knew I'd never know the answer to that.

The drive back to her dad's wasn't too far, but by the time I pulled into his driveway, Clara was fast asleep.

I shut off the engine and sat there a second, just watching them both, a smile on my face.

The two people I'd lost and found in the same breath.

It was selfish, maybe, the way I let myself imagine it, me walking them inside, staying the night, waking up to mornings that felt like family. But reality pressed against me hard. Trust wasn't rebuilt in a day, and Eric didn't know the truth yet. For now, all I could do was be here.

When Clara stirred, I cleared my throat. "I'll carry him in."

She nodded, voice thick with sleep. "Thank you."

Inside, I tucked Eric into bed, brushing his hair back like I'd done when he'd fallen asleep on my couch weeks ago. He didn't stir. Clara lingered at the doorway, watching with an expression I couldn't read, soft, heavy, like she wanted to say something but didn't.

I kissed Eric's forehead before stepping back. "See you tomorrow, buddy."

The words tasted strange, but right.

I said goodnight to Clara, letting my eyes linger longer than I should have, before pulling her in a hug that lasted too long, and bolted before I did something stupid like kiss her goodnight.

The drive home should've been enough to quiet me, but it wasn't. The day—the fair, the laughter, Eric's small hand in mine. This was too much and everything at once. And beneath it all, the weight of everything I hadn't said to Dad pressed harder. We didn't really speak after the confrontation with Heleen. I thought space and time were needed. I don't remember a time I'd gone without speaking to him.

So I didn't go home. I turned down his street instead.

* * *

Dad was out back, sitting with a beer, the night stretched wide around him. I didn't bother knocking. Just walked through and sat down across from him.

For a long time, we didn't speak.

Finally, he said, "Back then, I thought what I saw between you and Clara was just… loyalty. Siblings looking out for each other. I never imagined it was more." He paused, his jaw working. "But now, I see it clear as day."

I swallowed, then forced the words out. "I love her. Always have. That hasn't changed."

His eyes found mine, steady. "And the boy?"

I leaned forward, elbows on my knees. "He's mine. Doesn't matter how late I found out. I'll be there. However, I can. However she'll let me."

Dad nodded slowly, turning his beer in his hand. "I can live with that. What I can't live with is what Heleen did. That's going to take me time."

I didn't answer. My silence was enough. That might've been his wife, but she wasn't a factor in my life anymore. I couldn't bring myself to forgive her for what she did.

He set the bottle down, leaning forward. "So… what now?"

I shook my head, half a breath leaving me like it weighed a hundred pounds. "I don't know. She's in New York. I'm here. Eric's caught in between. I'll keep showing up. That's all I've got for now until I figure out my next move."

Dad studied me. "And the band? You've built something there. Can you keep it going with all this? Fatherhood isn't something you can half-ass. You have to be one hundred percent."

I rubbed the back of my neck, staring past him at the dark stretch of trees. "Music's the only thing that kept me sane all these years. I won't walk away from it. I'm talking to the guys and Sadie about it, so we'll figure it out. I'm going to be there for him one way or another. Music won't get in the way of that. It's not about chasing stages or drowning in crowds of fans. Now, it's about having something to give to him. Songs he can grow up hearing, knowing his dad wrote them with him in mind."

Dad tilted his head, listening. I wasn't sure he fully understood the pull music had on me, but he understood the weight of responsibility.

"You're saying you're ready to grow up," he said after a long pause.

"I'm saying I don't have a choice. He's eight years old, and I've already missed enough. I'm not missing any more." My throat tightened, but I forced it out. "If it comes down to choosing between a tour and being with him, I'll choose him. Every time."

Something shifted in Dad's expression then. Not forgiveness, not entirely, but a kind of respect I hadn't seen in years.

"I can live with that too," he said quietly.

We sat there in the heavy air of what had been broken and what might still be put back together.

Later, when I slid back into my truck, I thought about Clara in the passenger seat earlier, her lashes low as she drifted off, and Eric in the back, clutching his guitar like it was part of him. My son. My blood.

The ache of lost years sat heavy, but watching them like that made something shift in me. It wasn't forgiveness. It wasn't a clean slate. But it was a beginning.

And maybe a beginning was enough.

Forty-Five

Closing Chapters

C LARA
Eric's laughter filled the living room, wild and triumphant as his character on the screen defeated Denver's.

"Yes! I win again," Eric shouted, nearly bouncing off the couch.

Denver shook his head, trying to hide a grin. "Enjoy it while it lasts, bud. Next round's mine."

"Not a chance," Eric shot back, eyes glued to the TV.

I leaned against the doorway, my cup of tea warming my palms, and just watched. Denver sat shoulder to shoulder with Eric, guiding him through the game with the same patience he had when he'd shown him guitar chords. It looked so natural, like he'd always been there. Like this had always been his place.

Something inside me pulled tight.

Denver finally tossed the controller onto the couch cushion. "Alright. Time-out. I'll get breakfast going before your stomach starts growling louder than the TV."

Eric giggled, already setting up the next game.

I followed him into the kitchen, setting my cup down on the counter. For a moment, I just listened to the clatter of pans, the steady rhythm of him moving around like he belonged here.

"Have you thought about it?" I asked quietly.

He paused, spatula in hand. "About what?"

"Jamie. She's called me again."

His jaw ticked, eyes cutting to mine. "You don't owe her anything."

"I know. But this isn't about her, it's about me. I need to face it, hear her out. Otherwise, it'll feel like something unfinished."

He set the pan down, leaning against the counter. "She doesn't deserve your time."

"I'm not doing it for her."

Silence stretched, heavy but not hostile. His eyes searched mine, and though I saw his reluctance, I also saw understanding.

He let out a slow breath. "Then I'll go with you. But I'm not stepping inside."

Relief loosened something in my chest. "That's enough."

* * *

Jamie was already late.

I sat at a small table tucked near the back window, my hands wrapped around a lukewarm tea I'd barely touched. The air smelled like cinnamon and burnt espresso, and I wasn't sure why I agreed to this.

Probably because Denver refused. Maybe I needed to know why. Maybe I needed to look her in the face and feel nothing.

That was the difference now. I needed nothing from Jamie. Not an apology or an understanding. Just a clean end to a chapter I never wanted to live through in the first place.

The bell above the door chimed, and she walked in, looking around before spotting me. The same short cut hair she couldn't stop tugging behind her ear. Same clipped steps. She was different in contrast to the woman who screamed at me accusingly a few weeks ago outside the hospital. She looked smaller somehow. Not physically. The brightness she used to carry was gone. Like the world had finally taken something from her, too.

Jamie slid into the seat across from me and gave a tight, awkward smile. "Hey."

I nodded.

There was a long pause before she said anything else. She didn't meet my eyes when she spoke.

"I know I don't deserve to be here. But thank you for letting me talk to you."

She took a breath. "I was angry and jealous. I think… I have always loved Denver since we were kids. Deep down, I knew he didn't see me the way I wanted him to, but seeing how you wrote about your relationship with him, I guess… I just lost it."

Her eyes flicked to mine.

"I couldn't handle it. You were supposed to leave, Clara. You were supposed to be the girl who left and never came back."

"I did leave," I said, voice quiet. "But I never really got to stay, did I?"

She looked down at her hands.

"I told myself if I could ruin it, it wouldn't hurt as bad," she whispered. "Maybe he'd even see me as something other than the girl next door. Instead, I only made it worse. For you. For him."

As she spoke, I saw it all. The moments I'd missed. The glances I hadn't paid attention to when we were younger. She offered to get him water after practice, laughing a little too hard at his jokes. Sitting closer on the couch when we watched movies. How close to him she'd always try to be.

I looked at her now and saw none of the power she'd tried to hold over me. Just a girl who made the worst kind of mistake. I pitied her. Not because she lost him. But because she'd never had him to begin with.

"You ruined nothing." I wouldn't let her take my mother's credit any more than she deserved.

She squinted, surprised I'd said that.

"I hope you know I never hated you. I envied you."

I let that sit for a moment.

"I'm not mad. I won't pretend like I understand, but I get it," I told her.

"I've made mistakes. We all do. Sometimes we choose what feels right in the moment, and it shatters everything. But we're human. We were never meant to be perfect, just honest enough to grow."

I'd learned that firsthand. It took me a long time to admit it, but it was the truth.

Jamie's eyes searched mine. "D-do you think we could ever be friends again?"

I gave her a tight-lipped smile. "Take care of yourself, Jamie." I pulled out cash and rested it on the table, stood, and walked toward the door.

I wasn't walking away in anger. I was done carrying what didn't belong to me.

When I stepped outside, Denver's truck was at the curb. He leaned against the door, arms folded, waiting like he'd promised.

I climbed in, exhaling the weight I hadn't realized I was carrying.

"It's over," I said.

He nodded once and pulled out onto the road.

* * *

We didn't drive straight back. Instead, he turned down a quiet road by the lake and parked. The water shimmered under the fading light, the air thick with silence.

"Thank you," I said, my voice barely above a whisper.

His eyes stayed forward. "For what?"

"For standing with me. Even when you didn't want to."

He turned then, really turned, and the look in his eyes undid me. There was hurt there, still raw, but also something steadier, something that hadn't let go, even after everything.

"I don't know how this works," he admitted. "You there. Me here. Eric is in the middle. But I can't stop wanting you. Wanting to be in his life."

My chest ached. "I want that too."

He hesitated, hand twitching against the console, like he wasn't sure if he was allowed to touch me.

He closed the space first. Our lips met, soft at first, then heavier. It wasn't forgiveness. It wasn't a promise. It was something in between, grief and longing tied up with hope.

When we finally broke apart, our foreheads stayed pressed together, our breaths uneven.

With our ragged breathing filling the space between us, truth hung there. Whatever this was, it still mattered. It always will.

Forty-Six

Goodbye, Hello

CLARA

The lake was so peaceful in August.

I stood barefoot on the dock as the sun dipped low behind the trees, and for a moment, it felt like everything in me had settled.

The smell of charcoal and grilled meat drifted across the yard, mingling with bursts of laughter.

It had been a few months since I returned to Seattle. Weeks since I last saw my mother, and I was happy where I was with that.

I felt freer than I had in the last eight years.

Dad joined my side with a beer in hand, looking at the scene in front of us. It was Denver's official homecoming. It wasn't a coincidence that it was the day Eric, Ethan, and I were leaving.

Eric and Claire chased Denver across the yard with a water gun. Laughter rang out, Mason's unmistakably loud and dramatic, followed by Eric's higher-pitched squeal of victory. Sadie and Eli fought over a tong as the grill sizzled, begging for the meat to be turned. Ethan and Tom sat on the steps, deep in conversation, as they sipped their beers.

I smiled.

Dad wrapped an arm around my shoulder. "You've done well, kiddo."

That was the thing about love that didn't have to be earned. It didn't ask for anything but the truth. Dad has been supportive since I told him the truth. Always held me a little tighter whenever I was leaving the house. One thing I was grateful for was repairing our relationship.

"Thanks, Dad." I leaned my head on his shoulder.

When Claire and Eric found a new target and Denver headed our way, Dad excused himself.

I bit down on my bottom lip as Denver used his shirt to wipe some of the water off his face; the sun was shining down just right on him. Sometimes I lie awake and think about our last time on this dock, the one I was standing on right now.

"You okay?" he asked.

"More than just okay," I said, looking up at him and smiling.

We stood there in silence for a while, just watching our family. His fingers grazed mine, and I had the urge to take his hand in mine. I didn't.

"I meant what I said," he murmured. "I'll keep showing up."

We didn't plan on telling Eric the truth yet. Not because I didn't want him to know, but because I believed he needed time. Denver was a natural when it came to Eric and spent every chance he got with him.

"I know."

I wasn't leaving here with a clear path for our future. It would've been selfish if I demanded more than what he was giving me. What I did know was that I loved him and he loved me.

When it was time to go, I helped Eric into the back seat of our car. He was already half asleep, clutching his little guitar. *A parting gift from Denver. I swear it's the seventh one he bought.*

Ethan gave me a look before he rounded to the driver's seat.

"I love you," I said.

He kissed the top of my head. "Always."

I'd said my goodbyes to everyone else before they packed up and left.

I stood as Denver came up. He headed to where Eric was and, with hesitating steps, he kissed him on the forehead before popping back out.

This was the goodbye I was dreading. He'd promised to call Eric every day before making his next move. If it wasn't for school and my job, I'd stay. I'd do anything to be closer to him. For Eric to be closer to him. But one summer wasn't enough to make those drastic changes.

We looked at each other. As if a string was pulling us, we closed the gap and took each other into an embrace. He held me as I did him, wishing we could just stay like this. It felt like years since we'd held each other. I took in his scent, letting it cling to my clothes.

When we pulled apart, he looked at me, and I saw it in his eyes, the same thing I'd been carrying since we were kids.

It was always you.

We both knew it.

He said little, just stepped closer, his voice low and steady.

"Just in case you ever wonder, angel," he said, slipping something into my hand.

A guitar pick. Worn and familiar. The kind he always carried in his pocket, like a piece of his own skin.

I turned it over.

Still yours.

My chest ached.

I looked up at him, eyes stinging. He said nothing else. Didn't have to.

We weren't whole yet.

But we weren't lost anymore.

Just like he'd waited eight years for me, I'd wait for as long as he wanted.

I smiled, closing the pick in my palm.

He pulled me in again, his soft lips brushing my forehead.

For as long as he wanted.

Epilogue

CLARA

4 Years Later

I hadn't been to a club in years. Not since the version of me that wanted to disappear. Not since I knew what it felt like to be seventeen and terrified, leaving without saying goodbye.

Tonight, the lights were low; the bass pulsing under my heels. The scent of sweat, perfume, and cheap champagne clung to the air. Somewhere nearby, someone laughed too loudly. Strobe lights flickered above, casting everyone in a haze of motion and shadow. I could feel the music rumble through me.

Around me were the people who helped stitch the pieces back together. A few close friends, including Sadie and Ethan.

He leaned against the booth in his usual laid-back way, sipping something non-alcoholic and pretending he wasn't monitoring me like a big brother with a clipboard.

"I'm the man of honor," he'd reminded the bartender when we walked in. "That means I get to veto anything that smells like grave decisions."

Sadie rolled her eyes and handed him a lemon drop. "And I thought Denver was protective."

"Denver gave me the job," he yelled over the music. "You want to challenge it, take it up with him."

They bantered like this now. Somewhere along the way, Sadie grew on me. It hadn't been easy. She was Denver's friend before she was mine. Time does strange things. It softens people and makes space for the ones who stay.

Sadie nudged my side and gestured toward Ethan, who was now deep in conversation with one of my coworkers. "Is he still single?"

"You're asking this at my bachelorette party?"

"I'm asking because the answer matters," she whined, pulling her straw with her teeth. Then louder, across the table: "Hey, New York's Bravest, are you done playing hard to get? You know I love a man in a uniform."

Ethan nearly choked on his drink. He shot me a glare, like this was somehow my fault.

"Is this what I get for attending girls' night?"

She shrugged. "Flirting doesn't count at a bachelorette party."

I laughed and leaned back in my seat. My eyes drifted toward the entrance, half-expecting to see Denver walk through the door. I missed him, even if it had only been a day. That was the rule: no contact the night before.

Four years ago, there were no rules. Only distance and silence, and the long ache of waiting.

Denver didn't move to New York right away. When I left that summer, heart bruised but still beating, it took nearly a year before he followed. We did long distance. We argued. We figured out how to raise Eric across state lines, how to rebuild something real without losing ourselves again.

When he finally came, it wasn't some big dramatic gesture. He just showed up one Tuesday, suitcase in hand, and said, *"I'm tired of pretending I'm not already yours, angel,"* and unpacked like he never planned to leave again.

It wasn't perfect at first. There were long nights, hard conversations. Quiet dinners. Stupid jokes. Music in the kitchen. Intimacy that doesn't always look like romance, just two people slowly remembering how to trust.

He proposed two years after that. It was just me, him, and Eric at the lake house. The very first home he owned, and took me to when no one else knew about it. He kept it, and when we visit Seattle, we stay there.

Eric was the one who handed me the ring box. He'd helped pick it out.

Of course, I said yes. For as long as I could remember, Denver had been it for me. We cried. We have come a long way. From little kids hiding their love to being able to show it without a care in the world.

You asked me why I'm so sure. It's because when I think about the future... It's always you in it, angel. He'd told me that once. To this day, I believe it.

That night was also the night we sat Eric down and told him the truth. We held our breath for a reaction as he stared between the two of us. The only response we got was, "Okay. But I still want waffles."

We laughed and gave our baby what he wanted.

I didn't know what I expected his reaction to be, but it was as if he already knew. Like he had a feeling, and he was just waiting for us to say it.

Eric's twelve now. Smart, loyal, always humming one of Denver's unreleased tracks. He's just like him. He joined the band at school and plays guitar, the way Denver does. All feeling, no fear. He still calls Ethan when he gets stuck on a science project or needs someone to talk to about something awkward.

There's no competition. Just family.

I haven't spoken to my mother in four years. Not once. I don't miss her.

Sometimes I wonder if she ever thinks about me. If she regrets it, though, I stopped needing her to understand. She chose silence. I chose peace.

Tom tried. Therapy, long letters, meditation. In the end, even he had a breaking point. They divorced last year. He couldn't get over what she did. He still checks in on Eric. I think he's proud of the man Denver became, even if he doesn't always know how to say it out loud.

My dad and I... we've come full circle. He visits. Sends text updates on my little sister, who's fifteen now and somehow already cooler than me.

"Can you feel it? Now it's coming back..."

Sadie's eyes lit up. "Oh, my god. Geronimo? Really?"

"I requested it," I admitted, fixing my stash.

When the chorus hit, loud and reckless, I didn't bother putting on the heels I'd abandoned. I grabbed Sadie and Ethan's hands, dragged them to the floor, and let the music take it from there.

I danced like a girl who survived the storm and came out standing.

This was the end of the night before.

Tomorrow, I'd marry the boy who tore me open and helped me rebuild.

Tomorrow, I'd walk forward, not toward a clean slate, but toward one that held every mark we ever earned.

Say, I Do

DENVER

I was staring at my reflection, working the knot of my tie over and over until the fabric went stiff. My hands weren't shaking, but they weren't steady either.

"You're overthinking," my dad said from behind me.

I hadn't heard him come in. Still didn't stop me from stepping back, letting him take over like he used to when I was a teenager in a rush to make things worse.

He tugged the knot loose and started again. "You've got the same jaw clench you had before your first real gig."

I huffed. "This one matters more."

He finished the tie and smoothed the collar. He looked at me, tears in his eyes. "I'm proud of you, son."

I nodded. I tried to speak. Couldn't quite get anything out.

He'd always shown up in my whole life. Little league, talent shows, and hospital waiting rooms. The past four years cracked both of us open in ways neither of us could've seen coming.

He trusted and believed in Heleen. Believed in us. When it all unraveled, it hit him hard. Hit our relationship, too.

He didn't shut down or disappear, just sat with me countless nights in silence. Made space for the hurt and kept showing up until I met him there again. I still kept a close eye on him. I knew the divorce was a tough decision for him. I didn't fault him for it.

I got lucky in the dad department. I always knew that.

I still haven't forgiven Heleen. I never will. All that 'forgive and forget' didn't cut it with me when it came to Clara's expense. She and Jamie could go to hell for all I care. I cut contact with both of them when I found out about everything. Jamie tried reaching out a few times, but there wasn't anything to say to her.

Eric was stretched out on the couch in the hotel suite, eating dry cereal out of a cup and watching me like I was on stage.

"You're gonna mess up your tie again if you keep touching it," he said.

"I thought I looked alright."

"You did. Until you started pulling on it again."

I grinned. "Thanks, fashion expert."

He smiled and tossed a piece of cereal at my chest. "Just trying to help, old man."

I caught it midair and threw it back. "You're not too old to ground."

I missed out on most of his life, but my boy was twelve and mouthy, smart, half-grown, and all heart, all in one. He still had a framed photo of Ethan on his dresser, and I never asked him to take it down. Ethan was there for the years I wasn't, and I won't ever forget that.

But Eric calls me Dad now. He chose it himself. No prompt or nudge.

One night last year, I picked him up from band practice, and he climbed into the car, dropped his bag in the backseat, and said, "Hey, Dad, can we get pizza?"

I sat frozen in my seat until he snapped his fingers in front of my face to get my attention.

It was one highlight of my life.

I stayed back in Seattle for a while. Played shows, rebuilt, and faced the mess we were in. I'd needed time to figure out where the hell to go from there. Needed to rebuild my trust. When I couldn't take it anymore, I moved to New York. It was different, but the people I loved were there.

I still make music and write. Still tour now and then. It doesn't own me anymore. I come home to something that means more than the noise ever did.

The rest of the guys are still around.

But this, Clara, Eric, they're my life. Nothing will impede us.

Dad clapped a hand on my shoulder. "Time to go. They're ready for you downstairs."

Eric stood, smoothing his jacket. I took one more glance in the mirror. The knot was clean. The only nerves I had were getting through my vows without crying.

I was ready for everything else.

* * *

The chapel was warm, full of light. Summer spilled through the tall windows, catching the bright, open smiles of our guests.

My palms were sweaty, my tie too tight again. I kept shifting my weight, trying not to lock my knees like someone who didn't belong in front of the room.

Eli, my best man, stood next to me, giving me a look that said, *Breathe, man.* Mason, behind him, smirked. Sadie flashed a peace sign from the row behind as if this was a soundcheck and not the biggest day of my life.

The music changed. John Mayer's "Slow Dancing in a Burning Room" started playing as the man behind the piano played.

Her choice, I swear. *It's not traditionally romantic, but it's honest. It's about a love that's survived pain, and still they choose each other.* I couldn't agree more.

Everything stilled when the doors opened.

There she was.

Clara, in white, hair pinned back, eyes fixed right on me, even with tears threatening to fall.

She looked ethereal. Like everything I'd imagined she would look like on this day. My angel.

Her dad walked beside her. I thought when I asked his permission, he'd tell me no, but the man surprised me when he opened his arms and gave me his blessings.

I pulled at my tie, my black suit tight, and I watched my bride walk down the aisle toward me. That was *my Clara.* Not just the woman I'd loved for years, but the girl I fell for at fourteen, the one who made me believe in forever before either of us knew what it cost.

I didn't just cry. I broke quietly. Right there at the altar with the entire world watching.

She saw and smiled.

Eric stood tall beside the officiant, clutching the ring box. He gave me a brief nod, lips pressed to hide his nerves.

I mouthed, *You're killing it, buddy.*

He gave a thumbs-up.

When Clara reached me, I took both her hands.

"You look like a dream," I said, voice low. I wanted to kiss her right then and there.

"You're crying," she whispered, a little stunned smile curving her mouth.

"I've been waiting to cry like this for fourteen years."

The officiant gave the speech. The whole thing. Something about love not being perfect, but being real. About how family isn't always what we expect, but it's what we choose. I don't remember most of it. I couldn't take my eyes off her. It seemed as if I blinked, all this would disappear, and I'd wake up from a dream.

Now and then, she'd squeeze my hand, reminding me we made it and it wasn't just a dream.

I cleared my throat when it came time for our vows.

"I met you when I was a kid. Back then, I understood what love really was. Even then, it was you. It was always you.

"I thought I'd never deserve you after what happened. Thought I lost my chance. But you let me come home to you and our son, and I'll never stop being grateful for that.

"You're my peace. My fire. My anchor. My chaos. You're the song I've been trying to write my whole life.

"And I promise to spend every day learning you again. Loving you better than I did yesterday, and coming home to our family, always."

There wasn't a dry eye in the crowd, followed by a few 'awes'.

She cried through hers. Spoke through the tears like she was speaking straight to that boy she fell in love with, too.

"I don't believe in perfection," she began, "but I believe in us. In what we made of broken pieces. I believe in the way you never gave up on me, even when I did. I believe in the way you love our son so openly and don't shy away from it. I believe in the way you carry such grace with everything that you do. I believe you see everything beautiful about my life… It started with you. I vow to cherish, protect, and love you through thick and thin… I promise."

We both smiled, shaking our heads as our pinky fingers came up and closed around each other. *I promise.*

We exchanged rings. Eric handed them off like a pro. I squeezed his shoulder before I turned back to her.

"You may now kiss the bride."

I didn't hesitate. I kissed her like it was the first and last time. Like a man starved.

The room erupted, but I only heard her.

* * *

The reception was at a vineyard near the chapel. String lights everywhere, music in the air, surrounded by our loved ones.

Later, I took the stage with the guys and Sadie. It was always going to happen that way.

"I'm gonna need a little backup," I said into the mic. "C'mere, Eric."

He strutted up with the guitar we bought together last year, dark wood, broken in, his name carved into the strap. He tuned it without looking, nodding at me, and grinned like he was born for it.

Clara danced on the floor with her dad, eyes shining with glee as we played a few songs.

My wife.

We ended the night slowly. She and I, swaying in the middle of the dance floor. Just the two of us. Her head rested against my chest.

"I used to wonder how it would end."

I held her tighter. "It didn't end. It just took a while to begin."

Broken, Beautiful Lies

CLARA

The city was still.

Not quiet. New York was never quiet, but it still has that early morning quality. The kind of quiet one earns.

I stood on the balcony of our hotel room, wearing Denver's dress shirt. The fabric skimmed my thighs in the breeze. The mug in my hand had gone cold, but I hadn't noticed. I was watching the sky shift. My ring reflected off the light above me. I smiled. *Mrs. Stone.*

Somewhere in the room, a guitar pick clinked across the hardwood.

Behind me, the glass door slid open.

"Hey, wife."

I smiled without turning around. "Hey, husband."

His arms slid around my waist from behind. His body was warm against me, chest bare, skin kissed with sleep. I leaned into him. He kissed the back of my neck, then rested his chin on my shoulder.

I shuddered.

"You disappeared."

"I couldn't sleep. Too much adrenaline."

"You looked unreal yesterday, walking toward me like that."

"You cried," I teased.

He didn't deny it. "You've been it for me since I was fourteen. I just knew I'd spend my life catching up with you."

I turned in his arms and looked at him.

His hair was messy, swept back, but already falling forward again. His eyes were still heavy from sleep, a deeper brown than usual. There was stubble along his jaw, and ink crossed his chest and down his arms. One of the newer tattoos wrapped around his ribs, a small fox with a paper crown, drawn from a sketch Eric left on our kitchen table.

He looked at me without expectations. Without hunger. Just that quiet reverence I'd only ever seen in him when he was writing music or holding our son.

"I look at you and I remember every version of me that was waiting for this."

My throat ached. I reached for him without a word.

He undressed me with all the patience in the world. The fabric lifted from my skin. His hands followed. There was no rush. No weight to carry. He kissed my collarbone, my shoulder, then the center of my chest.

"I need you right now," he whispered against my skin. He hiked my legs up, and I wrapped them around his waist. "Like, right now, angel."

He laid me down on the silk-covered bed, shoving his pants off without taking his eyes off my bare skin. My tongue ran across my lips when his cock ran free.

"My beautiful wife." His green eyes bore into mine as he sucked my nipple, running his hand over the other.

I whimpered. "I need you in me now, baby," I heaved.

"So greedy." He kissed me as his hand traveled down between my legs. "And wet already? I fucking love it."

My back arched as he fingered me, running his thumb over my clit.

"Now," I hissed with impatience.

Smirking, he pulled out and replaced his finger with his cock. "Better?"

"Fuck yes."

There was nothing loud about it as we made love. His hands stayed locked in mine over my head, our grunts and moans tangled in the love we shared.

"I love you, angel. Forever."

"I love you."

He hit the spot I loved one too many times, and I was right on the edge.

"Cum for me, beautiful. You look so fucking good like this," he grunted, pace slowing down.

When I came apart, it was quiet. His name fell from my lips, and my body curled into his. He held me close.

"Angel," he whispered, right against my mouth.

When he followed, his hands trembled against mine.

Later, we stayed curled into each other, his fingers tracing circles into my hip. I dragged my hand along his chest and paused at the ink running down his arm.

A lyric I hadn't seen until last year.

Peace doesn't always come softly.

"We didn't get here by luck," I said.

"No. We bled for it. And we're still standing."

Eventually, I sat up and pulled the blanket with me. He watched me move, that slow smile spreading across his face.

"What do you want to do today?"

He reached for me, fingertips brushing my thigh. "Pack."

"For?"

"Our honeymoon. We leave at sunset. I got us a view that'll ruin you."

I leaned back into the sheets and laughed. "You already ruined me."

"Good."

I walked back onto the balcony while he stayed tangled in the bed. The city had come to life now.

This was home.

Him. Eric.

The life I never thought I'd be brave enough to have.

I didn't feel broken anymore. I didn't feel like a girl waiting to be forgiven.

I felt like someone who chose her story. Someone who stayed.

I looked out at the light.

"I think this is it," I said.

"What is?" he asked from behind me.

"The part where the story doesn't have to hurt anymore."

We were in chaos. We were heartbreak.

We were *broken, beautiful lies.*

But somehow, we became something real. Something whole. Something worth everything.

The End

Author's Note

Thank you so much for reading Broken, Beautiful Lies.

This book was one of the hardest for me to write. Not just because of Clara and Denver's messy, aching journey, but because it forced me to dig into themes of family, grief, forgiveness, and the way love can survive even when everything else falls apart.

To every reader who made it to this page, thank you. Your support, your review, your shares, your messages mean more than you'll ever know. Independent authors like me wouldn't be here without you.

Until Next time.

With love and gratitude,

Mary Jaay

Bonus Chapters

The Day Everything Fell Apart

JAMIE

Clara's door was closed, as always.

I should've walked past it. Said goodbye to Denver, went home, pretended the knot in my chest didn't exist. But every time I came over lately, I noticed how guarded she'd gotten. Like she was hiding something from me.

We used to tell each other everything. Now, half the time, she barely looked at me.

That thought gnawed at me as Denver ducked into the kitchen. He called over his shoulder that he'd grab a drink before we left, but I wasn't listening. My eyes were fixed on her door.

It wasn't planned. Not really. But my hand was already on the knob before I could stop myself.

Her room smelled faintly like her perfume. "What are you hiding, Clara?" I muttered, like the walls might answer.

I checked the desk. Empty. The closet. Shoes and folded clothes. Almost too neat. Almost like she'd gone out of her way to make sure nothing was out of place. Which made me think harder about where she'd hide something real.

The bed.

Half daring myself, I lifted the pillow.

There it was.

The diary was thick, worn, packed with her handwriting. My heart kicked against my ribs. I told myself I'd peek—just enough to feed the curiosity she'd been dangling in front of me for weeks.

I flipped to a page.

Pregnant.

Terrified.

Denver's.

The words punched me in the gut. I skimmed faster, unable to stop. Each line spilled with panic and shame, but under all of it, his name came up again and again. Denver. Denver. Denver.

My throat closed. My palms were slick against the paper.

They hadn't just been close. They'd been everything.

And suddenly, every laugh, every secret glance, every night they disappeared from the group when we were teenagers came into focus. I'd told myself I imagined it, that it was just them being protective, like siblings. But it hadn't been.

It had always been him.

The diary snapped shut in my hands, the sound loud in the quiet room. I shoved it back under the pillow, chest heaving. Then, like some sick instinct, I yanked it out again. My hands shook as I flipped to another entry about the pregnancy, about him. I left it open on her bed, the ink screaming up at me.

I told myself she deserved it. That if she wouldn't tell the truth, someone had to.

At first, I thought I wanted her to walk in and see it. To know someone knew. To feel the same gutting panic I felt.

But when I headed downstairs, my plan twisted.

Heleen was standing by the door, a mug in her hand. Surprise flickered across her face when she saw me.

"Heading out already?" she asked. Her tone was casual, but her eyes weren't. They were sharp, watching.

"Yeah." I forced a smile, shifting my bag on my shoulder. My voice came out too light, almost joking. "Actually…I think I left something in Clara's room. Could you check for me?"

Her expression shifted, a flicker of hesitation. Then, slowly, she nodded and went upstairs.

I waited at the bottom of the stairs, nails biting into my palms, pulse drumming in my ears.

When she came back down, her face was pale. Her mouth pressed thin.

She didn't say a word. She didn't have to.

I knew.

I'd given her the weapon without ever having to swing it myself.

"Everything okay?" I asked, voice thin, pretending I didn't already know the answer.

Her eyes locked on mine, sharp and cold. She only said, "No."

That single word cut through me, final and merciless.

I slipped out the door, the cool air rushing over my skin. My heart raced, but it didn't clear my head.

I should've felt guilty. I should've gone back, grabbed the diary, taken it all back. But I didn't.

Instead, I told myself this was justice. If Clara wanted to play with fire, she could burn for it.

But as I walked away, the hollow in my chest told me the truth.

I hadn't won anything.

Not Denver. Not Clara's trust. Not even peace.

All I'd done was make sure none of us would ever be the same again.

Haunted

<u>DENVER</u>

Dad and I pulled into the driveway like it was any other day. He'd taken me out, grabbed food, run a couple of errands, joked around like things were normal. And they were, at least until we walked through the door.

I didn't even head to my room first. My feet carried me straight toward Clara's. Habit, I guess.

Heleen was already in the hallway, her arms folded tight across her chest like she'd been waiting.

"Denver," she said, and something in her tone stopped me cold.

"What?"

"She's gone."

I frowned. "Gone where?"

"She said she needed a new start. She packed her things and left."

The floor tilted beneath me. I shoved past her, straight into Clara's room.

Empty. The bed stripped. The closet bare except for a single hanger. The desk cleared of her notebooks, her pens, her clutter.

The only thing left was a stretched pink hair tie sitting on the windowsill.

I picked it up with shaking fingers. My chest burned, like someone had jammed a fist inside and squeezed. She hadn't even told me goodbye.

* * *

One week later

The world kept moving. I didn't.

* * *

Two weeks later

* * *

Three weeks later

I barely slept those first nights. When I did, I woke up in a sweat, convinced I'd heard her voice. Every creak of the floorboards, every slam of a door, I thought maybe it was her. It never was.

I carried that hair tie everywhere. I pressed it in my palm until the elastic bit into my skin.

Jamie showed up on the third night, slipping into my room without knocking. She sat on the edge of the bed, handing me a soda and chips like it was just another Friday night.

"You've been quiet," she said gently.

"She didn't even tell me she was leaving." My voice cracked.

Jamie squeezed my arm. "I'm sorry. I'm here, okay?"

I nodded. And I was grateful. She couldn't fix the hole Clara left, but she filled the silence enough that I didn't drown in it.

* * *

One month later

Mason and Eli tried to pull me back into music.

"Just one song," Mason said, tossing me a pick in the garage.

I caught it, but didn't play. The guitar sat heavy in my lap, my hands frozen. Every chord I thought about strumming carried her shadow. She'd always been there—singing along, humming, teasing me when I messed up. Without her, the notes felt like static.

"Not today," I muttered, setting the guitar down.

They didn't push, but I could feel their worry pressing in on me.

I still wrote lyrics sometimes, late at night. Words that no one saw, scribbled out before I could finish them. Every line was about her, even when I tried to pretend it wasn't.

* * *

The summer

I went through the motions. Packed for college. Worked shifts I didn't care about. Pretended I was excited.

I even tried dating once, and let a girl from school talk me into going out for ice cream. She was nice, she laughed at my jokes, but every time she smiled, I thought of Clara. The guilt sat in my throat until I finally ended it before it began. No one compared. No one ever would.

Jamie stuck close. She was steady, dependable, the friend I leaned on when I didn't know how to stand on my own. Sometimes I caught the way she looked at me softly, searching, but I didn't have space in me for anything else.

* * *

College – Florida University

Clara and I had picked Florida together. We'd walked around the campus on a tour, both buzzing with excitement. We'd talked about dorms, classes, late nights filled with music.

It was supposed to be us.

Instead, it was just me.

I moved into the dorm, unpacking in silence. My roommate tried to make small talk, but the words slid off me. The room felt wrong, empty, like half of it was missing.

Mason and Eli came too, choosing Florida with me, like they knew I couldn't do it alone. We played some gigs around campus, wrote new songs, and tried to find our rhythm again. On the surface, it almost looked normal.

But nights were the hardest.

I sat on the edge of my dorm bed with my guitar, strumming until my fingers ached. Sometimes I'd sing until my throat went raw, the lyrics breaking apart as tears blurred the strings. I hated her for leaving. I missed her so much it hollowed me out.

Every plan we'd made together played on a loop in my head. Every memory haunted me.

She was supposed to be here. With me.

Instead, I was alone.

And I didn't know if I'd ever feel whole again.

Save Me

ETHAN

College

Grief never left me. It just changed shape. I could laugh with friends, write an essay, play a game—but underneath it all, there was always the shadow of her. My mom. And my little brother, who never got to be born.

She'd wanted to name him Eric. I was twelve when I lost them both. Old enough to remember, too young to understand. It felt like watching a storm roll in while you're locked inside the house, helpless, trapped. For years, I blamed myself for not seeing how bad it was. For not saving her.

That's why, the first time I saw Clara, I recognized it instantly.

We were in some required class, one of those big rooms where no one knows anyone. She sat near the back, hunched into herself like she wanted to vanish. Her eyes weren't focused on anything, not the professor, not the notes. It was that faraway look, the same one I used to see in my mom's eyes when she thought no one noticed.

I couldn't ignore it. I couldn't let myself.

The first time I spoke to her, she brushed me off. The second time, too. But I kept trying. I wasn't pushy, just… there. A question, a joke, an offer to share notes. She never encouraged me, but she didn't scare me off either. That was enough.

Eventually, she started answering. One-word replies at first. Then a little more. And one day, when she was pale and shaky outside class, she whispered, "I'm pregnant."

She looked at me like she was daring me to flinch, to run. But I didn't. I just said, "Okay. Want me to grab you some water?"

Her whole body softened, like she hadn't expected kindness.

From then on, I stayed. Played the part she needed me to.

When she had doctor's appointments, I went with her. I sat in the waiting room, sometimes beside her, sometimes just close enough that she knew she wasn't alone. I carried her backpack when she was too tired. I made sure she ate something before class, even if it was just a granola bar I shoved at her.

And slowly, something changed. She smiled more. Not a lot, but enough. Enough that I knew she was letting in light again.

We never talked about everything. She kept her secrets, and I didn't pry. She never asked about my mom, and I didn't force it on her. We just…existed side by side. I held her up when she was too tired to stand, and she gave me purpose when I was sinking in my own grief.

Months later, when she went into labor, I sat outside that hospital room with my head in my hands, praying to a God I wasn't even sure I believed in anymore. I don't know how long it was before someone finally told me I could go in.

And then I heard her voice.

"Ethan," she said, her face tired but glowing. She tilted her head toward the tiny bundle in her arms. "This is John Eric."

For a second, I couldn't breathe.

Eric.

My throat burned, my chest tight with something I couldn't name. She didn't know, not really. I'd never told her the name. But somehow, she'd given it back to me. A piece of what I lost.

I looked at her, at the baby, at the life she'd fought for even when everything in her screamed to give up. And I realized she wasn't just surviving. She was building something new. Something better.

"Hi, Eric," I whispered, leaning close to the little boy. He blinked up at me, and for the first time in years, the weight in my chest felt a little lighter.

Clara smiled, tired but real. And I knew then, I'd stay. As long as she needed me, I'd be here.

Not because I wanted anything in return. But because we'd both lost too much already. And maybe, together, we could make sure neither of us ever felt that alone again.

Big City, Big Lights

<u>CLARA</u>

New York was louder than I ever imagined.

The second I stepped off the bus, the city swallowed me whole. Horns blared, people shoved past me without so much as an apology, and for the first time since leaving home, I felt small. Invisible. Like I could disappear right there on the sidewalk and no one would even notice.

I clutched the strap of my suitcase tighter, the other hand resting unconsciously against my stomach. My stomach. Mine, but not only mine anymore. That thought both steadied and shattered me at once.

The dorm room they gave me was bare and sterile, two beds shoved against opposite walls. The other side was empty for now. I dropped my bag, sat on the mattress, and stared at the chipped paint until my eyes burned.

At night, it was worse. Too quiet, even in a city that never stopped moving. My mind filled the silence with voices I missed, Denver's laugh, my mom's scolding tone, the echo of everything I'd run from. I pressed my face into the pillow and let myself cry, muffling the sounds so no one down the hall could hear.

I'd told myself that leaving was a strength. Independence. Freedom. But it felt like punishment. I missed Denver so much it made my chest ache, like someone had carved out a piece of me and left the wound wide open. I missed home, even the broken pieces of it. And I hated myself for it.

Classes start next week. I dragged myself there, half-present, trying not to let anyone notice how my jeans were getting tighter, how I avoided eye contact, how I wrapped my hoodie around me like armor.

That's when I saw him.

He sat two rows behind me the first day, fire red hair, watchful eyes. At first, I thought nothing of it. But the second day, he moved closer. By the third, he was next to me.

"Clara, right?" His voice was quiet, careful.

I nodded, not looking at him.

"I'm Ethan."

"Okay." My tone was sharper than I intended, but I didn't care. I couldn't afford new people. I couldn't afford to let anyone in.

He didn't push. Just smiled faintly, like he'd expected me to brush him off. And the next day, he was there again. And the next.

It annoyed me at first, his persistence, the way he acted like sitting beside me was the most natural thing in the world. But there was something about him… a steadiness in his presence. Like he wasn't waiting for me to give him something. Like he just wanted to exist beside me.

One night, rain poured down as I left class. My umbrella snapped in the wind, useless. Ethan appeared at my side, holding his over both of us.

"You'll get sick," he said simply, nudging me closer beneath it.

I should've told him to go away. Instead, I let him walk me back to my dorm.

The wall between us cracked a little more a week later. I'd pushed myself too hard, skipped breakfast, sat through lectures, climbed four flights of stairs, and when I reached the top, my vision blurred. My knees buckled.

I don't even remember pulling out my phone. Just that Ethan was there within minutes, panic in his eyes but no judgment in his voice.

"Hey, hey, you're okay. I've got you."

From then on, he was just there. He started walking me to class, carrying my books when I got tired. He sat with me at appointments, even when I insisted he didn't have to. When the nurse asked if he was the father, he didn't flinch, just looked at me, waiting for me to decide what I wanted him to be.

One night, after weeks of silence, I couldn't bear it anymore, so I told him something, just a sliver of the truth. That I'd left more behind than I could explain. That there was someone I couldn't stop missing. I was terrified of failing before I even began.

He didn't ask for details. He just nodded and said, "You don't have to tell me everything, Clara. But whatever you tell me, I'll carry the weight of it with you."

I hadn't realized how badly I needed to hear that until the tears came, unrelenting.

For the first time in months, I laughed again, with him. He made stupid jokes, brought me snacks when my cravings got weird, and sat with me in silence when the weight of it all felt crushing.

Slowly, I started to believe I could do this. That maybe I wouldn't break.

When Eric was born, I thought I'd never survive the pain. Hours of labor left me shaking, crying, begging for it to be over. When the nurse placed that tiny, perfect boy in my arms, the world shifted. My son. My Eric.

"John Eric," I whispered, tears streaking my cheeks. "That's his name."

I glanced at Ethan. He froze, his eyes wide, wet with sudden tears. For a moment, I didn't understand. And then I remembered. His brother. The one he'd lost before he ever got to meet him.

"Eric," he whispered, his voice breaking. He smiled then, broken and beautiful. "Clara… thank you."

Watching him hold my son for the first time, I realized what he'd become to me. Not a replacement for the love I'd lost. Not someone I'd chosen in place of Denver. But a friend. A brother. A lifeline.

New York hadn't saved me. Ethan hadn't saved me.

But together with Eric, they reminded me that I was worth saving myself.

About the Author

Hi, I'm Mary Jaay, and I write romance with all the twists, tension, and emotions that make love unforgettable. My stories dive into complicated relationships, messy entanglements, and characters who don't always make the right choices, but who love with everything they have.

I'm the author of Never Have I Ever and Let Us Burn, with my newest novel, Broken, Beautiful Lies, releasing soon. Each of my books can be read as a standalone, but they all share one thing in common: raw emotion and romance that lingers long after "The End."

Also by Mary Jaay

Let Us Burn
"You're mine."

India was supposed to spend the summer healing, not falling for the one person she's sworn off.

The plan was simple: sun, sand, and the comfort of her four childhood friends. The same beach house, same routine, same people.

Except now, her ex is just down the hall…
   And his best friend, the arrogant, insufferable heartbreaker she can't stand?
   Yeah, he's the only one she can't stop thinking about.

One stolen kiss turns into sleepless nights. Secrets build, and tension snaps.
   The safe summer getaway becomes a ticking bomb of forbidden chemistry, emotional fallout, and everything they've kept hidden for years.

***Let Us Burn** is a fast-burn, high-heat forbidden romance packed with childhood friends, enemies-to-lovers sparks, and the kind of desire that doesn't ask permission. It sets everything on fire.*

Never Have I Ever
He wants him. But he's fighting it.

One game. One kiss. One night that changes everything.

Zach and Kane were supposed to be off-limits—just friends. Best friends. No crossing the line, until one reckless night, a few too many drinks, and a game of Never Have I Ever ignites something they can't take back.

Now, Zach can't stop thinking about Kane's mouth. Kane's hands. He looked at him like he was the only one in the room.

Kane knows what he wants, and it's Zach. But Zach? He's spiraling, scared of what it means to want a man. Scared of what it means to want him.

Their friendship was solid. Until it wasn't.

Now, every glance is loaded. Every touch is electric.

And if they give in again… there's no going back.

A friends-to-lovers M/M novella full of heat, heart, and messy, beautiful first love.